FOL Follett, James,
1939-

Churchill's gold

7.01
4-88

## Date Due

|  |  |  |  |
|---|---|---|---|
|  |  |  |  |
|  |  |  |  |
|  |  |  |  |
|  |  |  |  |
|  |  |  |  |
|  |  |  |  |
|  |  |  |  |
|  |  |  |  |
|  |  |  |  |

# CHURCHILL'S GOLD

By the same author

*The Doomsday Ultimatum*
*Crown Court* (novelization)
*Ice*
*U–700*

# JAMES FOLLETT

# CHURCHILL'S GOLD

Houghton Mifflin Company Boston
1981

First American edition 1981

Copyright © 1980 by James Follett

*Library of Congress Cataloging in Publication Data*

Follett, James, date
Churchill's gold.

1. World War, 1939–1945—Fiction.   I. Title.
PR6056.O44C5   1981      823'.914      80–27177
ISBN 0–395–30526–8

Printed in the United States of America

P  10 9 8 7 6 5 4 3 2 1

# FOREWORD

All the facts concerning Churchill's gold during 1940 and 1941 may never be revealed. The reason for this is that the Bank of England did not become a public concern until after the Second World War and therefore are under no obligation to transfer their wartime archives to the Public Record Office. All attempts to obtain information through official channels have been met with a polite but nevertheless very cold stone wall. For this reason I am grateful to those individuals in the United States, England, South Africa and Germany who told me what little they could, and I'm especially grateful to the very few who told me more than they should.

James Follett
February 1980

*For Christine*

*who got frightened in the African Bush*
*in the search for informants.*

# PART ONE

## KILLING

# 1

It had been sixteen months since the female sperm whale had copulated briefly with the old bull amid an excited welter of near-freezing foam in the lonely, icy wastes of the Southern Ocean. Now the moment of birth of her first calf was at hand.

It was a difficult birth; the tail of her firstborn was protruding from her body but the repeated muscular spasms that could crush a man to pulp were failing to complete the expulsion of the fourteen-foot calf.

The female rolled on to her side and thrashed the water white with her great tail flukes in a frantic attempt to dislodge the infant that was in danger of suffocation. Her herd sisters sensed the cow's distress. They abandoned their meal of squid and drove upwards through the warm layers of the Indian Ocean towards the sparkling sunlight.

'There! There! She blows – five sperm!'

Robert Gerrard pushed his mop of dark, curly hair out of his eyes and squinted up at the spotters' platform to get a bearing on the Malay boy's outstretched arm. He quickly focussed his binoculars on the sea and picked out the arching backs of the great beasts and the silvery plumes of their blows shining like fountains of pearls in the setting sun. The blows burst into the air at an angle ahead of the mighty creatures. They were definitely sperms – only sperms blew like that. And in December 1940 sperm whales were the only reason for the *Tulsar*'s presence in the Indian Ocean for the brief whaling season off South Africa's Natal coast.

Piet van Kleef, Gerrard's first officer, was leaning over the bridge rail, bellowing and cursing in Afrikaans at the men manning the derricks that held one of the *Tulsar*'s two high-speed whale-catcher launches.

'Hold it, Piet,' said Gerrard crisply, not taking his eyes away from his binoculars. 'Don't launch the catchers.'

The giant Afrikaner gaped at his captain in amazement. 'There's a hundred barrel of sperm out there, cap'n,' he protested, having already calculated his share of the bonus that the whales represented.

'I don't give a damn if there's a thousand barrels of sperm oil out there,' Gerrard growled. He jerked his finger at the reddening sun. 'It's too late. Sundown in two hours.'

Piet scratched his beard with a grimy thumbnail. 'Okay. So we barrel-line the bastards and pick 'em up in the morning.'

'And give every Goddamn shark around a free overnight dinner?'

Piet had served with Gerrard for ten years – long enough to learn the uselessness of trying to win an argument with the quick-tempered whaling captain from Boston. Despite his slight build Robert Gerrard possessed a wiry strength, was incredibly fast on his feet, and was accustomed to winning disputes either by use of his deadly fists or his quick thinking – two characteristics he had inherited from his Huguenot grandparents on his father's side. The American rested a sinewy arm on Piet's shoulder and gave the Afrikaner a friendly push.

'They'll feed tonight when the squid rise, Piet. They won't be far away in the morning.'

As Piet started shouting orders, Gerrard returned his attention to the small group of whales. They were cows. He guessed that the bull would be some miles seaward protectively quartering his wives. One of the cows appeared to be in difficulty for she was rolling on to her side, presenting her underbelly to her companions. It was then that Gerrard realized that she was giving birth. The huge waters thrown up by the majestic creatures suddenly cleared as the struggling cow rolled virtually on to her back, exposing the eight feet of her half-born offspring's body protruding from her belly. For a moment the fascinating scene was obscured by foam and broken water, then Gerrard, to his astonishment, saw one of the cows gently grasp the infant's passive tail and draw the creature from its mother's body.

In the twenty-five of his forty years that Gerrard had been hunting whales this was an event that he had never witnessed

4

before, and he knew it was something that he was unlikely to see again. He suddenly felt miserably alone: the birth of the whale was something that Cathy would have loved to have seen.

Some marauding seabirds, sensing the unusual, altered course and circled the scene speculatively. Two of the cows carefully eased their massive, blunt heads under the one-ton newborn sperm whale and held its head above water to enable it to suck down its first lungfuls of air. The movement snapped the duct-like umbilical cord that was as thick as a man's arm.

More seagulls joined in the lazy circling above the whales – their harsh, uneven cries plainly audible above the suck and hiss of the Indian Ocean's swell against the *Tulsar*'s steel hull. The whale calf's tail gave an uncertain flick. Immediately it was swimming, nosing its sensitive lips along its mother's curving flanks seeking the life-giving nipples.

Gerrard tried to forget Cathy as he watched the whales resume their northward migration, their backs arching black and grey in the ochre sunlight, wind-whipped blows scattering into the air like clouds of steam from strange locomotives of the deep. For once Gerrard was glad that he wouldn't have to kill them.

There was a reddening in the water in the whales' wake. The seabirds traded height for speed and spiralled down to investigate. Gerrard adjusted the focus of his binoculars and could distinguish the purple half-ton of placenta meat on the surface, expelled from the mother whale's body a few seconds after she had given birth. The seabirds were undecided – they cautiously circled the feast at wave-top height. One albatross had no reservations; it dropped straight down, its wings flogging the air to brake its descent. But the giant seabird never reached the water; it suddenly changed its mind and wheeled sharply into the air. The other seagulls did the same while uttering shrill cries of alarm.

Puzzled, Gerrard kept his binoculars trained on the mass of meat. The dorsal fin of a Mako shark closed on the meal like a miniature Genoa sail and abruptly sheered away.

At that moment Gerrard saw the reason for the birds' uncertainty: a long, low, menacing shape moving northwards at

5

about two knots. There was no mistaking that half-submerged profile. To Robert Gerrard it was the most despised shape in the world: the shape of one of the obscene things that had taken Cathy from him.

He lowered his binoculars. The shape was impossible to see with the naked eye. He guessed it to be about six miles distant, and checked the position of the late sun hanging blood-red above the horizon like a bloated, over-ripe fruit. The *Tulsar* was between the shape and the sun. There was a chance; a faint, impossible chance. He dived into the wheelhouse and pushed Brody away from the helm.

'What the hell?' the New Yorker protested. As a former middleweight prizefighter, and now the *Tulsar*'s coxwain, Brody was not an easy man to push.

'Sorry, Sam,' said Gerrard, spinning the chromium wheel and watching the rudder indicator slide round the scale.

'I thought we weren't going after them whales until morning?'

'We're not.'

There was a tense, dangerous note in Gerrard's voice that dissuaded Brody from pressing further questions. The coxswain watched Gerrard press the key that sounded the engine-room interphone. The *Tulsar* was the most advanced whaling factory-ship in the world – there were no voice-pipes.

'Bridge,' said Gerrard curtly. 'Listen, you guys, when I sound the telegraph for full ahead on both, I want just that and not a lot of dispute about your Goddamn turbines or I'll kick your asses all round the engine-room. Okay?' Gerrard listened to the brief reply and returned the receiver to its hook.

'Anything I can do, boss?' Brody inquired.

Gerrard felt in the top pocket of his grimy sweat-shirt for a crumpled Havana and lit it. The acrid bite of the stale cigar steadied his thoughts and nerves. The raw hatred that had erupted in his guts was replaced by the low cunning of a hardened hunter.

'Sure, Sam,' he murmured in answer to Brody's question. 'Follow my helm orders and signal for full speed ahead on both the instant I say.'

With that, Gerrard handed the wheel back to Brody and left the wheelhouse. He leaned on the bridge rail and trained his binoculars straight ahead. The shape was nearer and still moving north at the same speed. He studied it casually without a flicker of emotion on his weathered face to betray the brute savagery he felt towards the thing out there – the thing that had killed Cathy the year before on the first day of the war against Hitler. America was not at war with Germany, but that changed nothing.

'Left a bit, Sam,' Gerrard called through the open door. He was surprised with himself at how calm he knew his voice sounded.

Brody eased the gleaming wheel through his stubby fingers, correctly interpreting Gerrard's helm order as 'port ten degrees'.

'Fine, Sam. Hold her there.' Gerrard kept his quarry in focus through the binoculars. He sensed Piet's presence at his side even before the mahogany rail creaked as the huge Afrikaner leaned his bulk against it. Piet was built like the door of a bank vault: large, round, heavy and dependable. The six-inch wide elephant-hide belt that encircled his huge gut, supporting his shapeless denims, was in perfect proportion to his floppy *Voortrekker* hat. It took little imagination to picture Piet van Kleef riding a stinkwood wagon, driving an ox team across the jagged teeth of the Drakensberg Mountains as his Boer forebears had when they had pushed north from the Cape to escape British rule.

'So what are we chasing, cap'n?' Piet inquired.

Gerrard handed the binoculars to the Afrikaner and pointed. The giant scanned them back and forth for a moment before freezing their action. His outsize thumb moved delicately on the knurled focussing wheel. He stiffened. 'Jesus Christ,' he breathed. 'A submarine.'

'A German U-boat,' Gerrard murmured under his breath, taking the binoculars from Piet, ignoring the Afrikaner's worried expression.

'Are you planning what I think you're planning?' Piet demanded.

'Yep.'

'You're crazy.'

'That's right.'

'Jesus Christ,' Piet muttered. He rested his great paw of a

hand on Gerrard's sinewy wrist. 'Listen, man – how in hell do you know it's German? Here? In the Indian Ocean?'

Gerrard pulled his hand free of Piet's friendly grip. He gave a crooked smile. 'An anti-aircraft gundeck aft of the conning-tower, Piet. Only the Germans build subs like that.' He turned to the wheelhouse. 'Left a notch, Sam!'

The *Tulsar* turned one degree to port.

'What good will it do, cap'n?' Piet pleaded. 'It won't change anything – it won't bring her back.'

Gerrard stared through the binoculars. Piet noticed that his fingers were white from the tightness of their grip.

'You touch that sub and you'll be strung up so high, we'll need them binoculars to see who you are.'

Gerrard continued to ignore Piet. The Afrikaner became desperate. 'You'll be in big trouble with your government, and your government will be in one whole heap of shit with the Germans.'

The American lowered the binoculars. His grey eyes were glazed as he stared across the water but his voice was devoid of emotion when he spoke. 'Thank you, Piet. Those yellow bellies in Washington are ten thousand miles away, and that U-boat is less than four. I'm going to sink the bastard.' He suddenly wheeled round. 'Sam! Full speed ahead on both now!'

The engine-room telegraph clanged. The two languid bow-waves began climbing the hull as the whaling-ship's finely-balanced Parsons turbines poured ten thousand horsepower into the twin propellers. There was a ripple of excited commotion among the whalemen gathering along the bulwarks. Darting Malay boys were pointing and shouting; lithe, naked bodies swarmed on to the seaplane derrick for a better view. The deck began to shudder beneath Gerrard's feet as the *Tulsar*'s speed crept up to her maximum twenty-six knots. The boy who had spotted the whales was dancing up and down on the spotter's platform and yelling, 'There! There!' while pointing frantically with a skinny, outstretched arm.

The U-boat was now less than three miles away and was obviously unaware of the charging apparition bearing down on it from out of the rapidly-setting sub-tropical sun. Gerrard could even discern the outline of two men on the submarine's bridge.

8

'They must hear us if they've got hydrophones,' breathed Piet.

Gerrard clutched the rail in silence while staring straight ahead at the hated U-boat. The random knotted lines of blue veins on his muscular forearms pulsed visibly against a tattoo that depicted a Boston whaler harpooning a blue whale. There was a sudden flurry of movement on the submarine's bridge. The two men ducked out of sight. A Klaxon wailed faintly and the water astern of the U-boat was suddenly whipped to foam. Geysers spouted from the U-boat's deck casing vents as the craft began submerging at speed.

'Four left!' Gerrard bellowed.

The whalemen and Malays were whooping with delight. They had no idea what it was all about except that it was great fun. The U-boat captain tried a desperate move by turning his bows towards the charging ship – a move which Gerrard guessed was intended to reduce the size of the target. It was a mistake; the ill-conceived manœuvre cost the U-boat vital speed at the crucial moment. By the time the error was realized and the U-boat had regained lost way, the *Tulsar* was less than two hundred yards away and closing the gap at nearly fifty feet per second.

'Close the watertight bow doors, Sam,' Gerrard called to Brody.

Water was creaming past the conning-tower which was now the only part of the U-boat above water. Even Piet, normally the phlegmatic Afrikaner, was beating the wooden rail with a ham-like fist and roaring excitedly.

Only Gerrard was silent as he watched the stricken U-boat disappear from view beneath the *Tulsar*'s bow. 'Hard astern both!' he rapped out at Brody.

There was a shuddering blow that caused the whaling-ship to lose way abruptly. The *Tulsar* lifted her head as her terrible juggernaut momentum carried her over the U-boat. The scream of metal on metal set Piet's teeth on edge. 'Jesus Christ,' he whispered to himself. 'Jesus Goddamn Christ.'

The hideous shriek of twisting steel plates became a dull grating sound as the whaling-ship stopped and began going astern.

'Stop engines,' Gerrard ordered.

9

Brody's hand groped for the telegraph lever while staring ahead through the wheelhouse window. Gerrard leaned over the rail and gazed down at the sea where wreckage was surfacing in the centre of a spreading, evil-smelling oil slick. There was no sign of the U-boat. The Malay boys stopped their excited chatter.

Piet met Gerrard's eyes. The American was silent for a moment. He relit his cigar and flipped the match over the rail. Piet knew Gerrard well enough to recognize contrived casualness.

'Say whatever you want to say now,' said Gerrard. 'And then we forget it. Okay?'

But Piet could think of nothing to say.

Jack Colby, the *Tulsar*'s lanky, easy-going Canadian radio operator, appeared on the bridge and moved to Gerrard's side. He was holding a slip of paper which he studied for a moment before passing to Gerrard.

'It managed to transmit some sort of message,' said the Canadian. 'In code, I guess, because I couldn't make no sense of it – all except one word.'

Gerrard glanced at the confused jumble of letters scrawled on the paper in Colby's sloping hand. There was one clear word that virtually jumped off the paper: TULSAR.

Piet looked over Gerrard's shoulder and swore softly.

Colby grinned. Canada was at war with Germany; he had no objection to Gerrard sinking U-boats. 'Reckon there's going to be trouble, skipper?'

Gerrard returned his attention to the rainbow hues caused by the oil slick that were dancing on the water. He nodded. 'Yeah – I reckon so, Jack. Big trouble I guess.'

Two miles to the north the baby whale, with its toothless gums firmly fastened to a rubbery nipple, was greedily drinking its first meal of fifty gallons of its mother's rich, warm milk.

# 2

Josephine ignored the impatiently-flashing light on the Benjamin D'Urban Hotel's switchboard and disbelievingly read through the telegram for a second time. The cable from her mother in New York had been written like a letter with no attempt at word economy:

> DEAR JO I DONT KNOW HOW TO BEGIN THIS TO SOFTEN THE BLOW BUT PA HAD ANOTHER STROKE LAST WEEK STOP I GUESS I OUGHT TO HAVE TOLD YOU ABOUT HIS FIRST STROKE IN MY LAST LETTER BUT HE SAID I WASNT TO AND YOU KNOW HOW MAD HE CAN GET IF HE DOESNT GET HIS OWN WAY STOP THIS TIME HE IS IN A BAD WAY STOP HE CANT MOVE ON ONE SIDE STOP HE ASKED AFTER YOU LAST NIGHT STOP I KNOW HES SORRY OVER WHAT HAPPENED BUT HE WONT SAY IT STOP IF YOU COULD WRITE HIM AND SEND THE LETTER TO ME SO THAT I CAN READ IT TO HIM I KNOW HE WOULD BE PLEASED STOP YOUR LOVING MOTHER

'Is there a reply, mem?'

Josephine looked up. The Indian telegraph boy, hot and uncomfortable in his tight uniform, was watching her with dark, anxious eyes – sensing that this was one telegram that was unlikely to produce the customary sixpenny tip. 'Is there a reply, mem?' he repeated.

Josephine shook her head. The boy was half-way across the hotel's lavish rococo lobby when she suddenly decided on a course of action and called out: 'Yes! Wait!'

The boy returned to the reception desk. Josephine reached for a pad and pencil. Without hesitation she wrote:

> GIVE PA ALL MY LOVE AND TELL HIM IM COMING HOME ON THE FIRST SHIP STOP LETTER FOLLOWS LOVE JO

She ripped the note off the pad and gave it to the telegraph boy.

'Will it go today?'

'Yes, mem.'

Josephine opened the hotel's petty cash tin and realized that the tip should come out of her own pocket. She was always scrupulously correct where money was concerned. She watched the boy disappear through the revolving doors and wryly reflected that despite her resolution, her impulsive nature still ruled her life: an impulse had led to her storming out of her parents' home three years previously, ending up in South Africa, and now exactly the same sort of impulse was going to take her home again. Not even the grim news about her father's illness succeeded in overshadowing the sudden feeling of exaltation that she experienced.

She picked up the telephone and answered the flashing light.

# 3

At 9.30 am the black, chauffeur-driven Cadillac drew up outside the imposing Foreign Office building at the Brandenburg Gate end of the Wilhelmstrasse in Berlin. Ten minutes later, Douglas Napier, an assistant military attaché at the United States embassy, was shown into Joachim von Ribbentrop's ornate office. The Reich foreign minister was standing behind his absurdly large desk. His face tightened with anger when he saw who his visitor was and he curtly brushed aside Napier's opening pleasantries.

'I sent for the chargé. Where is he?'

'The chargé d'affaires regrets that he is indisposed, sir,' Napier replied, refusing to address the arrogant former champagne salesman as 'your excellency'. Relations between the United States and Germany had been decidedly sour since the brutal anti-Jewish Kristallnacht pogrom of November 1938 when SA rowdies throughout Germany had smashed and looted Jewish shops and businesses, and murdered their owners. Such was the outcry in America against the atrocities of that notorious night that the American government had recalled its Berlin ambassador and handed the German ambassador in Washington his passport. Relations between the two countries had further deteriorated with the torpedoing of the ocean liner *Athenia* which had caused the death of nearly thirty United States citizens.

Von Ribbentrop glowered at Napier for some seconds before picking up a paper from his desk. 'I have yet to receive an answer to my note concerning the deliberate sinking of one of our U-boats by the *Tulsar* in the Indian Ocean. Why?'

Napier stared straight back at von Ribbentrop without flinching. 'I understand that the chargé has made it clear that a reply will be forthcoming when my government is in full possession of the facts, sir.'

'You've had forty-eight hours,' Ribbentrop icily pointed out.

'The *Tulsar* is still at sea, sir. It is impossible for my government to reply to your note until we have talked to its captain.'

Ribbentrop's face paled as he listened to Napier's reasoned objection. He smashed his fist down on his massive oak desk. 'You've received a copy of the signal broadcast by the U-boat!' he shouted. 'The ramming by the *Tulsar* was a deliberate, unprovoked act of piracy! If the United States government feels that it is unable to deal with *Tulsar*'s captain, the Führer has stated that it may be necessary for him to reconsider his attitude to American warships escorting enemy merchantships carrying strategic war material! Good day to you!'

Napier stood his ground despite the dismissal; he had been given a specific instruction not to leave with his 'tail between his legs'.

'Minister,' he said politely, 'the secretary of state has made clear that *any* country may avail itself of the cash and carry scheme to purchase arms from the United States, and that any merchantship calling at United States ports to collect such arms is entitled to protection by our warships while in United States waters.'

'Rubbish!' Ribbentrop screamed. 'The cash and carry scheme is a cheap trick by Roosevelt to help Britain and her Allies! He knows only too well that Germany does not have the merchantships to take advantage of the scheme. And what if we did, eh? Supposing we sent ships into New York to buy arms? Would the American navy defend our ships against the

Canadian navy? Would American warships fight Canadian warships? I think not.'

'I doubt if Britain and her Allies would think of the cash and carry scheme as a cheap trick,' Napier observed quietly, surprised how easily it had been to side-track the pompous Reich foreign minister from the central issue. 'They're paying a fair price in dollars and gold for all the armaments supplied by the United States.'

Ribbentrop snorted. 'By its total disregard of the laws of neutrality the United States is needlessly prolonging a futile war and adding to the misery and suffering! How can the Führer seek peace while America insists on feeding the flames? Destroyers! Tanks! Field guns! Bombs! Ammunition!' Ribbentrop seemed to realize that he was in danger of losing complete control. He sat abruptly and pressed a button on his intercom. 'It is obvious that Roosevelt, like the captain of the *Tulsar*, has scant respect for human life. Your government has another twenty-four hours in which to compose a reply to our note. Good day.'

Napier gave a slight bow. 'There will be no reply until we have heard the captain's version of what happened, minister.'

Napier left the Reich Foreign Office building at 10 am. As he climbed into the back seat of his car he reflected with some satisfaction that at least he hadn't left with his 'tail between his legs'.

# 4

Gerrard and Piet watched the approaching launch with well-founded anxiety; the *Tulsar* was fifty miles from Durban and it was unheard of for the pilot's vessel of any port to travel such a distance to meet an inward-bound ship.

'Piet,' said Gerrard slowly, keeping his binoculars trained on the fast-moving craft, 'have you ever known a British pilot's boat to fly a Stars and Stripes courtesy pennant?'

'No.'

'Nor have I.'

'Trouble, cap'n?'

'I guess. Something tells me that that guy sitting in the cockpit hasn't come out to wish us a merry Christmas.'

That guy turned out to be Ian Boult – the austere and humourless acting United States consul in Durban – a man with a profound dislike of the sea and an even deeper dislike of those sailors among his fellow countrymen whose exploits occasionally obliged him to venture out on it. He climbed awkwardly up the *Tulsar*'s Jacob's ladder and looked about him suspiciously while wrinkling his nose at the pervading smell of whalemeat. His temper and his lightweight tropical suit had not travelled well. He glared at Piet and Gerrard, introduced himself and demanded to be taken to Captain Gerrard.

'I'm Gerrard,' said Gerrard shortly.

Boult's gaze took in Gerrard's ragged denims and stained sweat-shirt. 'Is there somewhere we can talk in private, captain?'

'I saw the damage to your bow, Captain Gerrard,' Boult stated when he and Gerrard were alone. 'Therefore we can take it the German claims that you collided with one of their U-boats are correct?'

'Yep.' Gerrard was leaning back on the chair in his day-cabin with his feet on his desk and his hands thrust into his pockets.

'Were there survivors?'

'Nope.'

Boult tried not to show his irritation at the sailor's casual attitude. He produced a notebook and pencil. 'How did the accident happen, Captain Gerrard?'

'It didn't.'

Boult was puzzled. 'But you said –'

'It wasn't an accident,' said Gerrard. 'I rammed it deliberately.'

Boult's notebook nearly slipped from his fingers. He stared at Gerrard aghast. 'You what!'

Gerrard repeated his statement. The gaunt consul strived to contain his temper.

'Why, for God's sake?'

15

'I don't like German U-boats.'

Boult closed his notebook. This was one meeting that wasn't going to be recorded. He sat forward in his chair and regarded Gerrard with undisguised hostility. 'Listen, captain, it may have escaped your notice, but it just so happens that we're not at war with Germany.'

Gerrard gave a sudden smile. 'Don't blame me, Mr Boult – I'm doing my damnedest.'

Boult was not amused. 'Did you know that the U-boat got a radio message out before it went down saying that it had been deliberately attacked and that it named this ship?'

Gerrard shrugged. He felt in his sweat-shirt pocket for the frayed remains of a Havana and lit it.

'Did you also know that the government have issued a statement discounting the German claim as hysterical propaganda?'

Gerrard inhaled boredly on his cigar.

'Do you have to put into Durban?' Boult inquired.

'Well I sure as hell ain't going no place else the state my bow's in,' Gerrard observed.

'The place is crawling with journalists waiting to interview you.'

'So?'

'So you tell them it was an accident.'

'That wouldn't be truthful, Mr Boult.'

'Goddamn it – we're concerned with diplomacy – not truth!' Boult exploded. 'You'll brief your crew: you were chasing after whales and you didn't see the U-boat because it was half submerged! If you don't agree to that, Captain Gerrard, you will, in the crude parlance that you sailors indulge in, find yourself up shit creek. At the least, you'll lose your ticket; at the worst, the German government could kick your ass through the Massachusetts maritime courts and pin a bill on you for several million marks for the loss of their Goddamn U-boat.'

Gerrard gazed levelly at Boult through a haze of cigar smoke. The diplomat was virtually trembling with rage and clearly wasn't bluffing. It didn't take much imagination to visualize the flurry that the U-boat's signal had created in the Berlin and Washington dovecots.

'Okay,' Gerrard agreed after a face-saving pause.

Boult relaxed. 'How will you pay for the repairs to your ship?'

The question puzzled Gerrard. 'She's insured.'

'Like hell it is,' Boult growled. 'The New Bedford Whaling Corporation are in trouble, captain – big trouble. It seems that their attempt to revive commercial whaling in the United States hasn't worked out. Hardly surprising if the skipper of their largest whaling-ship goes charging about sinking U-boats.'

The information Boult had was sketchy but he was able to tell Gerrard that the NBWC was in the process of being wound up. The news confirmed Gerrard's suspicions and accounted for the cryptic replies he had recently received from the owners in response to his radioed progress reports.

'Cheer up, captain,' said Boult five minutes later as he steadied himself on the Jacob's ladder. 'She's a fine, modern ship. Your owners won't have trouble finding a buyer. Whether or not they'd be prepared to keep you on as her captain is another matter.'

Gerrard watched the pilot's boat draw away from the *Tulsar*. He flipped the cigar butt into water and muttered one, heartfelt word to express his feelings. But he had no regrets for his action in destroying the U-boat. That was something that would never change.

# 5

Simon Gooding stared out of his office window at the haze-shrouded hills that separated Durban's Port Natal from the Indian Ocean before turning to Josephine.

'It's difficult, Miss Britten – very difficult.' He mopped his forehead with a spotted handkerchief. Thirty years in Durban and still he wasn't accustomed to the temper-sapping humidity. 'All shipping has to be convoyed from Cape Town, and the departure times of the convoys are kept secret. I could easily sell you a ticket and send you down to the Cape, but

17

you might have to wait anything up to three months for a United States bound ship, and even then there's no guarantee that you'd get a passage.'

The shipping agent loosened his tie. The slow-turning fan in the centre of the ceiling made no impression on the suffocating heat in the office. He wondered how the American girl managed to look so cool and composed. She was sitting on the edge of her chair and regarding Gooding with a half amused expression.

'My country isn't at war with Germany,' Josephine gently pointed out, well aware that the sarcastic edge in her voice was causing the shipping agent some embarrassment.

'Two US-registered ships have already been sunk on the Cape route, Miss Britten.' Gooding toyed with Josephine's passport to avoid having to meet her disturbing almond eyes and found those same eyes regarding him from her photograph. He snapped the passport shut and pushed it across his desk. A tug siren wailed across the harbour and the tentative quickening of the late afternoon breeze flooded the office with the thick, heavy scent of the sugar terminal. He shut his window; it was something to do while he thought of something to say. 'I'll make some inquiries among my contacts at the Cape, Miss Britten, but I can't make any promises.' He realized that his visitor wasn't listening – she was staring past his shoulder out of the window. Her eyes refocussed on him and she gave him an acid smile.

'A United States ship is just entering the harbour, Mr Gooding.'

The shipping agent spun round. Two tugs were nudging a whaling factory-ship across the harbour. There was no doubt about the new arrival's nationality: an enormous Stars and Stripes banner that extended down to the waterline was painted amidships on the side of the hull. The lower half of the ship's bow was a mass of torn and twisted plates.

'A male driver,' Josephine drily observed.

'It's the *Tulsar*,' said Gooding hastily.

Josephine smiled. 'If it's an American ship, am I wrong in thinking that it might eventually be sailing for America?'

Gooding mopped his brow again. 'It's a whaling-ship, Miss Britten – they never carry passengers.'

Josephine stood and pulled on her white gloves. 'Are you the owners' Durban agent, Mr Gooding?'

'Yes. But –'

'That's marvellous.' Josephine dropped her passport in her handbag and snapped it shut. 'You can make the arrangements.'

'You don't understand, Miss Britten. The *Tulsar*'s been involved in collision – she has to undergo repairs and –'

'Call me occasionally at the hotel to tell me how the repairs are progressing, Mr Gooding.' Josephine paused in the doorway and gave the hapless shipping agent a disarming smile 'It will save me having to pester you night and day with phone calls. A merry Christmas to you, Mr Gooding.'

The scent of her perfume lingered in the office and was more noticeable than the usual smell of sugar. Gooding opened his window and watched Josephine thread her way with a determined step through the throng of chattering Indian women crowded round the market stalls. He sighed wistfully and reflected that Josephine Britten was a very remarkable young woman.

# 6

Of all the intelligence organizations operating in Berlin towards the close of 1940 the Institute for Market Analysis occupying all six floors of a large, drab building on the Fasanenstrasse was the least prepossessing. Unlike the modern headquarters of RSHA VI Foreign Intelligence on Berkaerstrasse or the RSHA VIF Technical Group on Delbruckstrasse, there were no armed guards at attention either side of the main entrance and, more surprisingly, no blood-red Nazi party banner to relieve the dreary monotony of its bleak granite façade. The IMA was an anonymous organization that made up for its deliberate lack of grandeur with a quiet and deadly efficiency.

It had started operating ten years earlier as a study group

within the Reich Statistical Office issuing economic and military reports and forecasts based on information culled from the most abundant sources of intelligence in the world: newspapers, technical press reports and specialist journals. Under the direction of Professor Ernst Strick, lecturer in economics at Kiel University, it had grown steadily in size and influence and now had a team of two hundred researchers, translators and collators, a fourteen thousand volume library that was expanding each day, and an annual budget approaching one million Reich marks. If Strick's powerful agency was hated by its rival intelligence units it was at least held in high regard; time and again the IMA had demonstrated its ability to produce accurate, well-formulated forecasts and surveys. It had, for example, submitted reports to the OKW the previous February that detailed the level of arms, men and time that would be required to overrun the Low Countries. It had turned out to be an astonishingly accurate forecast.

Consequently, when Dr Strick was shown into the office of Walter Funk, the effeminate economics minister, he was confident that his latest report would be taken seriously.

'Dr Strick,' said Funk warmly, shaking his visitor's hand and indicating a chair. 'A rare pleasure. A drink? I have some excellent cognac.'

Strick sat and unfastened his briefcase. 'Thank you, no, Herr Minister.' It was eleven in the morning; the economics minister's passion for drink was equalled by his passion for men. Preferably young men. 'My secretary told you why I wished to see you?'

Funk poured himself a generous slug of brandy from an incredibly ugly cocktail cabinet. 'A matter of the utmost importance, doctor? An exaggeration surely?'

Strick placed his ten-page report before Funk and said calmly: 'This document is the result of a thousand hours' work by myself and my foreign economics monitoring unit. I personally have tested all the forecasts and found them conclusive. Provided we act swiftly now, Allied resistance will collapse by mid-February and the British will be forced to sue for peace by the end of February: the war against Britain and her empire will be over within the next eight weeks.'

For some seconds the only sound in the office was the slow tick of the bronze wall clock. Strick rested both arms on Funk's desk and leaned forward confidingly. 'As I'm sure your own intelligence agency has discovered, Herr Minister, this war will be won on the balance-sheet and not the battle-ground.'

Funk's minions had told him nothing of the sort but he had no intention of letting Strick know that. He gave a faint smile and said: 'I presume you're referring to the supposed drain on Britain's gold and dollar reserves as a result of their so-called cash and carry scheme with Roosevelt?'

'It's hardly a supposed drain, Minister,' said Strick politely. He had to be careful; Funk was one of the most powerful men in Germany and was vainly proud of his own over-staffed economic intelligence unit.

'It is if the British can get fifty destroyers out of the Americans in exchange for a vague promise to allow the US navy the use of Caribbean bases that it doesn't need,' Funk replied pointedly. 'Hardly a drain on Britain's gold and dollar reserves.'

'That was an isolated instance that Roosevelt dare not repeat,' said Strick. 'My information is that the Allies are having to pay in dollars or gold before they can take away a single round of ammunition. I have exact figures from the US Treasury. An isolationist official has revealed that the British Crown Agents are quietly selling off large tracts of Crown-owned land in New York and the mid-West. The sale of Courtaulds investments in the US is well known, of course.'

Funk looked at his watch. 'I don't wish to hurry you, doctor, but I have an appointment in ten minutes. If you could get to the point –'

'The point,' Strick cut in, 'is that Britain will have exhausted all her gold and dollar reserves by the end of this month, with the exception of her emergency reserve in South Africa. Britain's $4,500 million she had at the beginning of the war is now down to less than $600 million and most of that is earmarked for Canada to pay for supplies now being freighted across the US border to Montreal.'

Funk turned over the pages of the report and came to a column of figures which he studied intently for some seconds before pressing a key on his intercom and asking for the analysis figures on Britain's gold reserves to be sent in to him.

'It will be interesting to see how your figures compare with ours,' said Funk, giving his visitor a frosty smile.

There was a tap on the door. A secretary entered and placed a single typewritten sheet before Funk. He glanced at it and smiled. 'There appears to be a wide discrepancy, doctor,' he said when the secretary had withdrawn. 'You say Britain has $600 million dollars – we say nearer $1,000 million.'

Strick frowned. 'May I see please, Minister?'

Funk pushed the sheet of paper across his desk and gazed boredly up at the ceiling while mentally preparing a case to have Strick's budget slashed for the new financial year.

'Ah yes,' said Strick, unable to conceal the relief he felt. 'I've found the error. You've assumed that the French bullion that fell into American hands when the Vichy aircraft carrier *Béarn* fled to Martinique was credited to the British by the US Treasury. In fact that has not happened. We have established that the Americans intend holding the gold in trust for the French.'

Funk's gaze dropped from the ceiling to regard the slightly-built doctor. 'Then what is the true figure according to you?'

'That Britain will be absolutely broke by mid-April. The Lend-Lease bill that Roosevelt has laid before Congress is unlikely to become law before mid-June – and only then if Colonel Lindbergh's isolationist lobby does not manage to sway Congress against Roosevelt, as seems likely.'

Funk was no fool and could see immediately what Strick was driving at. He knew that Britain was conducting the war on a desperate hand to mouth basis. She had blood and steel in plenty but that was no good without the gold to pay for oil imports, food and munitions. Assuming that the Lend-Lease bill before Congress – enabling the president to hand over to the British all the arms they wanted without payment – became law, there would still be a period of two months in which Britain would be penniless. A few well-placed rumours in those neutral countries still trading with the British would be enough to exhaust her overseas credit. There would be a month when the Führer would be able to force the British to sue for peace. But Funk could see a snag.

22

'You mentioned the emergency gold reserves in South Africa,' he reminded.

Strick nodded emphatically. 'Allowing for a fifteen per cent increase in gold production at Johannesburg's Germiston refinery since the last figures were published in 1939, we have estimated that gold stocks in South Africa are in the region of $200 million. Strick paused. 'Four dollars each for every man, woman and child – that's all that's left of Great Britain's wealth. . . . Herr Reichminister – the British are defeated now as we sit here talking. Those figures prove it. But for Churchill to recognize that they are defeated it is absolutely imperative that we stop at nothing to ensure that the last of Britain's gold does not leave South Africa.'

# 7

Gooding brought his fly-swat smartly down on his desk in the South African shipping agency and scraped the remains of the insect into his wastepaper basket. The diversion gave him time to think. He had learned from previous visits by the *Tulsar* that Gerrard required careful handling; the tough, leathery-skinned American had a mercurial temper that could erupt without warning when things were not going his way.

'Well?' Gerrard demanded.

Gooding fingered the marine architect's report on the damage to the *Tulsar's* bow. 'It's not an unreasonable estimate, captain.'

'Like hell it is.'

'It includes the hire of the floating crane to lift the bow clear of the water while repairs are carried out,' Gooding pointed out. 'Look at the welding and riveting involved – the entire bow has to be rebuilt from forefoot to waterline.'

'Six thousand dollars,' Gerrard muttered. 'Jesus Christ.' He brooded for a moment. 'Have you worked out how much I need to get the *Tulsar* home?'

Gooding had the information in front of him. 'You'll

23

need four and a half thousand dollars to cover a skeleton crew's pay, bunkering, victualling, freshwater and harbour dues.'

There was a brief silence apart from the hum of the fan. Gooding mopped his face with a handkerchief.

'Harbour dues,' Gerrard muttered 'Jesus Christ – I sink a U-boat and the ungrateful bastards hit me with harbour dues.'

'I'll have a word with the port captain,' Gooding promised. 'Maybe we can get a waiver.'

'Listen, Gooding, cable the owners again and tell them straight – if they want the *Tulsar* back in New Bedford then they've got to wire the money.'

The shipping agent shook his head. 'There's no money to wire, captain. The creditors want to get their hands on the *Tulsar* but none of them are prepared to put up the money.'

Gerrard ran his fingers through his unruly mop of hair. 'Jesus Christ – what a fucking mess.'

'We could try the United States consul,' Gooding suggested. 'A loan from their contingency fund.'

'Not a chance – I'd sooner take the *Tulsar* out and scuttle her.'

'So we have an impasse. Unless ...' Gooding smiled and left the sentence unfinished.

Gerrard gave Gooding a sharp look. 'Unless what?'

'I don't think you'd be interested.'

'If you have an idea, then for Chrissake let's hear it.'

It was the capitulation that Gooding had been waiting for but a tactful opening was called for. 'If you sail home with a skeleton crew, you'll have about twenty empty process workers' cabins.'

'Yeah – I guess.' Gerrard's tone was pregnant with suspicion.

'There are American citizens scattered all over South Africa who want passages home. There are hardly any passenger services operating, and the US government won't take them out because they say their citizens are safer here than on the high seas.'

Gerrard stared at the shipping agent. 'The *Tulsar*? Carrying passengers? Jesus Christ – she's a whaling factory-ship!'

'She's modern,' said Gooding, talking quickly. 'She could

24

easily be cleaned out – smartened up. A US ship sailing with US passengers – the Board of Trade can't object provided your lifeboats are up to scratch, which they are. And there's something else: the longer the *Tulsar*'s hanging about here, the greater the chance that the authorities might take it into their heads to commandeer it.'

Gerrard opened his mouth and shut it. 'Well ... I guess it's an idea,' he grudgingly admitted after a moment's thought. 'How many passengers could we carry and how much could we charge them?'

Gooding made a note on his pad. 'I'll contact Hutchins at Cape Town. He's got about twenty Americans waiting to go home and there's one I know of right here in Durban. Allowing for two cooks, three stewards and a purser, I'd say that a thousand dollars per head would be a reasonable fare to New York.'

Gerrard stared at Gooding and shook his head slowly. 'Jesus Christ,' he muttered. 'Passengers!'

# 8

'You asked to see me, Mr Thorne?'

The manager of the Benjamin D'Urban Hotel half rose from his desk and gestured to a chair. 'Come in, Miss Britten. Please take a seat.'

Josephine perched on the edge of the chair and regarded Thorne with an icy expression. She had guessed the reason for the summons to his office.

'We were sorry not to see you at the guests' new year's eve party last night, Miss Britten.'

'I was very tired. 'I've been working double duties for a week.'

Thorne nodded sympathetically. 'Yes, of course. Actually, that wasn't the reason why I called you in. I was glancing through the telephone log-book this morning and I noticed that you've been making a considerable number of long distance personal calls during the past –' He never completed the sentence because Josephine jumped to her feet, her eyes blazing with unbridled anger.

'I've entered every call on my time sheet, Mr Thorne. You can check; I haven't been cheating you and don't you say I have.'

Thorne held up a consoling hand. 'Please, Miss Britten – you're the last person in the world I would ever dream of accusing of cheating the hotel. It's not that at all.'

Josephine remained standing, staring down at the hotel manager with open hostility. 'What then?'

Thorne gave an embarrassed smile and opened a ledger. 'Calls to East London, Cape Town, Port Elizabeth. I thought you were trying to find another job until I discovered all these numbers are for shipping and travel agents.' He closed the ledger. 'Why do you want to go home? And don't say it's none of my business, because I think it is if I stand to lose the best receptionist this hotel has ever known.'

'I've been here long enough for you to realize that I'm immune to flattery,' said Josephine coldly.

Thorne nodded, 'I know that only too well. I was merely stating a fact – we'd be sorry to lose you. If it's a question of more money...'

'It's not that.'

'No. I didn't think it was.' Thorne hesitated and said encouragingly: 'There's a stupid saying – you must've heard it – a trouble shared is a trouble halved.'

Josephine met Thorne's eyes. The hotel manager appeared to be genuinely concerned. But then she had known men before who had pretended to be worried about her. It meant nothing. Perhaps Thorne was concerned. To his credit he had never made a pass at her. She sat down and watched the hotel manager carefully to gauge the effect of her words.

'Two weeks ago I received a cable from my mother telling me that my father had been taken ill. Last week she wrote to me saying that the specialists have categorically stated that he has less than six months to live. Mid-June at the latest.' Josephine stopped abruptly and toyed self-consciously with her handbag strap. 'I've not been able to find a ship sailing home. What few ships there are are fully booked until August.

26

I've tried everywhere – even Lorenzo Marques. There's nothing ... nothing ...'

Thorne suddenly realized that Josephine was on the verge of tears. He was embarrassed – certain that to offer comfort involving physical contact, such as putting an arm round her shoulders, would be vehemently rejected. The American girl solved this dilemma by moving quickly to the door and pulling it open.

'You're right, Mr Thorne,' she said, not looking at him. 'It is a stupid saying. Damned stupid.'

# 9

Kurt Milland guessed the impending disaster when he saw that the small, training U-boat was running on its diesel engines instead of its electric motors. His warning shout was too late; there was a sickening crunch as the U-boat's bows ploughed into the massive timber pile that was designed to protect the stone jetty at Wilhelmshaven from such assaults. The timber was ripped from its mountings by the force of the impact and was brutally rolled between the U-boat's buckling outer hull and the unyielding granite of the jetty. Rivets chewed deep into the waterlogged outer layers of the pile, exposing the pale elm flesh below. The two men who had been standing on the U-boat's forward deck casing ready to heave a line to Milland jumped back in alarm and waved frantically to the men on the bridge. A group of children, well wrapped against the bitterly cold wind sweeping in across the North Sea, gave a lusty cheer of approval and were immediately silenced by Milland's withering glare as he took a threatening step towards them.

The U-boat came to rest with its battered bow gently nudging the stone steps. Milland caught the line thrown to him and dropped a clove-hitch over one of the stubby mooring bollards before stumping along the quay until he was level with the U-boat's conning-tower. The young officer on the bridge goggled at Milland in white-faced terror and followed his pointed gaze to the offending bow.

'Excellent, Herr Fischer. Excellent. If I were the enemy I'd be sinking now, would I not?'

Leutnant zur See Hans Fischer nodded miserably.

'But I'm not the enemy, am I?'

'No, Herr Kapitänleutnant.'

'I'm a friend, aren't I?'

'Yes, Herr Kapitänleutnant.'

'We shall have another discussion about what I am and what I think you are in my office at fifteen hundred hours.' Milland glanced at his watch. 'In three hours. It will be in addition to a general chat on our chances of winning the war if you partake in it.'

Milland swung his artificial leg round by pivoting his body on his sound left leg, and stumped away from the quay with a curious, rolling gait that gave him the appearance of being slightly drunk. He climbed behind the wheel of his elderly DKW and watched the trainee crew making the damaged U-boat secure in response to Fischer's orders.

A two-week-old copy of the daily newspaper the *Völkische Beobachter* was lying on the passenger seat beside him. He pulled off his mittens and reread the main story that had led to him keeping the newspaper for so long. It was beneath a banner headline:

US TREACHERY IN INDIAN OCEAN. AMERICAN SHIP RAMS U-BOAT.

Milland pushed the newspaper to one side and stared through the windscreen at the grey, windswept North Sea. His thoughts were with the forty men who had perished ten thousand kilometres from home and the man who had killed them. There was no doubt that the rest of the story would emerge in time. It was time to stop dithering and go straight to the Flotilla Commander.

Konteradmiral Hugo Staus, commanding officer of the 2nd U-boat Training Flotilla (Wilhelmshaven), was a gaunt, somewhat forbidding Prussian in his late fifties who had com-

28

manded a U-boat with distinction during the Great War. He was sitting at his desk signing defect reports when he heard the familiar squeak of Milland's artificial leg in the corridor outside his office. There was a firm rap on the door. Staus called out for Milland to enter and laid down his gold fountain pen, for he considered it the height of rudeness to continue writing when a visitor entered his office. He noticed that Milland was carrying a copy of the party newspaper.

'Good afternoon, Kurt,' said Staus. 'I hear that you've just had a little mishap with one of my precious Type II's?'

'Nothing serious, admiral,' said Milland, not for the first time marvelling at Staus' reliable intelligence – the crusty old bastard had his spies everywhere. 'One of my fledglings forgot that there's no reversing gearbox on a U-boat's diesel engines. The damage isn't too bad. I think a verbal reprimand will be enough unless you say otherwise.'

Staus nodded. The stocky officer standing before him was one of his best instructors and he had no intention of interfering in the way he ran things. Nor did Admiral Staus offer Milland a chair because he knew it would be politely refused. Milland was both courageous and stubborn. He made no concessions to the fact that he had an artificial leg and would allow no one else to make concessions for him. He knew that he would never be given his own command and yet he had thrown all his energies into the training of youngsters for their commands. Kurt Milland lived for U-boats to the exclusion of all else. Nor was he interested in women, although Staus knew from gossip that circulated around the headquarters building as freely as its draughts that there were a number of secretaries who found Milland attractive despite his disability.

'So what brings you to see me, Kurt?'

Milland unfolded the newspaper and gave it to Staus. 'It's about that story two weeks ago, admiral, when an American ship rammed and sank *U-497* in the Indian Ocean.'

'Yes indeed. A disgraceful incident. As I recall, the Americans claimed that it was an accident?'

'I don't think it was an accident, admiral.'

Staus raised his aristocratic eyebrows. 'Really?'

'I know the captain of the ship that sank the U-boat and I know why he did it.'

29

Staus' expression hardened. He looked down at the newspaper. 'You mean that you know this ... Robert Gerrard?'
'Yes, admiral.'
Staus thought for a moment and nodded to a chair. 'I think you ought to sit down, Kurt.'
Milland gratefully lowered himself into a chair and released the knee lock on his artificial leg so that he could bend the joint and sit without the leg thrust out. Staus waited patiently while Milland marshalled his thoughts.

'I used to be Gerrard's first officer on the *Tulsar* – that's the ship that sank the U-boat; I signed on with him at Spitzbergen after quitting a Norwegian whaler – the *Kraken* – in 1933.' A warm light entered Milland's eyes as he recalled his whaling days. 'She was brand, spanking new, admiral. The most modern factory-ship afloat and she still is. Parsons turbines, her own high-speed catchers, a spotter seaplane – everything. She was completely self-contained, a new concept in whaling.'

'Who does she belong to?' Staus prodded when Milland broke off and groped for words.

'The New Bedford Whaling Corporation. They were a Detroit consortium who wanted a guaranteed supply of sperm oil for car automatic transmissions that they were about to go in for in a big way. They financed the *Tulsar* because the American whaling industry was virtually finished and they didn't want to rely on Japanese supplies.'

'It was a success?'

Suddenly the warmth was no longer in Milland's voice. 'Gerrard was the sort of man to make sure it was a success.' He lapsed into silence. Staus noticed that Milland's hand had dropped to his right leg and seemed to be unconsciously tracing the outline of where Staus guessed Milland's stump was.

'Tell me about him,' the older man prompted.

'Nothing else mattered to him but catching sperm. Twenty – thirty – sometimes even forty a day if the hunting was good. He'd drive men to the point of suicide to fill the *Tulsar*'s tanks. If a flenser was careless and got cut badly when splicing up a carcass, then that was too bad. Flensing-knife cuts always turn septic but we never turned back to port.'

'But you carried a doctor?'

30

Milland gave a mirthless smile. 'We were supposed to. But Gerrard said that they did nothing but sit around earning other men's bonuses. Gerrard was the *Tulsar*'s doctor. No one ever complained because your bonuses were three times what they were on any other ship.'

Milland's knuckles were now white from where his fingers were digging into his thigh. He seemed to be forcing himself to speak; the memories were no longer sweet.

'I was with him for four years,' Milland continued. 'I returned to Germany in 1936 and joined the navy.'

Staus recollected Milland's medical card. The naval doctors at Kiel had passed Milland as 'one hundred per cent fit and one hundred per cent disabled'. His acceptance into the navy was the result of a tenacious battle by Milland with the officer selection board until, impressed by his courage and indomitable spirit, they had finally relented.

'He hardly ever wrote,' said Milland. 'Once in 1938 to tell me he was marrying a New Bedford girl. He sent me a wedding photograph. Then there was another letter that came on the day England declared war on us. It was postmarked Liverpool. He said that Cathy was going to have a baby and that he was sending her home via Montreal on the *Athenia*.'

The silence in the room was total.

'Cathy Gerrard was one of the twenty-eight Americans killed when *U-30* sank the *Athenia*,' said Milland. 'That's why I think Gerrard deliberately rammed that U-boat in the Indian Ocean.'

Staus remained deep in thought for some minutes after Milland had stumped out of his office, then he summoned a secretary and dictated a full report on the matter to the OKM – the naval high command in Berlin.

He imagined that his account would cause a brief stir in the higher echelons of the Kriegsmarine and then be forgotten. For once his normally sound judgement was seriously at fault.

# 10

Gooding disentangled himself from the hotel's revolving door and crossed the mosaic floor to the reception desk where Josephine was making up the bill for an elderly couple from Ladysmith. She smilingly bid the couple goodbye and signalled to a porter to help them with their luggage before turning to Gooding and treating him to a modified version of her smile that was normally reserved for the hotel's guests.

'Good morning, Mr Gooding.'

'Air-conditioning,' said the shipping agent enviously. 'What it is to be in a place with air-conditioning.'

'It always gives trouble in mid-February when the holiday season is in full swing. Did you really come here to admire our air-conditioning or do you wish to make a reservation?'

'Neither,' said Gooding, wondering if Josephine used her talent for making one feel uncomfortable on the guests. 'You remember that United States ship that entered the harbour while you were in my office the other day?'

A look of interest flickered briefly in Josephine's eyes. 'The *Tulsar* – yes – I remember.'

'She'll be sailing for New York just as soon as we can get her bow repaired and she'll be taking up to twenty passengers.'

Josephine regarded Gooding expressionlessly. 'That's very good news, Mr Gooding.'

'I thought you'd be interested.'

'I am. How long will it take to get the bow repaired?'

'We're not sure. The Dock Priorities Committee are insisting that repairs to Allied shipping come first.'

'It's important that I'm home before the end of May at the latest – much earlier if possible.'

Gooding chuckled. 'I think we can say that the *Tulsar* will be in New York long before then.'

The vagueness irritated Josephine. It offended those qualities of preciseness and efficiency that made her such a valued hotel receptionist. 'Can't you be more exact, please?'

'The only thing I can be exact about is the cost of the passage.'

'Which is?'

'Three hundred and ten pounds.'

Josephine's aloof composure deserted her. She stared at Gooding first in dismay and then in anger. 'But that's crazy – that's over a thousand dollars!'

'There's a war on, Miss Britten,' was Gooding's smooth reply. 'Things are different now. Oil, food, pay – everything's gone up.'

'Not that much they haven't. In two years working here I've had raises amounting to no more than one pound fifteen shillings a week.'

'Look, Miss Britten – we advertised for the first time yesterday in the morning papers and by ten this morning we'd sold nineteen of the twenty passages. We've one single cabin left so three hundred quid can't be that bad. I came to pick up my car from the garage and I thought I'd drop in to see if you were still interested in going home.' Gooding moved away from the reception desk. 'I'm sorry I wasted your time.'

'I *am* interested,' said Josephine sharply, resenting being forced to capitulate so quickly.

Gooding took a notebook from his pocket and scribbled briefly. 'Thank you, Miss Britten. I shall require your fare within forty-eight hours.'

'The full amount?'

'The full amount,' Gooding affirmed.

'But I haven't got three hundred in the bank,' Josephine snapped. 'Isn't it normal to pay a deposit first?'

'In peacetime it is,' Gooding replied, glancing in his notebook. The money he had collected so far was enough to buy steel plate for the repairs to the *Tulsar*'s bow but not enough to enable the shipwrights to start work. 'I'll keep the cabin in your name until the end of next week. If you can't pay by then I'm afraid that I'll have to let it go.'

He snapped the notebook shut and walked out of the hotel lobby without looking back at Josephine.

## 11

The landing area in Table Bay, marked by two lines of orange buoys, was clear of floating débris. The harbour boat that had carried out the inspection moved clear of the lane and fired a green signal flare into the cloudless blue sky.

As the huge, four-engine Empire flying-boat banked and began losing height, Ralph Holden had his first glimpse of the breathtaking splendour of Table Mountain rising like a mighty black bulwark out of the South Atlantic and dwarfing the sprawling lion shape of Signal Hill. There was a layer of perfectly white cloud spread over the top of the mountain like icing and spilling over the edge of the great escarpment like a vast avalanche that threatened Cape Town and yet failed to reach its target because the cloud was dissolved by the lower layers of warm air defending the city.

'The mountain's got a tablecloth on it today,' observed a cultured voice at Holden's side. It was the elderly admiral. He was peering out of Holden's window. 'Going to seem dashed odd being pitchforked into midsummer in a matter of a couple of days. Never have got used to it.'

Holden gave the sailor his customary charming smile and said nothing. He was well aware that his presence aboard the flying-boat had been the subject of endless speculation among the other fifteen passenger during the three-day flight from Falmouth in Cornwall. Their attempts to engage the fair-haired young man in conversation in the hope of learning something about him had been thwarted by his ability to side-track questions disarmingly and replace them with questions of his own, skilfully put, so that he had ended up knowing more about his inquisitors than they about him. After the first day of the flight they had learned to leave him alone. Most of the time he sat quietly in his seat nursing a leather, GVIR-crested briefcase that was handcuffed to his wrist.

The water became a blur beneath the flying-boat as its hull lost height. Then there was a tremendous bump followed by a deafening roar beneath the passengers' feet. After six refuelling stops since leaving Falmouth they were used to the unnerving business of a flying-boat's landing and few even bothered to look at the spectacular curtains of spray thrown up on each side of the hull. Even the ghastly sinking sensation when the flying-boat stopped planing and dug its wing-floats into the water no longer caused concern.

'Smooth landing' the admiral commented, eyeing the steel chain that linked Holden's wrist to the briefcase and wondering if Holden was one of His Majesty's couriers.

'Very smooth, sir,' Holden agreed.

The admiral grunted. At least the wretched fellow was polite, which was something these days.

Holden looked out of his window. The flying-boat was taxiing to meet the harbour patrol boat that would tow it to the safety of the inner basin.

'Mr Holden?'

A tall, distinguished-looking man in his late fifties approached Holden the moment he emerged from the passenger terminal and stood blinking in the bright sunlight. The porter, still smarting from Holden's refusal to allow him to take the briefcase, appeared to know the tall man for in response to a nod he carried Holden's suitcase to a waiting Rover and placed it in the car's boot. Holden realized that the Cape Coloured porter who had accosted him in the terminal was in fact the car's driver. Holden disliked other people taking the initiative; there was little warmth in his handshake.

'Plum,' said the tall man breezily, oblivious of Holden's coolness. 'Sir Max Plum. I expect your people gave you a photograph of me before you left. Prepared you for the worst.' He gave a booming laugh and steered Holden to the rear door of the car that the porter was holding open.

'Good flight was it?' Plum inquired, settling himself beside Holden in the back seat as the Rover drove through the dock gates and into Cape Town's waterfront sprawl of warehouses and seafood stalls surrounded by shouting women of every conceivable nationality.

'Very pleasant,' Holden murmured.

'No point in going to the bank. You must be pretty tired so I thought we'd go straight home. Mary will rustle up

35

something to eat.' Plum looked quizzically at his visitor. 'Is that okay with you?'

'Certainly – provided I can get down to work right away.'

Sir Max Plum, president of the Reserve Bank, gave a faint smile. A permanent under-secretary at the Treasury in London had tipped him off about Holden: 'Fellow's a glutton for work. For God's sake don't get in his way.'

The car sped through the Malay quarter and headed south-west into the pleasant Tuine Gardens suburb with white-washed bungalows overlooking terraced gardens with neat, Protea-filled flowerbeds.

Gradually the smaller bungalows abandoned the climb up Table Mountain's lower slopes and handed over the struggle to larger, more imposing residences.

Plum's house was a spacious, timber-framed chalet with a broad stoep – a veranda – overlooking Table Bay. The pincer-like arms of Cape Town's artificial harbour reaching out into the Atlantic resembled a series of taut silken threads laid on a flawless sheet of blue glass.

'Some view, what?' said Plum with a proud wave of his hand.

Plum's wife, an erect, greying woman, came down the steps of the stoep to greet Holden. She was a little surprised by his smart, lightweight tropical suit; visitors from England on the flying-boat usually turned up in heavy, unsuitable clothing. Obviously the fair-haired young man with the disturbing blue eyes was a careful planner.

'Mr Holden – how nice to meet you. Your room's ready and I'm sure you must be dying for a bath and a change. I know that you and Max have a lot of business to talk over, but I'd love to hear about London when you've got the time. It must be absolutely frightful with all that bombing. Some tea in thirty minutes.'

She bustled away to harangue hidden servants lurking in the depths of the house.

'How much does your wife know?' Holden asked the bank president two hours later. The two men were sitting on the stoep.

Plum put down his whisky glass and stared at Holden in

surprise. 'Nothing, of course. Only three people in South Africa know the reason for your visit: you and me, and Villiers at the Reserve Bank in Pretoria – he has to know because he has to authorize the release of the gold.'

Holden nodded and sipped his orange juice, then set his glass down on the table. 'You're aware that the gold has to be shipped immediately?' His tone was deceptively mild.

'Are things so bad?'

'If we don't get that gold to London within the next four months, the war will be as good as over for us.'

'The naval intelligence office in Simonstown have scoured every port in South Africa,' said Plum irritably. 'Everything that can float and move has been sent to Liverpool. There isn't a ship in South Africa capable of twelve knots, never mind twenty-five. Why the devil does it have to be so fast?'

'Our experiences so far with the *Queen Mary* and *Queen Elizabeth* have shown that a fast, unescorted ship can avoid U-boats and surface raiders.'

'Then send one of the *Queens* here to pick up the gold, damn it,' Plum muttered.

Holden nodded to the distant harbour. 'You can't move a ship in or out of Cape Town without the whole of South Africa knowing about it. The same applies to every other port. It only needs one of our pro-German Boer friends in the Ossewa-Brandwag to squawk on his radio-transmitter that one of the *Queens* has turned up here and we'd have every U-boat that Doenitz can muster lying in wait off Cape Town.'

'Smuts has had all the Ossewa-Brandwag fanatics interned,' Plum pointed out.

'The director of naval intelligence in London thinks otherwise,' said Holden. 'He's convinced that Ossewa agents are still helping surface raiders – possibly transmitting shipping movements to U-boats who relay them to Berlin. Only last month an American ship accidentally rammed and sank a U-boat off Durban. So what was the U-boat doing there if it wasn't relaying intelligence? There hadn't been reports of incidents between merchantships and U-boats.'

Plum remained silent. Holden had been well briefed.

'If we sent a warship to Cape Town or Simonstown,' Holden

continued, 'the Germans, knowing that all warships are desperately needed on the North Atlantic convoys, would guess what it's for and throw everything they've got at it.'

'Not if the gold was moved under the cover of a Cape convoy,' Plum pointed out.

Holden shook his head. 'We can't risk shifting the last of our gold a quarter of the way round the world in a convoy. We need a ship that is both fast and nondescript.'

'Well there isn't one.' Plum felt in his pocket and produced a sheaf of papers which he handed to Holden. 'That's a list of every ship lying in South African ports. There's nothing that fits the bill.'

Holden studied the list intently, slowly turning the pages as he finished scanning the columns that listed names, class of vessel, tonnage and performance, and where lying. He came to the last page.

'They're no good,' said Plum shortly. 'That's the appendix – ships belonging to neutral countries that are awaiting repairs.'

Holden's quick eye spotted a figure – twenty-six knots. 'There's a whaling factory-ship here that's more than fast enough,' he observed. 'Lying at Durban.'

Plum peered at where Holden's finger was pointing. 'But she's no use – she's American owned and registered.'

'So?'

Plum stared hard at his fair-haired visitor who was regarding him with an amused half-smile. 'Damn it, man!' he protested. 'We can't move the last of our gold on an American!'

'Why not?'

'Because it's unheard of, that's why not!'

'Which sounds like an extremely good reason for doing it,' Holden murmured. 'The *Tulsar*.' He frowned. 'The name sounds familiar.'

'She was the American that collided with the U-boat off Durban,' Plum replied stiffly.

Holden unhurriedly drained his orange juice and stood. 'I shall require a seat on the first flight to Durban, Sir Max. I'd be grateful if you would kindly make the necessary arrangements and book me into an hotel there.'

'Now?'

Holden smiled. 'I think so. It never ceases to amaze me just how quickly the present can become the past.'

# 12

A room key dropped without warning on the desk. Josephine quickly looked up and smiled at the Englishman – not flinching from the dispassionate blue eyes.

'Hallo, Mr Holden. Is your room okay?'

'I expect it will be adequate,' Holden replied. 'I shall be gone for a little over an hour. I've left two shirts on my bed. I'd be grateful if they could be washed and ironed please.'

Josephine promised that they would be ready the following day and watched the Englishman move across the lobby to the revolving doors. He moved silently, with cat-like grace. The discreet steel chain that she had noticed an hour before when he had first checked in was still in place, linking his briefcase to his wrist.

A girl entered the lobby through the revolving doors as Holden went out. She gaped after the departing figure for a moment before crossing to the reception desk.

'Wow,' she breathed. 'Who's that?'

Josephine stood and reached for her white gloves. 'A new guest,' she said coldly.

'He looks like Leslie Howard. Did he bring a wife?'

'You're three minutes late, Jenny,' said Josephine tartly. 'I made it clear that I had an important appointment.'

The Zulu looked old enough to have fought in one of Cetshwayo's *impis* at the Battle of Rorke's Drift. His magnificent ostrich feather head-dress almost fell off as he gathered up the shafts of his gaudily painted ricksha. He gave Holden a broad grin.

'Where to, baas?'

'The docks, please,' Holden replied. He settled in the cushions and repositioned the ricksha's straw sunshade.

The Zulu eased the ricksha out of the hotel forecourt and broke into an effortless, loping jog along the crowded seafront. Holden glanced back. Another ricksha was following a hundred yards behind. The passenger was the American girl from his hotel.

'Look, Mr Gooding,' said Josephine in what she hoped was a reasoning tone. 'I worked my passage from New York to Cape Town as a stewardess and I've worked as a receptionist in several large hotels since I arrived in South Africa, so I don't see what the problem is.'

Simon Gooding thoughtfully scratched his nose. 'Being a ship's purser isn't quite the same thing, Miss Britten.'

'It's not so very different from running a hotel,' Josephine retorted. 'And besides – most of the *Tulsar*'s passengers will be Americans – right?'

Gooding nodded.

'Okay then. It's going to seem pretty strange to them sailing on a whaling-ship – maybe they'd be glad to have a fellow American to turn to with their problems. Believe me, I know from running the Ben D'Urban Hotel that Americans seem to have more problems than most.'

'Why are you so keen to get home, Miss Britten?'

'That, Mr Gooding, if you'll forgive me for saying, is none of your damn business.'

The shipping agent thought for a moment and shrewdly said: 'Okay – I'll sign you on as the *Tulsar*'s purser for half the fare.'

'No,' said Josephine emphatically. 'That wouldn't be fair. If I'm worth employing as a purser, then I'm worth paying.'

Gooding conceded defeat. He knew from experience that a good purser was vital. 'Okay, Miss Britten. We'll pay you ten dollars a week as the *Tulsar*'s purser.'

'Twelve,' Josephine countered, 'and I'll look after the menus as well.'

'Twelve then,' Gooding agreed, wondering if his business might do better if he took Josephine on as a partner.

Holden stopped at the end of the quay to run his eye over every detail of the *Tulsar*. He knew little about ships but was

40

able to appreciate her fine lines. She was obviously of an advanced design and had represented a considerable act of faith by her now bankrupt owners in their chances of reviving New Bedford's whaling industry.

According to the specification that Holden had studied at length during the flight from Cape Town, the *Tulsar* had an overall length of 530 feet, a displacement of 7,000 tons, and her 27,000 shaft horsepower gave her a respectable top speed of twenty-six knots. The raised superstructure aft that housed the crew's quarters was divided by the canyon of the whale slipway that sloped down to the waterline at the stern. Forward of the crew's quarters was the open expanse of the flensing deck where the blubber was stripped from the whales. After that the carcasses were hauled under the seaplane platform to the lemming deck where the whalemeat was hacked from the creature's skeleton. At intervals around both decks were circular, hinged covers over the bone and blubber chutes. Immediately aft of the bridge were two high-speed whale-catcher launches slung from derricks. Mounted on the bow platform of each catcher was the ugly, business-like shape of a Svend Foyn explosive head harpoon-gun.

Holden moved to the crumpled bow and gazed at the damage. It seemed incredible that the ship could have sustained such a blow and remain afloat. He assumed that there was a watertight bulkhead in the bow. From what Holden had learned during the previous twenty-four hours about Captain Robert Gerrard, he wondered just how accidental the collision with the German U-boat had been.

He became aware that his presence on the quayside was attracting attention from the ship; a giant Afrikaner wearing a *Voortrekker* hat was watching him suspiciously from the top of the gangplank. Holden sauntered on, one hand thrust casually in his trouser pocket and the other holding the briefcase.

A shunting engine clanked across his path wearily pushing a long train of wagons loaded with beef. Through the intermittent gaps between each wagon and the next, Holden caught a glimpse of the hotel receptionist. She was near the administrative buildings but had vanished by the time the train had cleared from his field of view.

41

As far as Holden was concerned, the girl was following him, and it worried him.

When Holden was worried, he could be extremely dangerous.

Josephine returned to her room an hour after her successful visit to Simon Gooding and took a quick shower to cool off. She rarely ventured out of the hotel's air-conditioned interior on summer afternoons but the brief trip had been more than worth the effort.

She was half-way through a letter to her father when there was a tap on the bed-sitting-room door. It would be the page-boy with the cold drink she had asked him for.

'Come in.'

The door opened. Josephine turned to the door and immediately pulled her dressing-gown tightly closed – the fair-haired Englishman was standing on the threshold.

'Mr Holden,' said Josephine, quickly adopting the inane smile she reserved for hotel guests. 'You must've taken a wrong turning – you're in the staff quarters.'

Holden closed the door and leaned against it. He pushed his hands deep into his pockets and smiled lazily.

'I didn't take a wrong turning,' he said. 'I followed directions most carefully.'

It was a situation that Josephine had handled before, although this was the first time that a male guest had tracked her down to her room.

'Please, Mr Holden – I'll have to ask you to leave right now otherwise I could get into trouble and you could be thrown out of the hotel on your pink little ear.'

'We'd better keep our voices down then, Jo. Do you mind if I call you Jo or do you prefer Josephine?'

'Right now,' said Josephine, 'what I'd prefer is for you to beat it – or do I have to put it more crudely?'

Holden crossed his hands over his heart. 'I swear to go when you tell me what colour you're going to wear tonight.'

'Colour? Tonight? Just what the hell are you talking about?'

'We're dining together at the King Edward's Chart Room. I understand that it's the best restaurant in Durban.' Holden paused and added: 'I'm accustomed to the best.'

42

Josephine tried to pull the door open. 'So am I, Mr Holden – which is one reason why I won't be dining with you tonight. Another is that I'll be on duty.'

Holden's smile became a grin. 'No you won't, my lovely. The girl who's on duty at the moment has agreed to work some overtime.'

Josephine was confused. 'Joyce? Why should she do that?'

'She's susceptible to either my smile or my money' said Holden. 'Or both, maybe? Who knows?' He opened the door. 'I've hired a car for a few days, and I'll be ready at eight o'clock sharp. White would go well with your dark hair, I fancy.'

Josephine opened her mouth to protest vehemently at Holden's cavalier attitude but was too late.

Holden held his brandy glass up to the candle for a critical examination before tasting appreciatively. 'Brandy has suddenly become unaccountably scarce in London,' he commented.

'That's why you came to South Africa?' Josephine suggested.

'Can you think of a better reason?'

'What business are you in, Mr Holden?'

'Ralph,' Holden corrected. 'You have my permission to use my first name. Permission to use my second name is denied to everyone – even my mother. Have I told you about my mother? A remarkable woman.'

Josephine gave an acid smile. 'I suppose she taught you the art of dodging direct questions? Oh, please don't look surprised, Mr Holden – every time I've asked you a question about yourself, all I've received in reply is a compliment. You liked my dress during the soup; my hair during the fish; and my perfume during the main dish. It's fortunate that this isn't one of those twenty-course meals otherwise I might end up thinking I'm Jean Harlow.'

The eight-piece band finished their tuning up and proceeded to torment a Glen Miller slow number with an aplomb that tempted few couples to move on to the dance floor; the majority to remain seated.

'We shall dance,' Holden commanded, rising to his feet.

'Saved by the orchestra,' Josephine commented, also rising. 'And how could any girl refuse such a polite request?'

43

'My leg doesn't take kindly to being pulled,' Holden warned as he steered Josephine round the dance floor.

'And my foot doesn't take kindly to being trodden on.'

'Blame the band,' said Holden with cheerful arrogance.

The band standardized their music and improved rapidly. More couples crowded on to the tiny dance floor. To Josephine's relief Holden didn't take advantage of the waltz to press himself against her. Emboldened by their success, the band tackled a foxtrot. Josephine realized that Holden was an accomplished dancer, and, to her surprise, she made the unexpected discovery that she was actually enjoying herself.

'Why the smile?' Holden inquired.

'A friend of mine once said that there is no such thing as an Englishman who can dance.'

'Why did you leave home?' Holden asked abruptly.

It was a question that Josephine would have normally taken offence at, but the meal, the luxurious surroundings and the Englishman's not wholly unpleasant company had mellowed her defences. 'I wanted to see the world,' she replied. 'Does that sound corny?'

'Not unless you think it does. Did your parents mind?'

Josephine laughed. 'It was the second war of independence.'

'Which you won?'

'By default, I guess – I walked out.'

'Never to return?' Holden queried as he skilfully guided Josephine round a swaying couple who appeared more than a little drunk.

'That's what I said at the time,' said Josephine, avoiding the Englishman's eyes by gazing over his shoulder.

The band came to the end of their number. There was some desultory clapping. Holden led Josephine back to her table and poured her the last of the wine.

'Where was home?' Holden asked a minute later as they watched the couples.

'New York. Greenwich Village. My folks have a hardware store there.' Josephine regarded the Englishman thoughtfully. 'Why are you so interested in me, Mr Holden?'

Holden gave an easy laugh. 'You don't often find unattached American girls so far from home. How did you manage it?'

'By working, Mr Holden. By working hard. I joined a steamship company in New York, which was why I had the bust-up with my father – he didn't like his daughter working as a stewardess. That's what he said at the time.'

Holden was watching her carefully and noticed the sadness in her eyes at the mention of her father.

Josephine shrugged. 'I guess the truth was that he didn't like the idea of losing someone who was working for next to nothing in his run-down store.' She focussed her eyes on the glass of wine she was holding and wondered why she was telling everything to this stranger. It wasn't the wine. Wine was something she had learned to cope with, and she hadn't even approached the four-glass ceiling that she had decided on at the beginning of the evening.

'I was pretty good at running the hardware store, Mr Holden.'

'I'm sure you were, Josephine,' Holden murmured, sensing that the time was approaching when he would be able to manipulate the conversation round to the reason why he had taken Josephine out for the evening.

'While I did the buying, the store showed a profit. Not that that did much good because that meant more money for Pa to spend on liquor. I was worth more than Pa was prepared to pay me, so come 1936 when I turned twenty-one I took myself off to the General Navigation Steamship Company and got myself a job at four times what Pa was paying me. A year later I found myself in Durban and fell for the crazy Englishness of the place.'

'Even the docks?' said Holden casually.

Josephine stared at him. 'Hell, no. I never go near them unless I can help it.'

'A rough place for a woman,' Holden observed, his eyes fixed on Josephine.

'I can look after myself. What I can't stand is the stink of sugar. I was there today. It's getting worse.'

Holden was surprised by the unexpected admission. 'You went to the docks today?'

It was Josephine's turn to look surprised. 'Sure. I want to go home. I don't see what business it is of yours, Mr Holden, but I've fixed myself up with a working passage back to New

York.' She broke off and frowned at the Englishman. 'So what's so funny?'

Holden poured himself some more brandy. 'Forgive me, Josephine. I was smiling with relief. I too went to the docks today on business. In fact your ricksha followed me.'

'You thought *I* was following you?'

'At the time – yes.'

'Why should I do that, Mr Holden?'

Holden smiled disarmingly. 'My apologies, Jo – I jumped to the wrong conclusion.'

'My name is Josephine or Miss Britten. You haven't answered my question.'

Holden smiled disarmingly. 'My apologies, Jo – I jumped candour. 'To be honest, I thought you might be spying on me for my company's business rivals. So I thought I'd invite you out tonight in the hope that half a bottle of wine would make you confess. Instead I discover that you're looking for a passage.' He smiled ruefully. 'This evening's going to cost me a fortune. Serve me right.'

Josephine stared levelly at the impudent Englishman for some seconds before she allowed her icy expression to relax into a faint smile. 'I've enjoyed this evening, Mr Holden. It's the first time for a long time that I've been out with a man and not had to spend the entire evening fighting him off....'

'There's still time,' said Holden mischievously.

'... but there's something you ought to know,' Josephine continued, ignoring the interruption. 'One thing I've learnt since leaving home is not to expect favours, return them, or grant them.'

'Quite so, Jo,' Holden agreed.

'Just so long as we understand each other.'

Holden raised his glass. 'Let's drink to our understanding, Jo.'

# 13

'Telegram for you, sir,' said the pageboy, dropping the morning papers on the end of Holden's bed and holding out the buff envelope to the Englishman.

Holden pushed himself up on to his elbows and added a sixpence tip to his thanks. A sharp pain behind his eyes was a reminder that South African wine and brandy made unhappy companions.

'Breakfast in thirty minutes,' said the pageboy cheerfully before he left the bedroom.

Holden opened the telegram and spread it out on the coverlet. He removed a slim, black codebook from the briefcase that he kept under his pillow and proceeded to transcribe the meaningless jumble of code groups into plain text.

PURCHASING COMMISSION IN NEW YORK REPORT THAT TULSAR NOW ACQUIRED STOP   HAVE CONFIRMED THAT OWNERSHIP SECURED THROUGH USA HOLDING COMPANY THEREFORE TULSAR CAN REMAIN US REGISTERED SHIP AS INSTRUCTED STOP   VILLIERS AWAITING YOUR INSTRUCTIONS REGARDING SHIPMENT STOP   CONTACT YOU REQUESTED IS INSPECTOR HUGO MARGENT STOP   PRIVATE ADDRESS GOLF LINKS HOUSE MITCHELL ROAD DURBAN STOP   GOOD LUCK SEE YOU SOON LONDON STOP   LACY

Holden leaned back on the pillows. He was pleased with the information; Lacy was a colleague of his in London – an efficient but unimaginative civil servant who had dealt with everything and hadn't questioned why Holden should want the name of the officer in the Natal police who was responsible for tracking down members of the fanatical Ossewa-Brandwag. Even more important to Holden was that he now had absolute control of the *Tulsar*.

He composed a reply to London on the back of the telegram and encoded it.

THANKS FOR GOOD NEWS RE TULSAR STOP   URGENT YOU GET USA HOLDING COMPANY TO TELEGRAPH THEIR AGENT

HERE ADVISING HIM THAT I AM NOW ACTING FOR NEW
OWNERS STOP    AGENT IS SIMON GOODING STOP    TELE-
GRAPHIC ADDRESS GOODSHIP DURBAN STOP    HOLDEN

It would take at least six hours for Gooding to receive the
message from New York, Holden reasoned, therefore there
was little point in seeing him until the following morning.

The midday temperature edged over the hundred mark and
brought games of beach cricket to a standstill. There was little
movement among the holidaymakers on the crowded beach
and the only sounds were the thin cries of the sea's hemline
of children trying to encourage drowsy parents into the tepid
water.

Holden opened all four doors of his hired car to allow the
interior to cool and spread a street map of Durban out on
the burning roof.

'Mr Holden.'

It was Josephine. She came down the hotel's front steps and
approached the car. Holden folded the map and dropped it
on the car's front seat.

'Good afternoon, Jo. I'd be encouraged if you told me that
this is as hot as it ever gets here.'

Josephine glanced up at the clear January sky. 'It's the Goddamn humidity. New York can get like this. You should've
got the houseboys to put a mat over the car.'

'I'll remember in future,' Holden promised. He looked
expectantly at the American girl, waiting for her to speak.

'I enjoyed last night,' said Josephine awkwardly.

'Same here.'

'I vaguely remember talking about my plans to return
home.'

Holden felt in his pocket for his car keys. 'That's right, Jo.
To patch things up with your parents.'

'I don't normally talk about my plans with anyone, Mr
Holden. Perhaps it was the wine. I don't know. The trouble
is that the ship I'm returning home on isn't sailing for two
or three weeks. Perhaps even a month. In the meantime I still
need my job here, so I'd appreciate it if you told no one what
I told you.'

48

Holden slammed the car's passenger doors and sat behind the wheel. He ran his fingers through his fair hair and smiled up at Josephine. 'I usually stick to orange juice so the chances are that I might forget whatever it was you said. You're free tomorrow evening, so let's go for a swim and talk it over then. Okay?'

Holden started the engine and drove out of the hotel forecourt leaving Josephine smouldering with suppressed anger.

'I've heard of you, Mr Holden,' said Margent, folding the letter and returning it to his visitor. He was too much the experienced policeman to have missed Holden's slight start of surprise. He smiled and rested his chin on a set of knuckles that a prizefighter would have been proud of. 'Please don't worry. I know nothing of your business in South Africa – only that you've been given clearance to send and receive coded telegrams.'

Holden relaxed and sipped his orange juice. It was late afternoon but the midday heat still hovered persistently among the lengthening shadows of the acacia trees in Margent's garden. He set his glass down on the stinkwood table and came straight to the point:

'I want to know about the Ossewa-Brandwag.'

Margent absently drummed his powerful fingers while he considered his answer. 'Translated literally it means the "Ox Wagon Torch Watch" – a term which has little meaning to outsiders unless they understand the almost sacred esteem in which the ox wagon is held in Afrikaner folklore. To the *Voortrekker* families pushing up country into the unknown interior, the ox wagon was their home, their transport, their place of worship, and at night – when they inspanned their oxen and formed a laager – the ox wagon became their castle.' Margent paused to fill a briar pipe. 'Origins of the term Ossewa-Brandwag vary but the one I like was told to me by an old Boer when I was a lad. At night in the laager one small lamp would be kept burning by the night watch so that in the event of an attack the women would be able to light torches quickly and so provide light for them to see as they reloaded their menfolk's rifles.' Margent struck a match and lit his pipe. 'It's the story I prefer because it fits the concept of the

49

Ossewa-Brandwag story today – a torch kept burning by the night watch in readiness.'

'They're Nazis?' Holden queried.

'That's the label we give them for propaganda purposes. In reality they're a group of extremist Afrikaners who aren't necessarily pro-Hitler but totally opposed to South Africa being a British ally. To them it's a betrayal of everything that they and their parents fought for and died for during the Anglo-Boer War.' Margent examined the bowl of his pipe. 'I've arrested about twenty Ossewa-Brandwag kommandos so far – fellow countrymen whose parents, wives, children died in British concentration camps. Did you know that the British invented concentration camps and that sixty thousand men, women and children died in them?'

Holden countered the question with one of his own. 'How strong is the Ossewa-Brandwag now?'

Margent smiled. 'We've got about fifty in Internment Camp One at Koffiefontein.'

'In England they'd be hanged,' said Holden sourly.

Margent shook his head. 'Smuts has insisted on internment. He'll have to govern when the war is over and sees no point in providing the Nationalists with a load of ready-made martyrs. Anyway, the few we have interned so far seems to have deprived them of effective leadership – they were the really fanatical members of the *Broederbond*. Some of them were undoubtably Nazis.'

'Are there any big fish that you've not caught?'

'Not on my manor, there's not. They're mostly in the Cape Province. The Cape police operate differently – they prefer to keep the bastards under observation. They won't know what hit them if they start their blowing up power line stunts in Natal.'

'Who are they, inspector?'

'There must be hundreds of them.'

'The big ones – the organizers.'

Margent looked curiously at his visitor. 'Why is it so important, Mr Holden?'

Holden gave a slow smile. 'I'll be signing on a crew within the next few days to take a ship to England. And it's vital – absolutely vital – that we don't find ourselves turning an Ossewa-Brandwag fish over to the fifth columnists in England.'

Margent sucked on his pipe for a moment. 'There are two that I know of. One is a Port Elizabeth lawyer named John Voster. Son of a Karoo sheepfarmer in the north-eastern Cape. He went to Stellenbosch University, which is an absolute hotbed of Nationalism. He was the registrar to the Judge President of the Cape and before that chairman of the student branch of the Stellenbosch Nationalist Party. Right now he's a "general" in the Ossewa but I'd say his ambitions are more political than military. If the Nationalists should ever grab power in South Africa, then Balthazar Johannes Voster is the sort of man to climb to the top of the antheap. It's certain that the internment order against him will be signed before 1941 is out.'

'And the other one?' Holden prompted.

'Paulus Jan Kramer. A killer, and the most dangerous man not behind wire in South Africa today. He's German by birth. His parents were Prussians who settled in what was German South-West Africa before the League of Nations mandate took the colony away from Germany. In 1933, fired by the appointment of his hero Hitler as chancellor, he tried to organize a number of settlers into an armed uprising. He received a ten-year jail sentence at Windhoek but served less than two years and scooted off to Germany for a year once he was freed. We don't know what he did there but as soon as he turned up in Cape Town he started printing an anti-semitic newspaper that folded after its first edition. In 1938 he was accused of murdering a Jewish girl at Bantry Bay just outside Cape Town but the case was never proved. Now he owns a restaurant in Cape Town and has the outward appearance of being a respectable businessman. My guess is that he spent his year in Germany learning how to handle explosives, how to use a knife, a radio-transmitter, and so on.'

'Can you let me have the addresses of these two?'

'John Voster is in the Port Elizabeth phone-book, and Paulus Kramer is in the Cape Town book. You pay your money and you take your choice.'

Holden left Inspector Margent an hour later. He sat back in the car and considered the two names the policeman had given him. There was no hard evidence to suggest that the politically ambitious John Voster was a Nazi, but there was no doubt that Paulus Jan Kramer most certainly was.

His choice was Kramer.

# 14

Robert Gerrard leaned on the bridge rail and moodily watched the first sperm whales of the season being hauled up the whale slipway on the far side of Durban's harbour.

'I'll tell you something, Mr Gooding,' he said to the perspiring agent. 'As I see it, new owners means that they'll want this ship at sea working. And if they want it working – they'll have to pay to have her repaired. And if they can't afford to have it repaired then why the hell did they buy it in the first place?'

Gooding wiped his forehead. It was nine o'clock and already the cool of the morning was in retreat. He unfolded the telegram that had arrived from New York an hour earlier and read it through for the tenth time. 'I don't understand it,' he muttered. 'I just don't understand it.'

Gerrard took the telegram from him. 'So who's this guy Holden?'

'How the hell should I know, for God's sake?'

'Captain!' a voice bellowed from the flensing deck. It was Piet; he was gesturing to the gangplank. 'Guy here to see you, captain! The one who was nosing around yesterday!'

Gerrard told the Afrikaner to show the visitor up.

'Well now,' breathed Gerrard, watching Holden wearing a crisp white suit and holding a briefcase pick his way carefully along the lemming deck in Piet's footsteps. 'What in the world is that?'

'I have a suspicion that *that* is our Mr Holden,' said Gooding.

Holden dismissed Piet with a wave and raced nimbly up the companion-way two steps at a time.

Gerrard guessed that he was English before he spoke.

'Good morning, gentlemen,' said Holden, giving Gooding and Gerrard a perfunctory handshake. 'My name is Ralph Holden. I represent the new owners of this ship. I would be grateful if you would kindly show me to your day-cabin, captain, and order me some chilled orange juice. I have a great deal of talking to do.'

'First things first,' said Holden, spreading papers from his briefcase on Gerrard's desk. 'How much will the repairs to the *Tulsar*'s bow cost?'

'About one thousand five hundred pounds,' Gooding replied.

'And what about the total to get her ready for sea loaded with provisions and fuel?'

'Repairs, victualling and bunkering bring it to around two thousand five hundred pounds.' Gooding reached into a pocket. 'I've got the figures here.'

'I'll take your word for it, Mr Gooding. How soon can the *Tulsar* be made ready if work starts now?'

Holden's unblinking blue eyes made Gooding feel nervous. 'Five weeks.'

Holden opened a cheque-book, wrote briefly, tore out the cheque and handed it to Gooding. 'Five thousand pounds which you can draw from the Standard Bank here in Durban,' said Holden crisply. 'That ought to cover bonus payments to the shipwrights to have the *Tulsar* ready in three weeks. I've already squared the priorities committee.'

Gooding goggled at the cheque. 'Three weeks?' he said faintly. 'I don't think that's possible.'

'You may use the money to make any necessary incentive payments as you see fit. I shall expect a detailed account when the *Tulsar* is ready to sail and will make out a separate cheque for your commission. Right now I'd like a receipt, please.'

Gooding realized that he was dismissed. He pushed the cheque into his pocket and left the cabin mopping his forehead and muttering that he would be gone ten minutes.

Gerrard lifted his feet on to his desk, hooked his hands together behind his neck and regarded Holden almost sleepily.

'Now you're not going to tell me that you're interested in the *Tulsar* catching whales, are you, Mr Holden?'

'What's the *Tulsar*'s cruising range, captain?'

Without moving or taking his eyes off the Englishman, Gerrard replied: 'Eleven thousand miles at ten knots; eight thousand at twelve knots; five thousand at fifteen knots.'

'How about at twenty-six knots? The *Tulsar*'s maximum speed?'

'It would be pretty crazy thing to do unless we'd caught a lotta whale early in the season and wanted to be first in to get the highest prices.'

'But how far?' Holden pressed.

'Maybe two thousand miles if the turbines didn't blow up first.'

'Supposing you used your whale oil tanks for fuel oil?'

'Now I know you're not interested in whales.'

'Captain,' Holden's tone was icy. 'I'd appreciate it if you would answer my question.'

Gerrard was unmoved. 'And I'd appreciate it if you told me what all this is about. Why have you bought the *Tulsar*? She ain't much good for anything except catching and processing whales.'

Holden drummed his fingers on Gerrard's desk before replying. 'I have permission to tell you because of the U-boat you sank and because it is considered essential that you should know. The consequence of knowing is that your life is in constant danger should you show the slightest inclination to divulge the information.'

Gerrard's lazy eyes opened a little. 'Danger from whom?'

'From me.'

'That's interesting,' Gerrard observed. 'Back home I have a reputation for being what is known as a tough cookie.'

'I haven't killed enough people to have acquired a reputation,' said Holden mildly. 'But I'm willing to make a start.'

Gerrard suddenly sensed that there was more to the smartly-dressed Englishman than he had at first supposed. He met Holden's unwavering gaze and shrugged. 'Okay. I guess you'd best tell me.'

'The *Tulsar* is required to ship a large quantity of gold bullion to England as quickly and as discreetly as possible. Speed is of paramount importance, not only to avoid interception by surface raiders and U-boats, but because the gold is needed to maintain the flow of arms and food from the United States to Great Britain. Without it we're finished.'

Gerrard lifted his feet off his desk and lowered them to the floor. 'We?'

'The Allies. I represent the British government. The bullion held in Pretoria is worth US $240 million and it's the last of our gold reserves. Our holdings in London and Ottawa are now completely exhausted.' Holden watched the American dispassionately and noted that he appeared shaken.

'Jesus Christ,' Gerrard breathed after a pause. 'Two hundred and forty million bucks.' He whistled. 'Just how much gold is that?'

Holden smiled thinly. 'The gold refinery at Johannesburg mint it into 995-fine bars weighing twenty-five pounds each. We have to ship eighteen thousand bars. That amounts to a little over two hundred tons.'

Gerrard shook his head disbelievingly. 'Jesus Christ,' he repeated. 'Jesus bloody Christ. Two hundred tons of gold ...' His voice trailed into silence.

'Normally the bars are packed two to a box,' Holden continued. 'But because your cargo manifest will say that you are carrying lead, we will be using wooden crates normally used for pigs of lead. Each crate can hold ten gold bars making a total of eighteen hundred crates. Do you have plans of the *Tulsar*?'

Gerrard opened a drawer and pushed three sheets of paper across to Holden. 'Some rough sketches I did before our last refit. You can keep them.'

Holden studied the dimension drawing of the *Tulsar*'s below-deck layout. 'Each crate measures a foot high by a foot wide by five feet long – there's plenty of room. We can get the repair gang to insert two bulkheads here and here to create a hold.'

'There's something you've overlooked,' said Gerrard drily.

Holden raised his eyebrows. 'And what might that be?'

'We sold passages home to raise money.'

'Why should you think that that is something I've overlooked?'

55

Gerrard decided that he didn't like the self-assured Englishman. 'Because, if we're no longer sailing for the States –'

'How many passages have you sold?' Holden interrupted.

'Eighteen.'

'And they're all Americans?'

'Except for a Canadian couple.'

Holden gave a thin smile. 'Excellent. All of them will provide first-class, ready-made cover.'

'The trouble as I see it,' said Gerrard deliberately, 'is that they've purchased tickets to go to New York on the not unreasonable assumption that this ship is going to New York.'

'I'll have to announce a change of destination in mid-Atlantic,' was Holden's smooth reply. 'And I'll also arrange their passage from the UK to America on a neutral ship. Any more problems, captain?'

Gerrard shook his head reluctantly. 'I guess you've covered just about everything, but it's the craziest scheme I've ever heard of.'

Holden's answering smile was bleak. 'Of course it's crazy. Who in their right mind would think the British stupid enough to ship the last of their precious gold a quarter of the way round the world on a whaling factory-ship under a foreign flag?'

'No one,' Gerrard agreed. 'I guess you'll be coming along on this crazy trip?'

Holden nodded. 'I'm sure you can find an extra cabin, captain.'

'Sure,' said Gerrard dismissively. 'But there's one thing we must get straight first if you're coming along. You may own the *Tulsar*, Mr Holden, but *I'm* her captain and *I* give the orders. Okay?'

Holden shrugged. 'I don't see any problems there provided you follow my orders, captain. I know nothing about the day-to-day running of a ship.'

Gerrard didn't like the Englishman's answer. 'The smooth day-to-day running of the ship may mean that I'll be giving *you* orders, Mr Holden. I just want to satisfy myself that you'll obey them.'

Holden returned Gerrard's dispassionate smile. 'Let's deal

with that problem when it arises, Mr Gerrard,' he suggested amiably.


# 15

As the Lockheed Electra airliner passed over Durban Harbour, Holden could see that repair work was well under way on the *Tulsar*'s bows; the floating crane was alongside the whaler and two repair barges were in position. To his right the brutal escarpments of the Drakensburg Mountains rose sheer and forbidding out of the red soil of Africa.

The note of the two engines changed as the airliner levelled out at the top of its climb. Holden ordered an orange juice from the steward and glanced at his watch. It was 8.05 am. The Electra was capable of covering the thousand-mile flight to Cape Town in just under five hours and was scheduled to return to Durban the following day. Holden hoped that there would be no hitches to delay the aircraft's return because he had told no one of this trip and his absence from Durban for much more than twenty-four hours would hardly pass unnoticed. He had even purchased the ticket out of his own money and taken a seat at the front of the aircraft to avoid being seen by the constant procession of passengers visiting the aft toilet.

The Ford taxi bumped along Tafelberg Road high above Cape Town and deposited Holden outside the lower station of the Table Mountain cableway. The vast north-facing edifice of Table Mountain acted as a giant sun-trap, warming the air to an intolerable level so that after five minutes waiting for the cable-car Holden was sweating profusely.

The cable-car glided smoothly into its concrete niche. The attendant opened the door and held the gently bobbing car steady for the five passengers to disembark. A minute later, with only the attendant for company, Holden was aboard the car as it began its awesome one-mile climb up the precipitous sandstone slopes of Table Mountain.

'Bloody cold up there,' said the attendant, nodding to the thick layer of white cloud that covered the summit. 'Always happens when the sou'easter gets up. You won't be able to see anything.'

'I could hardly visit Cape Town without visiting Table Mountain,' said Holden.

The wind strengthened as the car maintained its steady climb like a money spider hauling itself up a cobweb. Holden instinctively braced himself as they neared the mighty avalanche of cloud spilling over the edge of the mountain. And then the car was into the 'tablecloth' and the temperature plummeted.

'Told you,' said the attendant as Holden turned up his collar.

Holden made no reply but stared upwards at the tower-like upper cable station that was looming out of the fog. It seemed that the car was stationary – that the broad lip of the mountain was sinking down to meet them. There was an almost imperceptible bump as the car came to a standstill.

'Don't go too far from the station,' warned the attendant, holding the car firmly against the platform for Holden. 'Come back if you hear the hooter. Stay on the paths otherwise you'll surprise yourself with how easy it is to fall off the edge.'

There was nothing to see on the mountain but the squares of yellow light that marked the windows of the small tea-room. Holden's footsteps sounded curiously dead as he moved along a narrow track that threaded its way through beds of wild belladonna lilies and crassulas. The path was so narrow in places that clumps of wet grass brushed against his trousers. He stopped and listened. There was no sound – not even the birdsong for which Table Mountain was famous – just a dead silence. Holden began to appreciate the cunning of the man who had selected this place for the rendezvous, for he had all the advantages – especially if he was familiar with the plateau's rocky terrain. He was probably watching him now – satisfying himself that Holden was alone.

A rock hyrax suddenly broke cover near Holden's feet and gave an angry cry as it scampered into the fog. There was a sound some yards behind Holden. He quickly followed the small rodent and crouched behind a rock, peering back along the

58

path. A figure of a man materialized out of the mist and walked past the rock where Holden was hiding. The man muttered a curse under his breath and quickened his step when he realized that his quarry had disappeared. That was enough for Holden: keeping his feet on the muffling clumps of grass, he darted behind the man and sent him sprawling on his stomach. The man tried to roll on to his back but Holden seized both his arms and doubled them up into the small of his back. It was a painful hold but the man made no sound.

'Mr Kramer, I presume?' said Holden pleasantly.

The man's face was pressed into the grass. He twisted his head sideways, swore in Afrikaans, and tried to throw his adversary off his back by bucking his powerful body. There was a sudden vice-like grip either side of his neck that sent a lance of pain stabbing into his head. He groaned.

'Please keep very still, Mr Kramer, and I won't hurt you.'

Kramer stopped struggling and the terrible pain mercifully eased. He felt the unseen fingers moving under his coat.

'I'm not armed.'

'Just making sure.' Holden stood. 'Okay – get up.'

Kramer climbed to his feet and sullenly regarded his smiling attacker while rubbing his neck.

'There won't be bruises,' said Holden. 'I didn't use enough pressure. Even so, you were as near to death just then as you are ever likely to be.'

'You're Holden?'

'How do you do, Mr Kramer? You're a disappointment to me. I imagined that the commander of the Ossewa Cape cell would be much too astute to allow himself to be ambushed so easily.'

'Who gave you my name and phone number?'

'Our mutual friends in Berlin,' said Holden. 'A long time ago. I've lost touch now which is why I've contacted you. I understand that you have a wireless transmitter. Now that would be useful because the authorities in Cairo are making difficulties for anyone who wishes to send cables to Germany.'

'I don't know what you're talking about,' Kramer growled.

'I have some useful information concerning the shipment to England of the last of the Allied gold from South Africa,' said Holden. 'Information that I'm prepared to part with in

59

exchange for two million Swiss francs paid into my account at the Bank of Montreux. Tell Berlin that the deal would be most profitable because the gold amounts to something like two hundred tons' worth or sixty million pounds, and its capture should not pose too many problems for the Kriegsmarine.'

Kramer pushed his hands into his pockets. 'I know nothing about you. I don't know who you are and I don't know if you can be trusted.'

'Of course you don't,' Holden agreed. 'But you must admit that we have enough information on each other to get ourselves hanged should one of us go to the police.'

Kramer noticed the quality of Holden's clothes. 'You're English?'

'With a higher esteem for money than my country.'

'Who do you work for, Mr Holden?'

'The Treasury.'

'Your address?'

Holden gave him his Kensington address.

'Tell me about this ship,' said Kramer.

'Not until I hear from my bank that half the money has been credited to my account.'

'Where are you staying?'

'The Benjamin D'Urban Hotel, Durban.'

Kramer asked disinterestedly: 'This ship ... it sails from Durban?'

'Full information when I've had half the money.'

Kramer considered. 'It is not for me to make decisions, you understand. I pass the information. Nothing else.'

Holden said that he understood. Kramer pointed into the fog. 'The cable-car station is that way, Mr Holden.'

Five minutes later, when he had made certain that the Englishman had gone, Kramer picked his way across the fog-shrouded plateau to the massive overhanging rock of the Silverstream Buttress near Platteklip Gorge where a party of Portuguese navigators had first climbed Table Mountain in 1503. He went down on his knees and cleared away some heather from immediately under the overhang, exposing a large, flat rock about two feet across. He strained briefly to push the rock to one side and lifted a small suitcase out of the hollow which he placed carefully beside him before releasing the two catches and opening the lid to reveal the neatly stowed headphones and the coil of antenna wire. The suitcase was a Telefunken Mark III 'Afu' *Agentenfunk* – or agent's transmitter-receiver.

He flipped the toggle switch to the 'I' position, pulled on the headphones and uncoiled the antenna wire. Being over three thousand feet above sea-level and with no obstructions, it was sufficient merely to toss the antenna wire over the edge of the gorge so that it hung straight down. Table Mountain made an excellent site for a low-power ten-watt radio such as the Afu. The faint hum in the headphones told Kramer that the set had warmed up. He watched the meter in the centre of the set and operated the Morse key in a random manner. The needle dipped which meant that the set was working satisfactorily despite the damp conditions it was stored under. The main advantage of the set was that its frequency was kept in tune by a quartz crystal and consequently required little skill other than a knowledge of Morse code to operate it.

Kramer's Morse had been hurriedly acquired during a crash course on his last visit to Berlin. It was poor, but that was an advantage for it enabled radio-operators on U-boats to identify his 'fist' quickly. He calmly transmitted a stream of Vs and waited for the U-boat's acknowledgement. The answering bleeps were sharp and clear, indicating that the U-boat had tuned in to him. He carefully keyed out:

ARE YOU READY FOR MY MESSAGE

Back came:

STANDING BY

Kramer's shaggy eyebrows knitted in concentration as he began keying his message for it would be necessary for him to make a deliberate error in the eleventh and twenty-second position of the text as a security check before the U-boat would accept the signal as genuine. An error in the thirty-second position would tell the U-boat that he had been caught and 'turned' and was being made to send false information.

Slowly, with painstaking care, he laboriously broadcast a full account of his meeting with Holden, remembering to make the deliberate keying errors in the right places.

# 16

'What puzzles me,' said Strick, 'is how he managed to open a bank account in Switzerland.'

'Difficult, but not impossible,' said Admiral Canaris. 'He works in the Treasury. The chances are that he has access to the London–Geneva radio-telephone link and has used it for his own purposes.'

Strick considered it likely that the British would keep a tight control on such a link but didn't contradict Admiral Canaris. As head of the Abwehr – OKW's vast intelligence and counter-espionage organization with ten times the budget and resources of Strick's own IMI – the prematurely white-haired admiral with his preference for scruffy civilian dress and his air of good-humoured indecisiveness, although not highly thought of in party circles, had nevertheless won for himself considerable power and influence by his uncanny ability to be in the right place at the right time.

'What have you been able to find out about him, admiral?' Strick politely inquired.

Canaris rifled vaguely through some papers in his filing basket and pulled out a document. 'Nothing much. There are several R. Holdens listed in the 1938 Treasury directory ranging from a clerical assistant to a principal officer.'

This was nothing new to Strick who had a copy of the same publication in his library. 'Have you found out anything by more direct investigatory methods, admiral?' Strick tried to sound tactful.

'Our South African contact arranged to have his hotel room in Durban checked. They didn't find much. A few unpaid bills that amounted to about two hundred pounds.'

The vagueness irritated Strick. 'I suppose the significance of that sum depends on whether he's a clerical assistant or a principal officer,' he commented sourly.

Canaris smiled. 'Either way, I think debts of two hundred pounds are significant. The British don't overpay their civil servants. Whatever his rank, such a sum would not be easy to pay off, and it does indicate that our Mr Holden is acquiring a taste for living beyond his means.'

'Perhaps,' said Strick unconvincingly. 'But do you really think we know enough about him to risk handing over a million Swiss francs? For all we know the whole thing could be a clever fabrication by your South African contact.'

Canaris shook his head emphatically. 'No. I know him. He's our most reliable man in South Africa. I'll see Funk in the morning and recommend that the first payment is made.' He chuckled and regarded his austere visitor with twinkling eyes. 'Cheer up, doctor. We'll be getting two hundred tons of gold at a bargain price.'

# 17

One of Simon Gooding's basic philosophies was that energy was something to be expended as sparingly as possible, especially during the humid months of Natal's summer. The daily presence of Ralph Holden in his outer office therefore made him feel decidedly uncomfortable. Every problem that arose in making the *Tulsar* ready for sea was dealt with by the young Englishman with a speed and efficiency that made the rotund shipping agent nervous and aware of his middle age. Whether it was a shortage of steel plate one day for the repairs to the hull, or difficulty in obtaining welding materials the next, all the problems were briskly steamrollered by a combination of Holden's short telephone-calls and long cheques. Another of Holden's characteristics that Gooding envied was his ability to maintain his almost icy detachment when things were not going his way.

Gooding was gazing out of his office window watching the dockside traffic while eating a sandwich when he noticed a neat, tropical-suited figure making his way quickly through the fish market. It was Holden. Gooding had never seen the fair-haired young man hurrying before. The shipping agent returned to his desk and was pretending to be industrious when Holden burst in. He looked up – hoping that his benign, welcoming smile cloaked his alarm.

'Good afternoon, Mr Holden. How's everything going?'

'I spotted an American girl on the *Tulsar*,' said Holden curtly. 'A Miss Josephine Britten. She works as a receptionist in my hotel and I'd like to know what she's doing on the *Tulsar*.'

Gooding mopped the back of his neck. 'She's our purser, Mr Holden.'

'Since when?'

'Since I gave her the job,' Gooding replied irritably.

Holden recalled that Josephine had told him that she had obtained a working passage back to New York although she had not told him which ship she was due to sail on.

'Her name wasn't on the passenger list you gave me,' said Holden.

'Because she's not a passenger. You told me to look after the crew, Mr Holden.'

'Why does she want to go home?'

'She's not the sort of girl one asks too many questions. Anyway, it's none of my business.' Gooding met Holden's blue eyes. 'Besides, she's been damned useful. She's fixed up the cabins – supervised the repainting and even scrounged some carpeting from a hotel that's being demolished. And she's got the carpenters to fix up a bar in the restaurant. That girl knows what she's doing. She's worked every minute of her spare time.'

Holden said nothing. Gooding's statement explained why he had hardly seen Josephine during the previous three weeks. 'I need her home address,' Holden said after a moment's thought. 'All I know is that it's somewhere in Greenwich Village.'

Gooding nodded and fingered through a number of papers impaled on a spike. 'How's everything with the ship?' He removed a slip from the spike and handed it to Holden.

Holden glanced briefly at the paper and thrust it into an inside pocket. 'The hull's finished,' he said in reply to the shipping agent's question. 'Gerrard says that the riveting and welding is not the best he's seen but it will have to do. The floating crane will be lowering the *Tulsar*'s bow tomorrow.'

Gooding was surprised. 'So she'll be ready to sail by next week?'

Holden smiled coldly. 'There are a few alterations to be

made. I'm having some of the forward oil separator tanks removed so that a hold can be created.'

'A hold?' Gooding echoed. 'What do you want a hold for, for God's sake?'

'We might as well earn some money on the New York trip,' said Holden. 'In addition to the passengers the *Tulsar* will be carrying a cargo of lead. The necessary papers will be with you by the end of next week.'

Gooding was about to point out that the cost of converting the *Tulsar* would hardly justify the return on the freight rate but decided that it would be wiser to remain silent.

# 18

The lobby of the Hotel Benjamin D'Urban was filling with the *Tulsar*'s passengers and their luggage when Holden entered after breakfast on 17 February. He watched with an amused smile while Josephine tried to placate an aggressive sugar magnate and his querulous wife.

'Mr Vanson,' Josephine was saying desperately, 'I'm very sorry but I can't give you a sailing date because I don't know it yet.'

'Know how long we've been stuck in this country?' Eli Vanson demanded. 'Over a year – that's how long. And now you say we're to be stuck in this crummy hotel.'

All the passengers had identified Josephine as having something to do with the mysterious shipping line that was supposed to be taking them home and were, with the exception of two smiling Ursuline nuns, all talking at the top of their voices. The most popular topic was the apparently far from ideal conditions aboard the train that had brought them from Cape Town.

Holden pushed his way through the crowd and leaned on Josephine's desk until she noticed him.

'I understand you're to be the purser on this ship, Jo. No wonder I've hardly seen you. I thought you were deliberately avoiding me.'

'I wouldn't dream of trying to avoid you, not unless you've caught something unpleasant that is. Is there something I can do for you?'

'You can fix me a comfortable cabin on the *Tulsar*, Jo.' Holden grinned at her look of surprise and added. 'You obviously haven't checked the passenger list that carefully, my love.'

'You're going to New York on the *Tulsar*?' said Josephine incredulously.

'That's right. I shall expect the best cabin you have.'

'Mr Holden,' said Josephine carefully. 'There are no classes on the *Tulsar*. All I can promise you is that your cabin will be adequate. I'm sorry but I can't make exceptions.'

'Not even for the owner?'

The mocking blue eyes annoyed Josephine. She looked suspiciously at Holden. 'I get the impression that you are trying to tell me something.'

'That's right, my angel – as the owner's representative I believe I'm entitled to a decent cabin. Check with Simon Gooding if you don't believe me.'

Josephine stared at Holden and nodded. 'I'll see what I can do, Mr Holden.' She turned to the honeycomb of pigeon-holes behind the desk and gave Holden a telegram. 'This arrived ten minutes ago for you, Mr Holden.'

Holden returned to his room and quickly decoded the London telegram.

JOSEPHINE BRITTEN SUBSTANCE OF YOUR 41 STROKE 3 CONFIRMED STOP   NO CONNECTION WITH ISOLATIONIST OR PRO-NAZI MOVEMENTS IN USA THEREFORE NO OBJECTION TO ALLOWING HER AS PASSENGER STOP   FATHER SUFFERING FROM KIDNEY DISEASE STOP   HAS LESS THAN FOUR MONTHS

Holden watched the flames curl the telegram into black flakes. He stirred the remains to dust and emptied the contents of the ashtray into the waste bin. For some seconds he sat perfectly still, gazing out of the window at the rash of sunshades on the beach. When he had informed the Treasury that the *Tulsar* would be carrying passengers they had insisted on being supplied with their names and addresses to enable them to

66

carry out security checks. Josephine's name and address had been the last. His immediate problem was Josephine's reason for wishing to return home which was obviously to see her father. He had no intention of getting involved in the personal problems of the *Tulsar*'s passengers but he liked the American girl well enough not to want her to embark on a voyage in the belief that she was going to New York when in fact the *Tulsar* was bound for England.

There was only one course of action.

Gooding had a certain strength of character that Holden hadn't bargained for. The shipping agent swept an armful of papers off his desk, crammed them into a box file and thrust it into Holden's hands.

'I can't stop you sacking Miss Britten,' said Gooding, glancing across his office at Gerrard in the hope of support. 'But I won't be party to it. I'll refund the commission you've paid me and you can find yourself another agent.'

The two men glared at each other across the desk. 'All I'm asking,' said Holden calmly, 'is for you to book the girl's passage home on another ship and I'll pay her fare.'

'There are no other ships,' said Gooding. 'That kid's worked damned hard getting everything fixed up – she's taken a big load off my shoulders and Captain Gerrard's, and I'm damned if I'm going to fire her without good cause.' Gooding pulled on a fedora and moved to the door. 'I have to go to the customs office about the cargo of lead. See if you can make him see sense, Captain Gerrard.'

'So what's the big trouble?' Gerrard asked Holden when Gooding had left.

'I had to clear all the passengers' names through London,' said Holden. 'They told me that Josephine Britten's father has less than four months to live. As I see it, that must be the reason why she wants to return home.'

Gerrard gave the Englishman a lazy grin. 'So you're going to tell her that the *Tulsar* isn't going to New York?'

'Don't be so damned stupid.'

'Seems that it's not me who's being stupid. I didn't figure you to be the sort of guy to lose his head over a girl.'

Holden ignored the American captain's familiarity. 'I just

don't want to see her hurt if her father dies before she gets home.'

Gerrard shrugged. 'I don't want passengers on my back. I've only spoken to the kid a couple of times but I got the idea that she could handle them.' He grinned again. 'They're going to kick up a helluva stink when they find out they're not going to New York, so I say she stays.'

# 19

Holden drove eighty miles down the coast from Durban and arrived at the nondescript, depressing little town of Port Shepstone at 1 pm. He parked outside the Duke of Bedford Inn, a small single-storey hotel, and entered the restaurant where Kramer was waiting impatiently for him at a corner table.

'You're an hour late,' complained the Afrikaner. 'You had a three-hour drive and I had a three-day drive from Cape Town, and I managed to be on time.'

'How safe is this place?' Holden demanded curtly.

Kramer shrugged. 'As safe as anywhere.'

The two men ordered a light lunch and waited for the waiter to withdraw.

'Your bank will have received the money by now,' Kramer began.

'I heard from them this morning,' said Holden guardedly.

'I thought the Swiss banks were difficult about sending out information?' Kramer inquired casually, as though he wasn't particularly interested in Holden's answer.

Holden realized that for all his faults, the rugged Afrikaner was no fool. 'There are ways.'

Kramer sank his teeth into a stick of celery and chewed noisily. He was very interested in means of sending communications outside South Africa. 'What ways, my friend?'

The waiter brought their order and departed. 'I have some information for you,' said Holden coldly.

Kramer grunted. 'About time. So what about the ship? What's its name?'

'The *Tulsar*. She's an American-registered whaling factory-ship.'

Kramer lowered his knife and fork and gaped at Holden. 'The *Tulsar*? Christ, man, isn't she the Yankee that rammed and sank a U-boat just before Christmas?'

'So I believe,' said Holden noncommittally. 'Which ought to make her that much more of an attractive target for your superiors.' Holden signalled the waiter and ordered a carafe of orange juice. 'She leaves Durban on 25 February – a week's time.'

Kramer nodded.

'There's one thing that I must insist on,' said Holden, watching the Afrikaner with hard, dangerous eyes. 'She's to be captured and not sunk. That must be clearly understood.'

Kramer grinned wolfishly. 'No one's planning to send sixty million pounds' worth of bullion to the bottom so what's the big problem?'

'*I* shall be on the *Tulsar*,' said Holden acidly. 'I shall expect to be taken off as a prisoner and sent to Switzerland.'

'You'll be interned.'

'I've made arrangements.'

'With the Swiss?' Kramer sounded disbelieving.

'It's none of your business, Kramer. Your job is to pass on the information I give you.'

The two men regarded each other with mutual distrust.

'There's the question of the passengers,' said Holden. 'They're all American citizens apart from two Canadians –'

'Passengers?' Kramer queried, his bushy eyebrows going up. 'What passengers, my friend?'

'They're the *Tulsar*'s cover. They think they're going to New York.'

Kramer bared his yellow teeth in a grin. 'Clever.'

'More by accident than design. They're to be repatriated as quickly as possible, you understand?'

Kramer nodded. 'Okay. How many of them?'

'Eighteen. Under no circumstances must they come to harm.'

'I can't see any problems there, but of course the Canadians

69

are British Allies. They'll have to be interned or imprisoned.'

'Which leaves one final question,' said Holden. 'The position of the capture. I suggest leaving it as late as possible – off the coast of France within range of air cover for the prize crew. If it's grabbed in the South Atlantic, the British will throw everything into getting it back or sinking it.' Holden hesitated before coming to the most crucial point of all – one that he had deliberately left until the end. 'You must tell your friends that the only chance they have of capturing the *Tulsar* is if they use one of their capital ships ... such as the *Tirpitz*.'

Kramer's eyes narrowed. 'Why, my friend?'

'The *Tulsar*'s fast – damned fast. Twenty-six knots. They won't catch her with anything else.'

Kramer stared hard at the fair-haired Englishman for some seconds before nodding his agreement. 'I will pass the information today. They will require the name of the *Tulsar*'s captain.'

'Her original captain – Robert Gerrard – the man who sank the U-boat.'

'And you have the drawings of the *Tulsar*'s layout?'

'You won't need them,' Holden replied. 'I'll show the prize crew where the gold is stowed when they come aboard.'

'In case anything happens to you,' Kramer murmured.

An icy tone crept into Holden's voice. 'What could possibly happen to me, Mr Kramer?'

'We have to cover ourselves, my friend. Insurance.'

The two men were silent – each convinced that one was double-crossing the other. Holden shrugged, reached into his breast pocket, and handed Gerrard's plans of the *Tulsar* to the Afrikaner. Kramer glanced briefly at the freehand drawings before thrusting them out of sight. They were exactly what he wanted.

After the meal, the two men drank a discreet toast to the success of the venture: Kramer with a glass of beer and Holden with an orange juice.

# 20

Kramer's 'Cuckoo to Alice' radio signal was picked up by his colleague 'General' Rudolf Messener of Ossewa-Brandwag Kommando VI Gruppe, Windhoek, South-West Africa, at field strength three. Messener screened the signal for the deliberate keying errors to ensure that Kramer hadn't been 'turned' and rebroadcast the message on the 15,460 kilocycles wavelength using the powerful 500-watt RCA transmitter that Kramer had brought back from Berlin in 1937 in shipping crates labelled 'electrical spares'.

*U-395* of the 2nd U-boat Flotilla was charging her batteries three hundred miles east of Montevideo on the far side of the Atlantic when her radio-operator intercepted Messener's signal. The keying error screen proved satisfactory so he re-encoded the message into Kriegsmarine 'Purple' on his Enigma cypher machine and relayed it on the 4,995 kilocycles wavelength – the standard frequency allocated to U-boats.

Quarter of the way round the world, at Treuenbrietzen, just south of Berlin, the antennae on the roof of a graceful, stucco country mansion that belonged to the OKW's Chiffrierabteilung listening-post, picked up *U-395*'s relay. The signal was quickly verified for authenticity in the listening-room and passed, still in its coded text form, to the dissemination-room where only the first four codegroups were decoded to establish the message's intended recipient. The suffix 'Alice' alerted the duty officer who immediately abandoned standard procedure and decoded the remainder of the signal himself without sending it to the appropriate room where it would have to await its turn.

Five minutes later, the red machine in the bank of Geheimschreiber teleprinters in Admiral Canaris' Berlin headquarters started clattering. It was the only machine that printed its text without a carbon copy.

The message's long and devious route did not substantially delay its journey; an hour after Kramer had stowed his Afu radio suitcase under the bed in his Port Shepstone hotel room, a pink flimsy was laid before Admiral Canaris in Berlin. Nor had the accuracy of the message suffered apart from the spelling of 'Durban' which had changed to 'Durbin'.

By 5.30 pm Canaris and Reichminister Walter Funk had completed their urgent briefing of Hitler that provided him with a detailed account of British plans. The real purpose of their visit was to persuade the Führer to agree to a capital ship such as the *Bismarck* or the *Scharnhorst* being sent into the Atlantic to intercept and capture the *Tulsar*. But Hitler would have none of it, for fear of another humiliating defeat similar to the loss of the pocket battleship *Graf Spee* in December 1939. His neurosis concerning Germany's capital ships had even led to the *Graf Spee*'s sister ship, *Deutschland*, being renamed because the Führer had ruled that no ship bearing such a name could be allowed to sink. *Deutschland*'s new name, *Lutzow*, had not brought the pocket battleship much luck – her stern had been blown off after Operation Weserübung in Norway.

'There are our surface raiders,' Hitler pointed out. 'We can send them into the Indian Ocean.'

'With respect, *mein Führer*,' said Canaris. 'Such a concentration will serve to alert the British and would be certain to lead to an alteration of their sailing plan for the gold. We think it best not to show our hand until the *Tulsar* is in mid-Atlantic with no friendly port to hand where she can off-load the gold. Also, even with a radio-observer on board, our surface raiders do not have the speed and radar to seek out a specific ship on the high seas – they are designed to engage and destroy enemy shipping that they come upon by chance.'

It was an argument that Hitler wasn't interested in. Once again he refused to allow the release of a capital ship, then launched into a long tirade about the uselessness of battleships and cruisers.

'Do you know how many extra U-boats we could have had if Raeder hadn't been allowed his Z-plan white elephants such as the *Tirpitz*?' he bellowed. Four hundred! And with four hundred extra U-boats at sea the war against Britain would be over now!'

Funk was tempted to point out that the war would be over within a few weeks if the *Tulsar*'s gold was prevented from reaching England, but decided that silence was more prudent when Hitler started raging about naval matters.

Hitler's voice rose to a shout as he harangued his visitors. Funk quailed before the onslaught while Canaris remained impassively silent.

'Those ships are more useful sitting at their anchorages where the British can't get at them than they would be at sea – their presence and the fear that they'll suddenly break out are tying down thousands of men and countless ships on convoy escorts that aren't preventing my U-boats from sinking merchantmen. The U-boats are our only effective naval force – ask one of them to capture Churchill's gold.'

An hour later Canaris and Funk were sitting in Strick's office gloomily outlining the gist of the interview to Strick. The economist listened attentively and asked Funk to repeat Hitler's final words.

'He said to ask a U-boat to capture Churchill's gold,' said Funk.

'Which is exactly what we'll have to do,' said Strick. 'It was an order, was it not?'

'It didn't sound like an order,' said Canaris doubtfully.

'You can be certain that Hess can make it sound like one if he wishes,' observed Strick. 'I presume the meeting was minuted?'

Canaris nodded.

'In that case I suggest we get Hess to ratify Hitler's statement as an order; setting a U-boat on to the *Tulsar* is better than doing nothing. Maybe they'll be glad of the opportunity. After all, it was the *Tulsar* that sank that U-boat last December. What was the captain's name?'

'Robert Gerrard,' said Canaris. 'An American.'

'I wonder if we have information on him?' Strick mused. 'If the British are crazy enough to use a neutral ship commanded by a citizen of a neutral country, it would be silly if we did not exploit their stupidity by at least checking to find out if this Gerrard can be either bribed or blackmailed.' Strick picked up one of his telephones and asked a collator in the central document library to check the indexes to see if Gerrard's name appeared.

'It's a faint possibility,' said Strick, replacing the receiver and pressing his intercom button to order coffee.

A few minutes later a clerk entered his office and placed a folder on his desk. Strick opened it and quickly read through the brief report it contained while Funk and Canaris looked on.

'Well,' said Strick, pushing the document across his desk to Canaris. 'We can rule out blackmail: Gerrard's wife was drowned when the *Athenia* was torpedoed.'

Canaris read carefully through the brief report and frowned. He turned to the front page to see who had originated it. He stiffened. 'But this is amazing! Your information on Gerrard has come from a former colleague of his who is now a U-boat instructor.'

'What is so surprising about that?' inquired Strick. 'Whaling, like the Foreign Legion, has always attracted men from every nationality under the sun.'

Canaris nodded his white head. 'You miss my point entirely, doctor. It occurred to me that if we're to hunt for Churchill's gold with a U-boat, what better choice to lead the hunt than a man who knows Gerrard, knows how his mind works, and who also knows the *Tulsar*?'

# 21

The giant 23 Class Henshel locomotive wreathed itself in clouds of hissing steam as it grated to a standstill beside the *Tulsar*. Robert Gerrard leaned over the rail and looked down with interest at the forty flat-top wagons that the 111-ton locomotive had hauled across the highveld from Pretoria. Each wagon was stacked with coffin-sized wooden crates – fifty to a wagon – each of which bore the stencilled inscription of the lead mining corporation at Broken Hill near Lusaka in Northern Rhodesia.

'No guards?' Gerrard queried.

Holden joined him at the rail. 'Why invite awkward questions by mounting guards on what is supposed to be a cargo of lead?' he countered.

A tide of black stevedores swept over the crates to unfasten the ropes while a mobile dock crane trundled into position. Five minutes later the first sling-load of crates was guided down through the gaping hole in the *Tulsar*'s deck. Holden preferred not to think of the consequences should one of the crates fall and break open, revealing the true nature of its contents.

Holden followed Gerrard down the steel ladder into the *Tulsar*'s sweltering hold. The two men moved along the narrow passage-way between the rows of crates that were stacked eight high and secured with skilfully-tied lashing. The sun burned down with furnace intensity through the open hold on to the gleaming, oil-black backs of a team of sweating Zulus who were packing heavy bales of coir wadding between the crates and *Tulsar*'s hull.

'They're to protect the outer skin,' said Gerrard in answer to Holden's question. 'The *Tulsar*'s not designed to carry cargo. If those crates were to break loose in heavy weather they'd smash through the side like dogs going through a paper hoop in a circus act.'

They completed their tour of inspection and climbed back on to the deck. Josephine saw them emerge and closed purposefully in on them clutching a clipboard that had become an indispensable part of her accoutrement as the *Tilsar*'s purser.

'Captain Gerrard,' she said briskly. 'I have worked out the restaurant seating plan for week one of the voyage which requires your approval.'

Gerrard gaped at her in alarm. 'Why me, honey?'

Josephine was nonplussed by his reply. 'Well – it's usual for the captain to approve the seating at the captain's table unless you're happy to let me –'

'I'll eat with the crew like I always do,' Gerrard declared, glaring at Josephine as if he was daring her to contradict him.

Josephine promptly accepted the challenge. 'You can't,' she retorted. 'Having a proper captain's table is part of the social niceties of shipboard life.'

Holden smiled thinly at Gerrard's discomfort. 'I doubt if Captain Gerrard has got any social niceties.'

'That's right,' Gerrard growled, grateful for Holden's perceptive observation. 'I ain't got no social niceties.'

'Or a tuxedo to go with them,' Holden added drily.

'That's right,' Gerrard affirmed, aware that Holden was grinning at him. 'I'll tell you what, honey. As Mr Holden's the owner, how about him doing the honours?'

Holden's smile vanished. Josephine turned to the Englishman and looked at him critically. She nodded to Gerrard. 'Okay, captain, that's fine – if you don't mind the passengers coping with second best.'

# 22

Gerrard stood on the bridge on the afternoon of 25 February and glowered down at the excited passengers and well-wishers who were crowding round the foot of the *Tulsar*'s gangway. Those who weren't clamorously seeking Josephine's attention were either buying last-minute souvenirs from the hordes of Zulu women peddling strings of brightly-coloured beads or tripping over the luggage that the porters were unloading from the coach. Two customs officers had set up a trestle table and were proceeding to chalk mysterious runes on the passengers' trunks – a process that could apparently be carried out without examining the contents of the trunks. The two Ursuline nuns created a black oasis of tranquillity by sitting quietly on a packing-case and saying their rosaries while the newly-wed couple who had arrived from Cape Town the previous night were content to sit in a cocoon of happiness, arms tightly around each other, ignoring the chaos around them. Josephine envied them as she tried to placate Mrs Rose Lewis without losing her temper.

'Please, Mrs Lewis – I promise you – you won't have to share a cabin and the cabin will be big enough.'

Mrs Rose Lewis was a stern Canadian woman who owned several large chins and one small, embarrassed husband who was at her side and wishing he wasn't.

'And it must have an opening porthole. Herbie and I suffer with our chests at night – we must have air. Mustn't we, Herbie?'

'Yes, Rose,' said Mr Lewis obediently. He didn't suffer with his chest, but his wife took the view that her ailments, like the debts for expensive clothes that she tended to acquire, were transferable to her husband.

Josephine pacified Mrs Lewis with vague promises and was immediately involved in a dispute between Mr Eli Vanson and one of the customs officers over a fifty-dollar gold piece that Mrs Eli Vanson was wearing round her neck.

'The regulations are clear, sir,' said the customs officer politely. 'The export of gold from Britain and the dominions of the Empire is forbidden under the emergency regulations.'

'It was one of my wedding-presents to her, for Chrissake,' Eli Vanson snarled angrily. The sugar magnate had discovered when he and his wife had first visited South Africa that British customs officers were the most cussed breed on the planet. He turned to Josephine. 'Will you explain that to this creep, Miss Britten?'

'The rules are very clear,' said the customs officer, unruffled. 'Personal jewellery is allowed but not bullion or gold coins.'

The argument was ended by the second customs officer, the more senior of the two. He produced a set of goldsmith's scales and weights and said that His Majesty's Customs and Excise were empowered to purchase the gold coin at the market rate, and added very apologetically that it was his job to ensure that the only gold that sailed that evening on the *Tulsar* was in the form of tooth fillings.

Josephine unlocked the cabin door and pushed it open. 'Number six, Mr Holden,' she announced cheerfully. 'Your home for the next few weeks.'

Holden surveyed the cramped cabin without enthusiasm. The cot berth fixed to one bulkhead took up most of the floor space. The opposite bulkhead consisted of a range of lockers surrounding a wash-basin and mirror. There was a chair and a small writing desk below the only porthole.

'It's not my idea of an owner's stateroom,' said Holden.

77

'It's the largest cabin on the ship by six inches each way. I measured it personally.'

'That's very considerate of you, Jo.'

'As you're used to the best, it's only right that you should have the best. Of course, if you don't like it, you can only blame yourself for not buying a bigger boat. The air-conditioning controls are beside the bunk, and there's a call buzzer beside the desk. One buzz for the cabin steward, two buzzes for the bar steward.'

'How many for you?'

'My cabin-cum-office will be open eight till eight each day. There'll be a pad for messages if I'm not there.'

'I'll make frequent use of it,' Holden promised.

Josephine dropped the cabin key on the bunk. 'There's a (card in the drawer which gives the times of meals.' She moved to the door. 'I hope you have a pleasant voyage, Mr Holden.'

Kramer was able to slip unnoticed aboard the *Tulsar* simply by walking up the gangway holding his Afu suitcase transmitter-receiver in one hand and a travelling-bag in the other. He chose a moment when there was a general mêlée of passengers, porters, ricksha boys and well-wishers clustered on the quay-side by the ship and crowded on to the flensing deck. He strolled casually around the ship, pausing now and then to examine details that interested him, and nodding to passengers who were doing the same thing. A small group were staring up at the Northrop seaplane and arguing among themselves as to its purpose. They took no notice of Kramer as he pushed past them and made his way aft to the port lifeboat that was nearest the stern and not visible from the bridge or the quay. The lifeboat was high above the deck, hoisted hard against the curved davit heads. Kramer prayed that it would not be used for lifeboat drill. He made sure no one was looking and reached up to slacken the ropes that held the lifeboat's canvas cover in place. He pushed the radio set and the travelling-bag into the lifeboat, grasped the gunwale, and hauled himself up. He rolled into the lifeboat and quickly pushed the cover back into position. He crouched in the darkness for some minutes, listening intently for sounds suggesting that his entry into the lifeboat had been noticed. Once satisfied that all was well, he pulled a torch out of his travelling-bag and examined the interior of his new home. The lifeboat was thirty feet long and equipped with five pairs of oars. The lockers at both ends under the short decks were well provisioned with tinned food and there was a full fifty-gallon freshwater tank under each of the five thwarts. There were even blankets provided in waterproof bags. He hid the plan of the *Tulsar*'s layout under the duckboards and set about making himself comfortable.

Josephine had said her goodbyes at the hotel and had deliberately kept them unsentimental. She therefore gave a brief frown of annoyance when Jenny tapped hesitantly on her open door and entered the cabin.

'A telegram came for you just after you left,' said the girl. She opened her handbag and gave Josephine the envelope. 'Mr Thorne sent me. He said that it might be very important.'

'Thank you, Jenny. It was very kind of you to come.'

'I'll miss you. It won't seem the same without you. I'm sure to get into a horrible mess and double-book all the rooms, or something.'

'You'll manage. Remember never to lose your temper with the guests. If you always remain polite when they get rude, they'll end up feeling stupid. It always works.'

'I'll remember it,' Jenny promised.

Josephine tore the telegram open the moment she was alone.

PA OVER THE MOON WHEN I TOLD HIM YOU WERE COMING HOME STOP    DOCTORS SAY ITS BEST THAT HE STAYS IN HOSPITAL BECAUSE I CANT MANAGE WITH HIM ALONE STOP HES STILL WEAK BUT HE HAS BEEN THINKING ABOUT YOU ALL THE TIME NOW STOP   HE IS VERY SORRY ABOUT ALL THE MISTAKES STOP   YOUR LOVING MOTHER

Josephine was prevented from re-reading the telegram by the sudden appearance of the newly-married husband in her doorway. He made some embarrassed small-talk before blurting out his unhappiness about the tiered bunks that he and his bride were required to come to terms with. It was one of those problems that never arose in a hotel or large ship. Josephine realized that being the purser of a ship like the *Tulsar*, while not easy, certainly wasn't going to be dull.

Kramer pushed his knife into the taut canvas of the lifeboat cover above his head and worked the blade back and forth until the slit was wide enough to give him air and provide enough light during the daylight hours to conserve his torch batteries. He unpacked his travelling-bag and placed a Walther P-38 pistol on one of the lifeboat's thwarts within easy reach of his sleeping-bag. If discovered, he intended to sell his life dearly.

At one minute to midnight the pilot ordered the *Tulsar*'s mooring lines to be singled up. Two dockers unhitched the fore and aft mooring springs and a small harbour tug gently nudged the *Tulsar* away from the quay. The pilot stood shirt-sleeved and motionless in the soft glow from the binnacle and called for slow astern port – slow ahead starboard. The *Tulsar* came about, pivoting on her keel until her head was bearing on the centre of Port Natal's natural basin.

There was only Gooding to wish her farewell at that hour. To the sweating blacks, labouring through the humid night to load ice into the ponds of the darkly-clustered deep sea fishing-boats, the *Tulsar* was merely another white man's ship off to the seas that they traditionally feared.

'Slow ahead both,' the pilot called to Brody at the helm.

'Slow ahead both,' Brody repeated, obeying the order.

'Saw your new bow today,' commented the pilot, feeling in the pockets of his peajacket for a packet of cigarettes. 'Looks smart, I must say, but a ship that's caught a clout like that is never the same again I say.'

' 'T'aint right, leavin' like this,' Mrs Eli Vanson said to her husband who was standing beside her on the weatherdeck.

'Why's that, sugar?'

'There should be a band, an' streamers, an' sirens instead of this sneakin' off in the night like a thief.'

'Sugar – just so we're heading for home, I don't give a damn just how we leave.'

Gerrard leaned against the bridge rail, smoking a tattered Havana, and watched the harbour lights slip by while allowing his senses to harmonize with the feel of the *Tulsar*. For once there was the muted hum of the turbines and the soft tinkle of the engine-room telegraph instead of the shuddering uproar of riveting-guns and welders' hammers. The *Tulsar* was a ship again – a living entity around him instead of a helpless mass of ironmongery at the mercy of indifferent shipwrights and equally indifferent landsmen who knew and understood nothing about ships.

Josephine awoke and realized that the ship was moving. She grimaced as she sat up in bed – the wine at the welcome aboard reception she had organized for the passengers had been a mistake. She drew the curtain back from the porthole and watched the dark, humped outline of The Bluff sliding silently past. The lighthouse swept the horizon with spokes of light. She gazed for some minutes at the departing land that had given her independence and taught her hard but gratefully-received lessons in survival. All she wanted now was for the *Tulsar* to speed her to New York so that she could make everything up with her father before it was too late; but she knew that she would return to South Africa again.

Hidden in the lifeboat, Kramer stirred and opened his eyes in the darkness. For a second the strange noises and the unfamiliar motion nearly caused him to panic before he realized that the *Tulsar* was moving. His hand reached out and touched the cold steel comfort of his pistol and knife. Reassured, he drifted back to sleep.

The *Tulsar* cleared The Bluff and lifted to the first rolling swell of the tepid Indian Ocean as if giving a sigh of relief at finally being freed from the imprisoning embrace of the brooding escarpment hills that guarded the sullen African continent.

# PART TWO

# FIGHTING

# 1

The stump of Kurt Milland's right leg ached abominably and he was certain that blood was beginning to break through the chaffed skin. Another five minutes of this infernal walking, he thought, and the leather socket of the artificial leg would be too wet to hold his stump firmly in place. He tried to tighten the shoulder harness through his shirt by pushing a hand under his greatcoat but that meant letting go of the handrail of the narrow boardwalk. His right foot caught on a coil of rope, causing him to stumble against the two men he was so desperately trying to keep up with as they made their way towards the four giant sheds of Krupp's Germania Werft U-boat construction yard. Admiral Staus steadied Milland with one hand and looked at him in concern.

'Are you all right, Kurt?'

Milland clenched his teeth and nodded, aware that the construction yard manager was regarding him with contempt.

'How much further?' Staus demanded.

The civilian pointed to a completed U-boat that was receiving its final coat of grey paint. It was less than fifty yards away, moored against the concrete quay and boxed in by the rust-streaked hulls of two unfinished U-boats that looked old before they were completed. The uproar of hammering and bursts of intense blue fire from arc-welders' torches in the open-sided sheds suggested that Krupp's were tearing U-boats apart instead of building them.

The three men moved slowly along the quay, stopped beside the U-boat and stared down at it. For the hundredth time that freezing morning Milland wondered why an important training programme had been interrupted to drag him to Kiel to look at U-boats under construction; he wasn't interested in their building – his job was the building of the fighting men who would have to take them to war.

'Some boat, eh, Kurt?' said Staus.

Milland tried to forget the pain in his right stump and ran an experienced, if disinterested, eye over the new boat. It was an ocean-going Type IXD with a surface displacement of 1,600 tons – double that of the current operational boats. Milland had read about the new boats and had doubted the wisdom behind their creation; the surface night attack technique by U-boats was proving effective. It was the method being taught by the training flotillas that depended on small U-boats with small conning-towers that were difficult for the convoy lookouts to spot. Milland decided that if the top brass had invited him to look at the new ocean-going cruiser submarines, to ask his opinion of them, then he would say exactly what he thought of them.

'Some boat,' he said to Admiral Staus. 'But too big to take part in massed attacks on convoys at night.'

Staus chuckled. Milland could always be relied on to speak his mind with candour. 'Actually, Kurt, that's not what they're intended for.'

'With respect, admiral, we should not be building boats for any other purpose other than for sinking enemy shipping. The fighting power of a submarine does not increase in proportion to its size as it does in the case of other warships.'

The manager glared at Milland. 'These boats are intended to carry the offensive into distant waters – the Pacific and the Far East.'

'I think we ought to go aboard,' Staus quickly intervened.

The manager led the way along the gangplank to the U-boat's forward deck casing. Milland was appalled at the expanse of deck and guessed that such a length of boat would pose particular problems in preventing its bow breaking the surface when at periscope depth. Maintaining correct trim was a U-boat chief engineer's biggest headache. They passed the business-like mass of an 88-millimetre gun mounted on the forward casing and climbed the steel rungs set into the side of the conning-tower. Ladders presented no difficulties to Milland for he had developed his arm and shoulder muscles so that he could climb any ladder by going up it hand over hand.

He swung his right leg stiffly over the rail that guarded the multiple-barrelled anti-aircraft guns and followed the manager and Admiral Staus down the bridge ladder into the new U-boat's softly-illuminated control-room.

'Welcome aboard *U-330*,' said the manager cryptically.

A thought occurred to Milland as he looked round the spacious control-room: 'Are the training flotillas to be issued with these boats, admiral?'

Staus smiled. 'I think not, Kurt. Especially not this boat. The aft tubes have been removed, so it wouldn't be much use for providing torpedomen with a full training programme.'

Milland was puzzled. 'Why take out the tubes?'

'To make room for the Maybach diesels,' said the manager. 'Big bastards – four thousand horsepower each. Twenty-five knots on the surface – the fastest U-boat ever built. Had thirty men working fifteen hours a day to get her ready. Radar, extra tanks to give her a twenty-thousand-mile cruising range, everything. And we haven't finished yet. We're unshipping that 88-millimetre later today and mounting a 104-millimetre quick-firing gun instead, and quadruple 20-millimetre anti-aircraft guns on the wintergarten deck.' The manager paused. 'This boat will have more hitting power than the *Tirpitz* by the time we're through, and be nearly as fast.'

Milland frowned at Staus. 'I don't understand, admiral. What has all this to do with me?'

Staus nodded to the manager. 'Leave us now, thank you.'

The manager accepted the dismissal and climbed out of the control-room. Staus indicated Milland to sit. The officer gratefully sat on the settee-berth and stretched his leg to ease the pressure on his aching stump. He looked questioningly at his superior officer.

Staus reached into an inside pocket and produced a sealed Kriegsmarine envelope which he toyed with while collecting his thoughts. 'Kurt,' he began. 'You remember telling me about your past association with Robert Gerrard – the man who sank *U-497* in the Indian Ocean last December?'

'Yes, admiral,' Milland replied cautiously, sensing trouble looming.

'I reported our conversation as a matter of routine. There was nothing that reflected on you, you understand. Naturally,

I thought the whole business would be a seven-day wonder and then be forgotten. But it wasn't.' Staus paused and tapped the envelope. 'What I have to tell you now, Kurt, is most secret and can be divulged only under the conditions given in these orders. On 25 February the *Tulsar* sailed from Durban bound for England with a cargo that consisted of two hundred tons of gold – the last of the Allied reserves. Without it they cannot continue with this senseless war. The Führer has issued a directive that a U-boat is to intercept the *Tulsar* and to capture it if possible or sink it if not. This U-boat.'

Milland suddenly realized why he had been hauled away from Wilhelmshaven. 'I'm wanted to brief the new captain of this boat, admiral?'

Staus shook his head. 'No, Kurt – you *are* the captain of this boat.'

Milland stared at the older man, the pain in his stump forgotten. 'I'm *what*!'

Staus repeated his statement and held out the envelope to Milland who accepted it with lifeless fingers. 'Despite your handicap, the OKM have decided that you should have command of this boat. I'll have your things sent from Wilhelmshaven. Your crew will be arriving just as soon as I can get one together at such short notice. There isn't time for a shakedown cruise which means that you'll have to carry out training *en route* to intercept the *Tulsar*.'

Milland stared at Staus, hardly taking in what the admiral was telling him.

'There's one thing I must know,' said Staus. 'You told me that Robert Gerrard was a determined man.'

'Ruthless,' said Milland, holding the envelope as if he was expecting it to explode.

'If that's the case, capturing the *Tulsar* won't be easy. You'll probably have to pump shells into her –'

'I think I know what you're trying to say, admiral,' Milland suddenly interrupted. 'If it's necessary for me to kill Robert Gerrard I won't hesitate.'

# 2

Milland stumped along the quayside on 5 March, his greatcoat collar turned up against the snow flurries and bitingly-cold north-easterly wind driving across the Baltic. He drew level with *U-330*'s bow and resisted the temptation to gaze at his first command. He spun his weight round on his left heel and walked back the length of the U-boat. The two men fitting a cluster of fixed radar antennae round the rim of the U-boat's conning-tower guiltily resumed work when they saw Milland scowl at them.

Milland tugged his peaked cap down more firmly on his head and looked at his watch. They were late. After three days of frustrating delays during which time the construction yard had run through their entire repertoire of excuses – sometimes inventing new ones – Milland had had enough. All he wanted to do now was take his boat through the Kiel Canal and into the North Sea to the war – away from the stupefying morass of stores requisitions, equipment defect reports, acceptance certificates and chart amendments. It was unbelievable how much paperwork had to be got through before a U-boat could be declared operational. Only one formality had been deliberately omitted: the commissioning ceremony. *U-330* was a ghost boat. Such was the importance of her secret mission that officially according to Kriegsmarine records, *U-330* did not exist.

A bus appeared at the far end of the quay near the entrance to the harbour and rumbled towards Milland over the puddle-splattered tarmac. The vehicle stopped. Twenty men in civilian dress disembarked and dragged their travelling-bags and suit-cases from the vehicle's stowage bay. Milland noted that someone had had the sense to see that the men did not use service-issue kitbags. He recognized some of them as men who had passed through his hands at the training flotilla. There was Munt – the chief engineer he had specifically requested from the 1st Flotilla, and Hans Fischer – unfortunate officer who had bent a U-boat at Wilhelmshaven.

One of the new arrivals spotted the white cover on Milland's

cap that was the emblem of a U-boat captain and cautiously
approached him. Milland eyed him warily. He looked too
young to be his new first officer. He returned the young
officer's salute.

'Captain Milland?'

'Yes?'

The young man smiled. 'Good morning, captain. I'm
Lieutenant Peter Sarne. I've brought you your crew.'

'Very good, Mr Sarne. Two lines please. Officers and petty
officers to the fore.'

'Yes, captain,' said Sarne crisply. He produced an envelope.
'A letter from Admiral Staus. He asked me to pass on his best
wishes for the success of your new command.' Sarne hesitated.
'And I would like to add my best wishes, captain.'

'You're a Bavarian, Mr Sarne?'

'That's right, captain,' was Sarne's cheerful reply. 'Munich
–pearl of the South. They were always telling me on my officer-
training course that my accent would be a blight on my career.'

Milland resisted an impulse to smile. 'Just make sure that
I don't become a bigger one,' he warned.

'I'll be very careful, captain,' said Sarne solemnly.

This time Milland smiled. Sarne's easy-going good humour
would prove an invaluable asset on the long mission that lay
ahead.

# 3

Gerrard flipped his cigar butt into the water and turned to
face Holden. The two men were standing on the *Tulsar*'s
bridge.

'Mr Holden,' said Gerrard slowly, 'I thought I made myself
plain – I'm the captain and if I say we zig-zag all over the
Indian Ocean then we zig-zag all over the Indian Ocean.'

'Which we've now been doing for ten days,' Holden
observed.

Gerrard shrugged. 'It's not my fault that there are two German surface raiders around the Cape. As soon as Simonstown give the all-clear we head for the Cape, and not before.'

'When was the last signal from Simonstown?'

'Two days ago.'

Holden regarded the American seaman dispassionately. 'In future I'd like to see all incoming signals.'

'They're routine warnings to all ships. You want weather forecasts as well?'

'I want to see everything please, captain.'

Gerrard shrugged again and pulled a battered cigar from his sweat-shirt pocket. 'Okay. I'll tell Jack Colby.'

'There's something else,' said Holden. 'Every morning you and I will agree a sailing plan for the following twenty-four hours.'

'Nope,' said Gerrard, lighting the cigar.

'That's an order, Mr Gerrard.'

Gerrard grinned. 'If you want to know in advance what I don't even know myself, then I guess the best thing is for you to take over the *Tulsar*.'

Holden remained unruffled. 'All I'm saying, captain, is –'

'And all *I'm* saying, Mr Holden, is that if you want to get this ship safely to its destination, then you leave the running of the ship to me. You worry about the cargo – I'll worry about the ship. Okay?'

'All I want is a measure of co-operation.'

Gerrard laughed. 'I'll tell you something, Mr Holden. You go into any waterfront bar from Sydney to Boston and ask them what Robert Gerrard knows about co-operation. They'll tell you – he doesn't even know what the word means. Maybe I'm not running a whaler now, but nothing's changed. I'm a loner, Mr Holden. I always have been and I always will be.'

# 4

Milland was massaging surgical spirit into his stump to harden the skin made tender by the endless walking at the construction yard when there was a tap on his door. An advantage of the ocean-going cruiser submarines was that there was sufficient room for the commander to have his own cabin.

'Come!'

It was Sarne. His eyes widened in quickly-concealed surprise when he saw Milland's truncated leg. 'Heligoland's on our quarter, captain. You left word to be told.'

Milland grunted and rolled on a new stump sock and motioned for Sarne to sit down. 'What do you think of our crew, Mr Sarne?'

'I'd rather answer that in two weeks, captain.'

'You'll answer it now,' said Milland mildly.

'We need a shakedown cruise. We need diving drill; silent running drill; gun drill –'

'We'll have plenty of time for that,' Milland interrupted.

'But we'll be in the middle of the convoy routes in a couple of days.'

'As we've cleared Heligoland I can now tell you the purpose of our patrol. We're not interested in shipping – what we're going after is one particular ship.'

As Milland quickly outlined *U-330*'s mission, Sarne's pale young face seemed to get even paler, but when Milland had finished, he demonstrated his ability to turn his mind quickly to the practical problems.

'The *Tulsar* is unescorted, captain?'

'Yes – because she's fast.'

'Then how can we possibly hope to find one ship in the whole of the Atlantic?'

'We have the DT apparatus – radar, and the latest hydrophone equipment which can detect propeller noises at a range of fifty miles.'

'Under the right conditions,' Sarne pointed out.

'There are two agents aboard the ship,' said Milland. 'One has a radio-transmitter which he will use to transmit the

*Tulsar*'s position every twenty-four hours, and the other is one of the passengers.' Milland smiled at Sarne's expression of astonishment. 'I think we have an excellent chance of capturing the *Tulsar*, Mr Sarne.'

Sarne returned to the control-room and climbed into oilskins and pulled on a sou'wester. He joined the four lookouts on the bridge who were quartering the horizon with binoculars, watching for the sudden appearance of a U-boat's deadliest enemy – aircraft.

*U-330* was making six knots to conserve fuel-oil but heavy seas were surging across the deck casing as if she was driving into them at fifteen knots. The leaden cloudbase extended like a shroud from horizon to horizon. The wind whitened the driving spray into ice that grew on the big 104-millimetre gun in a steadily thickening layer. One of the lookouts was obviously suffering from seasickness but Sarne did nothing; the best cure was to keep the man occupied.

He braced himself against the U-boat's rolling motion by holding on to the attack periscope standard. As he turned Milland's words over in his mind, a thought occurred to him: if their mission was so important, why had Milland been chosen to lead it? Why select a man who was virtually a cripple?

# 5

The only respite from the heat for Kramer came at night when he could risk folding back the flap of the lifeboat cover and gulp down cool, refreshing draughts of night air. He had endured two weeks in the lifeboat with the sun beating down unmercifully on the dark blue canvas above his head; two weeks of lying in his own sweat, hardly daring to move for even the slightest exertion made him giddy with heat sickness; two weeks of nagging worry, wondering why his compass was saying that the *Tulsar* was zig-zagging east when its course ought to be south-east to take it down to the Cape.

The luminous hands of his watch were showing 3.30 am

when he unlaced the cover and stood up. The night air tasted like champagne. His most pressing need was to visit the toilet. He listened carefully. The only sound was the faint hum of the turbines and the steady surge of the Indian Ocean creaming past the *Tulsar*'s hull. Satisfied that all was clear, he swung his leg over the side of the lifeboat and dropped silently to the steel deck plating.

Mrs Rose Lewis prodded the bulge that sagged down from the upper bunk. The bulge stirred. 'I can't sleep, Herbie.'

Herbie made a distinct snoring sound suggesting that he could sleep and, furthermore, was sleeping.

Mrs Rose Lewis sighed and pushed her sheet down to the end of the berth. It was unbearably hot in the tiny cabin and her bunk had run out of cool corners for her feet to explore. She had lost count of the number of times she had turned her pillow over. 'I'm thirsty,' she complained to the bulge.

'Call the steward for a drink,' Herbie muttered.

'They never answer the bell at night. It's a disgrace. Everything's a disgrace.' She swung her feet to the floor and stood. 'I'm going on deck for some air. I can't breathe in here.' She groped for her dressing-gown and pulled it on. A minute later she was climbing the companion-way that led to the port deck. The cold steel made welcome contact with her feet.

Kramer crouched in the shadow of a ventilator and listened for some seconds before making the fifteen-yard dash across the open expanse of the flensing deck. At that precise moment, with impeccable timing, Mrs Rose Lewis appeared in the crew entrance and gaped in surprise at Kramer's doubled-up figure racing towards her.

'Why, hello,' she said. 'I guess you can't sleep either, huh?'

Kramer's reactions were fast for his nerves were keyed for action. He swerved towards Mrs Rose Lewis and seized her by the throat before she could cry out. His fingers sank deep into her yielding flesh and closed hard round her windpipe. She struggled feebly as he dragged her backwards towards the galley. He pushed the door open and quickly pinned her to the floor with his knee across her throat while he fumbled for his knife. She made choking noises and then began fighting with amazing strength.

Kramer ripped her nightdress open and probed below her left breast, feeling with his fingertips for the gap between her lower ribs. The woman brought her knees up suddenly and struck him in the small of the back, nearly causing him to lose his hold.

Human ribs are arranged like the overlapping slats of a slightly-closed venetian blind, thus making a downward stab difficult; the tip of the knife is liable to be deflected from rib to rib. To succeed, as Kramer knew, the blow has to be upwards – delivered with considerable force to penetrate the tough tissue between each rib and the next.

Kramer positioned the knife against Mrs Rose Lewis' chest and thrust, quickly shifting his grip to drive the nine-inch blade home with the palm of his hand. He felt a sudden spasm shudder through the knife which told him that the blade had penetrated the heart. He held the knife steady so that the pulsating organ would destroy itself on the razor-sharp steel. The woman's body went limp. Kramer released the knife. The handle twitched for a moment and then was still. There was little bleeding from the wound after he withdrew the knife – most of the bleeding from the severed heart ventricle would be filling the chest cavity.

Kramer peered to the left and right and satisfied himself that the deck was still deserted. Terrified in case he was discovered, he quickly dragged the woman by her ankles towards the scuppers, taking care to keep the body on its back to avoid tell-tale blood streaks on the deck. He breathed easier once he had the body and himself concealed in the shadow of one of the towering ventilators. He debated what to do with the body. Obviously the simplest solution was to tip it over the side, but there was a snag: when the alarm was raised later that morning and it was established that the missing woman wasn't on the ship, there was a possibility that Gerrard would retrace the *Tulsar*'s course. He was a skilled seaman and would be able to make an accurate allowance for the effect of the Mozambique Current. The whaler was crewed by men with keen eyesight who were trained to study the sea. There was a chance that the woman's body might be found. Admittedly, it was an extremely faint chance, but one that Kramer felt he couldn't afford to take. It would be necessary to ensure that sharks found the body attractive. And with their ability to smell blood in the water, it was a task that shouldn't be too difficult.

He sliced the woman's nightdress right open and tore it from her body. He then made two deep, diagonal knife-slashes across her torso starting at her collar-bones and traversing down to the opposite thigh. To make doubly certain, he pushed her legs apart and stabbed upwards, twisting the blade viciously in her body before pulling it out. Blood oozed from the savage incisions. He rolled the body through the scupper with his foot. One final push and it tumbled out of sight into the white foam. The splash was inaudible.

Kramer used the nightdress to wipe his knife and the deck clean before tossing it over the side after Mrs Rose Lewis.

At 4 am Gerrard went on to the bridge to relieve Piet.

'New course for you before you sign off, Piet,' said Gerrard looking up from the gyro-compass. 'Two-two-zero. Time we headed south-west. Our Mr Holden is complaining. Who's on engine-room watch?'

'Midge,' Piet answered.

Gerrard grinned, crossed to the engine-room telegraph, and signalled for full speed ahead on both turbines. The interphone bell rang almost immediately. Gerrard lifted the handset off its hook and said: 'No arguments please, Midge. Time we got a move on.'

The *Tulsar* heeled gently as Piet spun the helm. Gerrard watched the twin hands of the turbine bridge repeaters gradually edging up to the maximum revolutions reading. The movement of the two pointers was matched by an increased hum from the turbines. The *Tulsar* began building up speed.

# 6

'What's the matter, Mr Lewis? You'll be late for breakfast.' Josephine discovered the little, bespectacled Canadian in the corridor outside her cabin. He was still in his pyjamas and dressing-gown, and looking very distraught.

'It's Rose, Miss Britten. I haven't seen her since I woke up. She got up in the night to go on deck for air.' Herbie watched Josephine appealingly as if the question of his missing wife was one that he hoped she would shoulder.

'What's the trouble?' Holden inquired as he stepped out of his cabin.

'Mr Lewis has lost his wife,' Josephine explained.

'She's bound to be somewhere. Mr Holden and I will look – you go on up to breakfast,' Josephine suggested.

Gerrard listened patiently to Lewis' account of the previous night and looked up at Josephine and Holden who were standing either side of the unhappy Canadian.

'Did you check the empty cabins?'

'We searched the entire ship,' said Josephine. 'Everywhere but the hold.'

Gerrard stood and glanced questioningly at Holden. 'Well, if it's okay with Mr Holden, he and I will check the hold but I don't see how she could have gotten herself in there.'

Holden shone his torch along the last of the aisles between the stacked wooden crates that were surrounded by bales of coconut matting. 'Nothing here,' he called out to Gerrard.

The American joined him and surveyed the narrow passageway. 'Maybe we ought to shift some of those bales.'

'We're wasting our time,' said Holden. He wrinkled his nose in distaste. 'And these overalls stink.'

A shadow fell across the two men. They looked up at Piet's head and shoulders framed in the open circular hatch against the sky. 'We've found something, cap'n,' said the Afrikaner grimly. 'But we've got to stop.'

97

The cessation of the turbine hum woke Kramer. There were excited voices near the lifeboat he was hiding in. He knew that the disappearance of the woman was bound to create a disturbance, but there was no good reason why it should be created so close to his lifeboat. Perhaps there was something he had overlooked? A smear of blood on the deck or perhaps there was something wrong with the lifeboat? But it was unlikely because he had taken such great care to leave no trace, and the lifeboat cover was in place. A cold wedge of fear suddenly thickened in his throat: stopped engines! A crowd round the lifeboat! It could only mean one thing: this lifeboat had been selected for lifeboat drill.

He reached for his gun and waited.

Less than four yards from where Kramer lay sweating in fear, the chattering Malay seamen helped their compatriot climb back on to the *Tulsar*'s deck where Piet relieved him of his trophy.

Gerrard spread the bloodstained nightdress on the chart table and stared coldly at Lewis. The Canadian fingered the garment for a moment and nodded.

'Where did you find it, captain?' His spectacles were misting up. He removed them and nervously polished the lenses with a handkerchief.

'Not far from where you threw it,' Gerrard replied. 'Except that you didn't throw it hard enough. It was caught on the port turbine condenser outlet.'

Lewis blinked and glanced at Holden. The fair-haired Englishman was regarding him thoughtfully and saying nothing. 'I don't understand, captain.'

'It's a short length of pipe sticking out of the hull.'

'No – I mean what you said about me throwing this.' Lewis' hand trembled as he touched the nightdress. 'And what are these marks?'

'Blood,' was Gerrard's cryptic reply.

'You can't be certain of that,' Holden observed.

'I know what bloodstains look like. Why the blood, Mr Lewis? Why not just give her a push? Or were you frightened that she might scream?'

The Canadian's eyes filmed with tears. 'I didn't kill her. If you accuse me, you'd be letting the real killer escape.'

Gerrard rested his chin on his hands. 'Mr Holden – what in hell are we going to do with him?'

'There's nothing we can do until we reach port,' murmured Holden. His mind was racing over the problem of why Mrs Rose Lewis had been killed and who her murderer was. He was certain that her husband wasn't responsible otherwise why had he identified her nightdress?

'I'm not having a killer loose on my ship,' Gerrard stated. 'Piet!'

Piet van Kleef appeared in the wheelhouse doorway. 'Cap'n?'

Gerrard jabbed a finger at Lewis. 'Have him locked in the bow compartment.'

Holden looked up boredly at the deckhead. 'I don't think you should do that, captain.'

'Dealing with murderers may not be part of the normal day-to-day problems aboard a ship,' said Gerrard, 'but it's still my responsibility.' The American turned to Piet. 'See that he has ten minutes exercise each watch.'

'But you can't do this to me!' Lewis protested as Piet gripped his arm. 'I swear before God that I've done nothing!' He tried to break free and realized that argument was useless. There was a silence in the wheelhouse after Piet had taken Lewis below. Holden decided not to intervene; there were more important battles ahead with Robert Gerrard that he was determined to win.

'You have anything to say, Mr Holden?' Gerrard inquired.

Holden pursed his lips and nodded. 'About agreeing a daily sailing plan, captain ...'

Five days after leaving the Kiel Canal and heading north, *U-330* reached the Arctic Circle and steered westwards on a course that would take her round Iceland to the north before entering the Denmark Strait and the North Atlantic proper. It was a long, tedious route but it reduced the risk of the U-boat encountering the numerous RAF Coastal Command Hudsons and Sunderland flying-boats on anti-submarine patrols.

As Milland had expected, the weather had ruled out opportunities for Sarne to meet the stringent training schedule of crash dives, gunnery practice, damage control drill and escape drill. Nevertheless, the crew were efficient and morale was high. Otto Munt, the U-boat's chief engineer, had submitted meticulous daily reports on the general state of the U-boat's machinery; and his fuel-oil consumption figures were scrupulously accurate. More important – he got on well with his petty officers, and his mechanics had familiarized themselves with the two non-standard Maybach diesel engines.

*U-330*'s radio-operator was Dieter Venner – a quick-tempered petty officer and a native of Cologne. He was also responsible for the ratings who operated the hydrophones and radar equipment.

Leutnant zur See Hans Fischer, *U-330*'s second watch officer, had admitted to once working in a top Frankfurt restaurant, a confesson that led to his appointment as the ship's *maître d'hotel*. As such he was responsible for drawing up the daily menu. The responsibility had gone to his head and his ambitious ideas on what could be achieved with the limited variety of the U-boat's supplies led to bad blood between him and the cook.

The main off-duty preoccupation of the watches was speculation about the purpose of *U-330*'s mission. From the secrecy surrounding their posting to the U-boat the members of the crew knew that it was something of extreme importance. An enterprising torpedo mechanic had opened betting on the possibility that *U-330* was destined to carry out a series of spectacular raids on Allied shipping in distant waters to emulate the successes of the surface raider *Atlantis*. When Sarne and Milland were together in the control-room their conversational exchanges were listened to with studied disinterest by the control-room watch in the hope of overhearing a hint as to the purpose of their voyage.

When Milland was told that *U-330* was an hour from the Denmark Strait, he decided that it was time to end the gossip and speculation. He entered the control-room and watched Fischer writing up the log at the chart table – a task made virtually impossible by the U-boat's rolling that even her present surface speed of eight knots did little to alleviate.

'Everything in order, Mr Fischer?'

Fischer looked up from the log. 'Yes, captain. Obermaschinist Koenig managed to trap his fingers in the inspection hatch to number four battery compartment. Sanitätsobermatt Steiner has stitched him up and given him a shot of morphine.'

Milland made a mental note to pay the unfortunate mechanic a visit. He had lectured often enough on the need for senior officers to show concern for their crewmen; now was the time to put this into practice. But first there was something else to attend to.

'Mr Venner!'

Dieter Venner leaned out of his radio-operator's compartment. 'Yes, captain?'

'Switch off the bridge loudspeaker. I don't want the lookout duty watch distracted.' Milland reached up and unhooked the crew address microphone. 'Men of *U-330*,' he began, his voice echoing back at him through the open watertight door from the various loudspeakers throughout the U-boat. 'You've all been wondering about the purpose of our mission for long enough. Now is the time to put you out of your misery. Our task is the greatest that the Fatherland has ever asked of its fighting men: we are to bring about a swift end to this senseless war!'

Milland spoke for five minutes, making no apologies for repeatedly stressing the Allied dependence on gold to finance their war effort. 'The British Empire is made up largely of under-developed countries with little or no industry; the factories of Europe are now denied to them therefore only America can supply their needs in tanks, ships and aeroplanes.

And America is insisting on payment in gold. Stop the flow of gold and their war effort will collapse overnight.... Gentlemen, I have given an undertaking the *U-330* will not fail in her objective of capturing the *Tulsar*'s gold! That is all.'

There was the sound of a muffled cheer from the engine-room followed by applause from the men in the control-room. Fischer was gaping at Milland in astonishment while Munt and his helmsman and hydroplane-operator were laughing and clapping each other on the back.

Milland thoughtfully returned the microphone to its hook and caught Fischer's eye. Milland knew enough about the serious-minded junior officer to guess what he was thinking: the Atlantic Ocean covered thirty-two million square miles. As a place to play a deadly game of hide-and-seek, the odds were stacked in favour of the hider.

# 8

Kramer listened carefully, sweat coursing down his face into his two-week beard, making absolutely certain that no one was near the lifeboat before cautiously lifting a corner of the canvas cover and peering out. It was mid-afternoon and the sun was beating down with unbridled ferocity.

As he expected, the deck was deserted. He slipped his binoculars round his neck and dropped to the deck. He leaned casually against the rail for some seconds, waiting and listening to ensure that he hadn't been seen. The weatherdeck where his lifeboat was situated came to a dead end at the stern where the whale slipway, guarded by safety rails, sloped down to the waterline.

For Kramer to see across to the starboard side meant walking forward to the flensing deck. There was no alternative. He moved openly – to be seen behaving furtively would be suicidal. He leaned forward against a ventilator to steady his grip and trained his binoculars on the lazy headland.

There was no mistaking the razor-ridged finger of rock

reaching out into the sea with the squat lighthouse at its seaward extremity: it was Cape Point. After a huge zig-zagging sweep round the Indian Ocean, presumably to avoid the usual shipping routes, the *Tulsar* had finally rounded the saw-edged reef of Cape Agulhas – the southernmost point of the mighty African continent – and was now entering the Atlantic Ocean.

Over seven thousand miles to the north, *U-330* was also entering the Atlantic Ocean.

Hunter and hunted were now on the same hunting ground.

# 9

The Purchasing Commission agent from London watched the steel grab drop into the hold of the British freighter. It emerged clutching a huge load of rubble in its massive fingers. Bricks and masonry escaped the grab's hold and fell into the East River but the bulk of the load remained intact. The operator swung the jib and pulled the lever that opened the grab. The falling masonry added to the great cloud of dust that was hovering over the New York waterfront between East 59th Street and 42nd Street.

There were twenty Allied-registered merchantships at anchor in line-astern waiting patiently for attention from the grabs. The cargo they had borne as ballast across the grey North Atlantic was thousands of tons of London rubble created by the Luftwaffe's blitzkrieg. The remains of pubs, warehouses, shops, factories and churches – many of which had been built when Broadway was still an Indian trail – were providing the foundations of what was to become reclaimed land in Manhattan. When their holds were emptied and cleaned, the ships were due to be loaded with aero-engines and spares, anti-aircraft guns, rifles and millions of rounds of ammunition, bomb-sights, machine tools, and all the innumerable accoutrements of industrialized warfare.

'So what's the latest?' the Purchasing Commission agent asked his companion.

The State Department official thrust his hands into his pockets and stared out at the ships. 'We can't release a single round of ammunition – even against a post-dated cheque – until the gold is in Fort Knox and fully accounted for.' He kept his gaze on the ships so that he didn't have to look at the British civil servant at his side. 'Our lawers say that "cash and carry" means just that.'

The agent remained silent. During a visit to Washington he had seen a demonstration outside the White House by women bearing placards that urged Congressmen and Senators to vote against 'Roosevelt's War Bill 1776'. There were other banners such as 'Lend-Lease is a lease on our freedom!' and 'Another Boston Tea Party – Kill HR 1776'.

But there was a gleam of hope: the isolationists were not having it all their own way; the Committee to Defend America by Aiding the Allies was waging an effective counter-campaign with emotive posters and full-page advertisements in newspapers. But despite the encouraging signs, it seemed to the agent that there was a very real chance that the only part of London not to end up under the jackboots of the Nazis would be beneath the feet of New Yorkers

# 10

At 0.02 am on 17 March, Kramer completed his observation of the moon and the Southern Cross with his sextant and took one final lower-limb and upper-limb reading of the moon to double-check.

He pulled the lifeboat cover back into place and settled down with a notepad, torch and nautical almanac to calculate the *Tulsar*'s position as best he could despite his inexperience in handling a sextant. There were two additional factors that prevented him from obtaining an accurate fix. Firstly,' he wasn't a hundred per cent certain after three weeks at sea if his watch was still giving the right time. Astronomical navigation – the measuring of the relationship between the moon and the stars, and their angle above the horizon – is dependent on an accurate timekeeper. Secondly, he was uncertain of his own height above the horizon in the lifeboat in order to make reliable angle of dip corrections.

Fifteen minutes later he had a position worked out, albeit a somewhat dubious one. The latitude fix ought to be within five degrees, which meant that the *Tulsar* was due west of Walvis Bay on the Atlantic coast of the former German colony of South-West Africa. His thoughts turned to his fellow Ossewa- Brandwag 'officer' in Windhoek. Every night General Rudolf Messener would be listening for messages broadcast by Kramer which he would relay on his powerful short-wave transmitter.

Kramer returned the sextant to its case and reached for his Afu suitcase radio-transmitter/receiver.

# 11

Milland hauled himself on to *U-330*'s bridge and gratefully inhaled draughts of air that weren't poisoned with the stench of sweat and diesel-oil. He pulled up the collar of his leather coat and rubbed his hands briskly together. Dawn was beginning its assault on the eastern horizon.

'Good morning, captain,' said Sarne, sensing that Milland was in good humour.

'Good morning, Mr Sarne,' Milland responded. 'Some good news to end your watch. HQ have relayed the *Tulsar*'s position to us. Their agent aboard the *Tulsar* is earning his keep.' He handed Sarne a blue signal flimsy. The junior officer examined it.

'Twenty-three degrees south – ten degrees east?'

'So?' Milland demanded.

'It's a bit vague for a position, don't you think, captain? Degrees in round figures – no minutes of arc?'

Milland chucked. 'It's better than nothing, Mr Sarne.'

Sarne said nothing. He could well understand his captain's

elation. The message was long overdue – the unspoken fear had been that the agent on the *Tulsar* had been discovered. 'Still a long way to go, Mr Sarne,' said Milland affably. 'But the great thing is that we know where the *Tulsar* is and they know nothing about us. She's as good as ours, Mr Sarne.'

# 12

Josephine nodded a good morning to the two Ursuline nuns who were leaning against the rail like a pair of benign crows. The newly-weds – not so newly wed now – were sitting at opposite ends of the flensing deck and pointedly ignoring each other while other passengers were sitting in small groups discussing in hushed tones the murder of Mrs Rose Lewis – an issue which for almost a month had proved a durable topic of conversation. Mr and Mrs Vanson were noisily conducting one of their frequent acrimonious disputes over Mr Vanson's long hours spent propped against the bar in the restaurant trying to forget Mrs Vanson.

Josephine could still hear the sugar magnate's wife's shrill voice as she made her way down the companion-way that led to the oil separator deck. The temperature rose noticeably below deck and she felt the covers of the two magazines she was carrying stick to her hands. The sides of the cavernous gallery closed in as she neared the bow. It was a trip she made a point of making twice a day. She rapped on the steel water-tight door that sealed the bow compartment from the rest of the ship.

'Mr Lewis? Are you awake?'

There was a movement on the far side of the door.

'Miss Britten?' answered a hopeful voice.

'Good morning, Mr Lewis. I've found you two more magazines. I'll leave them outside. The seamen will let you have them after your morning exercise.'

'Thank you, Miss Britten. You're very kind.'

'Did you sleep well?'

The voice that answered was apologetic. 'Not very well, Miss Britten... I could hear the noises. They're getting louder, I think.'

Josephine frowned. 'What noises, Mr Lewis?'

'I haven't liked to say anything before in case you thought I was being silly.'

'What noises?' Josephine asked again with some irritation.

'Well ... a sort of metallic, grating sound.'

Josephine listened. 'I can't hear anything.'

'It comes and goes.' Lewis paused. 'It's either me or maybe there's something wrong with the ship.'

'Mr Lewis, I'm going to speak to Mr Holden about having you moved out of here.'

'You mustn't make a fuss on my account. You promised that you wouldn't.'

'I promised that I wouldn't with the captain. Unlike the captain, Mr Holden isn't an unreasonable man.'

Holden closed his book when Josephine sat in the vacant deckchair beside him.

'You've got to do something about that poor man shut up in the bow compartment,' Josephine said without preamble.

'Me?'

'You're the owner.'

'I represent the owners,' Holden corrected.

'Which right now amounts to the same thing. It's inhuman shutting him up down there. He didn't kill his wife and you know he didn't.'

'Do I?' Holden asked blandly.

Josephine sensed that the fair-haired Englishman was mocking her. She broke her own rule and allowed the anger welling up to control her behaviour.

'Listen – if you were any judge of character you would know that Mr Lewis could not have possibly murdered his wife. My God, you've only got to look at him.'

'You mean his mild expression?'

'Yes.'

'Crippen had a mild, butter-wouldn't-melt-in-my-mouth expression, Jo. And I'll tell you something else – not one of the passengers or crew has a motive for killing Mrs Lewis.'

'How do you know?'

'Because I know all your backgrounds – even the backgrounds of those two nuns.'

Josephine stared at Holden. He was regarding her with a half smile that she found infuriating. 'Even me?'

Holden hooked his hands together behind his neck and gazed up into the clear sky. 'Even you, Jo. I know about your father's illness, and that he's not expected to live much longer which is why you're so anxious to return home. You must be as worried as everyone else about the time this voyage is taking and yet you've said nothing. I admire you for that.' He stood. 'I'll do my best with the captain.'

# 13

It was three hours after midnight on 8 April when Kramer edged back the lifeboat cover and gazed up at the arching splendour of the Milky Way vaulting across the clear tropical sky.

He swung his binoculars to the north in the direction the *Tulsar* was heading and quickly picked out the visible portion of the Plough in Ursa Major. Two of the stars were known to mariners as the Pointers. Kramer located them and followed the direction they indicated to the horizon. He found the point of light almost immediately. He had seen it before on his visit to Germany in 1936. It was a star never seen by those who spent all their lives in the southern hemisphere. Poised several light years above the North Pole to an accuracy of one degree, it was the star that had guided mariners through the ages from the first tentative wanderings of the Phoenicians and the Vikings. It was a star whose reliable presence had triggered the explosive spread of civilization, exploration and trade in the northern hemisphere, while culture in the southern hemisphere, with no equivalent accurate star, had stagnated.

It was Polaris – the Pole Star.

Its appearance told Kramer that the *Tulsar* had either

crossed the Equator or was very near to crossing it, a surmise
that was confirmed twenty minutes later when he completed
the calculations based on his sextant observations.

At one minute before his scheduled transmission time, he
switched on his Afu and waited for it to warm up. He
wondered how far away the U-boat was and whether it would
hear him.

# 14

'Captain to control-room! Captain to control-room!'

Milland was wide awake and strapping on his leg before
the loudspeaker on the bulkhead clicked into silence.

'This had better be good, Mr Sarne,' he growled when he
stumped into the control-room.

The first officer held out a signal flimsy. 'The best news since
we left Kiel, captain.'

CUCKOO TO EAGLE
TULSAR 2N 30W HEADING DUE NORTH 25 KNOTS

'The first signal we've managed to pick up direct from the
*Tulsar*,' said Sarne. 'The keying errors were in the right places
so there's no doubt that it's genuine.'

'Two degrees *north*!' Milland exclaimed jubilantly. He
moved to the chart-table and examined *U-330*'s position. The
U-boat was just below the Tropic of Cancer, six hundred miles
north-west of the Cape Verde islands. He plotted the *Tulsar*'s
position on the chart and measured the angle between it and
the U-boat with a pair of dividers.

'Twenty degrees,' Sarne commented, hoping his voice didn't
reveal his mounting excitement. 'One thousand two hundred
miles between him and us. We're on the same longitude – so
if he maintains his maximum speed on a northern heading and
we hold our maximum speed on a southern heading, we'll be
converging at fifty knots ...'

'And intercepting in twenty-four hours,' Milland finished.

'With luck. And if this weather holds.'

The two men studied the chart to confirm their deductions.

'Chief!' said Milland abruptly. 'Steer one-seven-five!'

*U-330* heeled gently as her bows came up to her corrected course.

Milland watched the gyro-compass with satisfaction. 'Okay, chief. Full speed ahead both!'

In the engine-room the diesel-mechanics stuffed cotton-wool in their ears and slid the throttles wide open.

# 15

Gerrard regarded the large black box with some suspicion. It was unlike any piece of equipment he had ever seen before and had been installed in the *Tulsar*'s radio-room by naval electronics experts from Simonstown during the whaler's Durban refit. Jack Colby, the *Tulsar*'s amiable Canadian radio-operator, had been given a brief training on the equipment's operation and maintenance.

'For Chrissake, Jack,' Gerrard muttered. 'Who in hell could be shadowing us at the speed we've been keeping up?'

'Colby shrugged. 'Search me, cap'n. All I'm saying is that I've picked up his signals two nights running. Always on the same bearing – astern of us – and at the same strength. Whatever it is, it's keeping up with us.'

Gerrard spun a chair round and sat astride it, resting his chin on the chair back while he stared at the black box. It was a recent British invention – High Frequency Direction Finding apparatus – known officially as H/F D/F and unofficially as 'Huff Duff'. It was a remarkable piece of equipment because it enabled the direction of radio signals to be pinpointed at sea without the need of shore receiving stations equipped with steerable antennae. Jack Colby had demonstrated to Gerrard how the apparatus worked. It was amazingly simple; in the centre of the black box was a tiny screen less than six inches in diameter. When signals were picked up by the Huff Duff's antenna, they appeared on the screen as a glowing ellipse. All the operator had to do was spin a wheel to tune the ellipse into a hard line, and the angle of the line across the screen gave the bearing of the source of the signals. Even short bursts could be quickly located. The British had developed the equipment to locate the position of talkative U-boats shadowing convoys. Hitherto, rapid radio direction-finding at sea had been impossible.

While Gerrard was prepared to accept that the equipment worked, he was not prepared to accept that it was possible for a ship to shadow the *Tulsar* without being seen during the clear weather they were enjoying, *and* for the ship to cling doggedly to the same position astern of the *Tulsar* irrespective of the *Tulsar*'s frequent course changes. It just wasn't physically possible and he told Colby so. The lanky Canadian gave another of his indifferent shrugs.

'Suit yourself, cap'n. But there ain't nothing wrong with that piece of fancy gear. It can pinpoint Rio a treat. Someone is following us, sure enough – sitting right on our tail.'

Gerrard woke Holden an hour before dawn. Despite the hour, the Englishman was alert and relaxed as he sat on his bunk listening to what Gerrard had to say.

'Colby is convinced that we're being shadowed,' said the American.

Holden raised his eyebrows. 'By what?'

'Search me. But Colby's certain from that Huff Duff thing that there's something sitting on our tail.'

Even Holden looked surprised. 'I would've thought it impossible.'

'That's exactly what I said.'

'So what do you plan on doing?'

'Nothing.'

'Is that wise?' Holden inquired.

'Okay – so maybe we start zig-zagging again.'

The suggestion pained Holden. 'Why not do the obvious?'

'And what's that?' Gerrard demanded suspiciously.

'Take a look.'

Gerrard levelled the Northrop seaplane out at fifteen thousand feet and circled to enable Holden to sweep the horizon with binoculars. In the clear, golden light of the early morning it was possible to see over a hundred miles at that altitude and yet the only movement Holden could see on the glittering blue expanse of the tropical Atlantic was the constantly-spreading V of the toy-like *Tulsar*'s shining white wake.

'Can you go higher?' Holden yelled above the roar of the engine.

Gerrard opened the Wright Cyclone's throttle and eased the tiny monoplane into a gentle climb. The horizon stretched further and further away and began hazing into a subtle blend with the flawless blue sky.

'Clearest I've ever known it!' Gerrard yelled to his companion.

And still there was nothing.

Gerrard levelled the Northrop out at twenty thousand feet. Holden became aware of the tightness in his chest caused by oxygen-depleted air. He kept searching with the binoculars. Visibility was excellent in all directions. The *Tulsar* was completely alone in the centre of a circle of ocean three hundred miles in diameter – an insignificant speck in the middle of a vast blue nothingness.

Holden lowered the binoculars and shook his head. Gerrard cut power and lost height in a series of wide, sweeping circles round the *Tulsar* while Holden kept searching. Gerrard was about to call Colby on the radio to tell him that he was coming in but returned the microphone to its hook when he saw the whaler losing way and stopping. He flew over the *Tulsar* at five hundred feet with the intention of landing the seaplane on the leeward side of the ship. It was then that he spotted something wrong with the cover on one of the port lifeboats. He opened up the engine, pulled the seaplane round in a tight turn, and flew back over the *Tulsar* for a closer look.

'Torn lifeboat cover,' he shouted in response to Holden's query.

'Serious?'

'Yeah – a lifeboat can fill with several tons of water from heavy seas and squalls. One crashed down on a deck damn near killing two men on my first trip.'

Gerrard carefully gauged a long trough in the ocean's lazy swell and quickly cut power when the seaplane's floats touched the surface. The tremendous water drag on the speeding floats hauled the seaplane to a stop in less than a hundred yards. He taxied the wildly bucking aircraft into the relative calm afforded by the *Tulsar*'s drifting bulk and anxiously watched the ship heaving ponderously towards them. The derrick was swung out with a Malay boy clinging precariously to the hoist. Gerrard cut the engine so that the boy would not be mangled by the seaplane's spinning propeller. For crucial seconds Gerrard and Holden were wholly dependent on the boy's agility, unable to taxi clear of the *Tulsar*'s looming bulk if trouble threatened.

The boy's feet landed on the wing. There was the sound of the hoist being shackled to the seaplane's lifting-point. A second later a pair of large intelligent eyes looked down through the clear canopy. The lad gave Gerrard the thumbs-up sign and repeated the gesture to the ship for the benefit of Piet who was manning the donkey engine.

The big Afrikaner engaged the donkey engine's clutch and lifted the seaplane clear of the water. Willing hands guided the floats down on to the seaplane's platform and held the canopy open for Gerrard and Holden.

'Nothing,' Gerrard announced to Colby who was watching quizzically from the circle of chattering Malays and Lascars. 'Absolutely nothing. Not even porpoises. You might as well toss that Huff Duff gizmo over the side.'

Gerrard jumped down to the deck followed by Holden. Colby looked at Holden for confirmation. The Englishman gave an expressionless nod.

'Piet!' Gerrard yelled. 'The cover on lifeboat six has got a rip in it you can drive a bus through. Have it fixed right now.'

Piet climbed down from the derrick operator's saddle and barked an order to the Malay boy who had secured the hoist to the seaplane.

The passengers had watched the seaplane's launching and recovery with great interest because it made a welcome break in the ship's monotonous routine. Josephine pushed through the small crowd towards Holden.

'Enjoy your trip?'

'Fine,' said Holden, brushing his lightweight suit with his

hands and looking in concern at an oil stain. 'Whale steaks for dinner had we spotted anything.'

Josephine was not amused. 'Have you spoken to him about poor Mr Lewis?'

'Have you got anything that will get this stain out?'

'What about Mr Lewis!' Her almond eyes went round with anger. 'Well?'

'There are other problems to deal with at the moment,' was Holden's unhelpful reply.

Josephine saw Gerrard moving towards the bridge steps. On an impulse she suddenly pushed forward and grabbed hold of his arm.

'Captain Gerrard –' But she got no further for there was a loud report from aft followed by a blood-chilling scream. Josephine followed Gerrard and Holden as the two men raced down the port deck towards the stern. There was a rush of passengers' feet behind her and then loud gasps of dismay. Josephine was dimly aware of Mrs Eli Vanson's screams as she was dragged away from the scene by her husband.

Gerrard's arm was round the shoulders of the half-naked Malay boy who had jumped down on to the seaplane. For a second Josephine thought she was going to faint when she saw his terrible injury. Blood was pumping from the boy's neck and coursing across the deck.

'My God,' she whispered. 'Oh, my God.' Despite her shock, she had the presence of mind to rip a panel out of her dress. With a fleeting, grateful glance, Gerrard tore the cloth from her fingers and rolled it into a ball which he pressed against the deep wound that traversed the boy's chest and ended in his neck. Josephine was dimly aware of Piet's booming voice behind her bellowing at everyone to get back.

'Hold it in place,' Gerrard commanded Holden.

Without hesitation, the Englishman pressed his hand against the sodden cloth while Gerrard tried to staunch the flow of blood by digging his fingers hard into the boy's carotid artery.

'Baas ... boat ...' the boy moaned. 'Boat ... boat ...'

Blood and spittle frothed between the boy's lips and flecked Gerrard's arms.

'Okay, sonny,' said Gerrard gently, sliding his free hand

under the lad's body. 'Don't try to say anything.' He glanced up at Josephine and Holden. 'We've got to get him down to the sick bay and we've got to carry him level. Okay – lift when I say.'

Holden supported the boy's back while Josephine carefully slid her arms under his knees. They lifted the boy when Gerrard gave the word and carried him through the silent crowd while Gerrard kept his grip on the carotid artery. A sailmaker's awl fell from the boy's fingers as he was lifted on to the stainless steel table in the sick bay.

Gerrard took his fingers away. The blood didn't resume pumping from the ghastly wound. He held the boy's wrist for half a minute before carefully placing the tiny brown hand across the still chest. He avoided looking at Josephine and Holden, and she knew that it was unnecessary for him to say anything.

One of the two Ursuline nuns appeared in the doorway. She looked anxiously from face to face and then at the still form on the table. 'Is there anything we can do?' she asked.

# 16

*U-330*'s speed was pushed up to an incredible twenty-seven knots in the ideal weather conditions that were prevailing in mid-Atlantic.

Chief engineer Otto Munt's calculations showed that the two roaring Maybach diesels were consuming fuel at the rate of quarter of a ton per hour. But Milland wasn't concerned; the *Tulsar* would have ample oil to enable *U-330* to replenish her tanks.

Despite the appalling bucking motion of the charging U-boat, Milland had plenty of work for the crew. Ready-use ammunition lockers by the 104-millimetre and 37-millimetre guns were filled and the guns themselves cleaned of saltwater deposits and greased. Even the quadruple 20-millimetre anti-aircraft guns were checked and loaded with long, snaking belts of tracer. Once Milland was in range of the *Tulsar*, he was determined to bring all the U-boat's considerable firepower to bear immediately – especially on the bridge and wheelhouse. With Gerrard dead there was a chance that the whaler could be persuaded to surrender. With Gerrard alive, there was no chance. Although Milland knew nothing of how Gerrard would behave under conditions of war, he knew enough about his adversary's character to make a shrewd guess that Gerrard would sooner scuttle the *Tulsar* than allow it to be captured – especially by a U-boat.

Milland thought of the times he and Gerrard had spent together: the long voyages down to the desolate, frozen wastes of the Southern Ocean – hunting amid the grinding nightmares of fog-shrouded icebergs in their relentless pursuit of the immensely profitable schools of mighty blue whales. On one occasion their bonuses had amounted to a thousand dollars each which they had blown in a memorable two weeks of warm Australian beer, hot-blooded Sydney waterfront prostitutes in dingy bedrooms who knew how to separate a man from his money painlessly, and chilly magistrates in austere courtrooms who knew how to do it painfully.

But that had been before his leg had been crushed by a blue whale breaking loose on the *Tulsar*'s slipway and Gerrard's greed had made him into a cripple.


# 17

It was thirty minutes since the murder of the Malay boy.

Holden reached the corner of the superstructure and dropped flat on his stomach, holding the *Tulsar*'s Lee Enfield rifle across his forearms, army fashion. He crawled behind a rearing ventilator shaft and peered cautiously down the weatherdeck to where the Malay boy had been shot. He heard Gerrard move behind him.

'You see anything?'

'He must be in the lifeboat,' Holden replied calmly and aimed the rifle at the lifeboat.

'Whoever it is, we want him alive,' Gerrard reminded Holden.

Holden said nothing. He had no doubt that the man in the lifeboat was Kramer. If Kramer was taken alive the chances were that with the ugly mood Gerrard was in over the recent killing, Kramer might talk to save his skin. Holden didn't know why Kramer had stowed away on the *Tulsar* but he did know that it would be dangerous to let Kramer live.

'You in there!' Holden shouted. 'I'm giving you five seconds to come out! You hear me!'

Silence.

Holden fired. The Lee Enfield kicked like a mule against his shoulder and the shot chewed into the heavy pulley block that secured the bow end of the lifeboat to the davit. He worked the bolt and sent two more rounds crashing into the ash block. The lifeboat swayed dangerously.

'Neat,' Gerrard commented admiringly. He raised his voice. 'Are you coming out or do we shoot you out?'

Holden fired again. The ropes holding the lifeboat parted. The bow crashed down on to the deck and twisted sideways, spilling folding oars and water tanks across the steel plating. There was a movement under the tangle of ropes and canvas. Kramer had lost his pistol when the lifeboat crashed down. He cursed and thrust his hands high above his head.

'Don't shoot! Don't shoot!'

He stood up. A wild, unkempt, filthy man with a savage look of defiance in his eye.

Gerrard lunged forward and knocked the Lee Enfield down just as Holden pulled the trigger. The bullet smacked against the deck near Kramer's feet and zinged skywards, causing Kramer to hold his hands even higher.

'Don't shoot, you bastards!' he snarled.

'I thought we wanted him alive, Mr Holden?' Gerrard observed caustically.

Holden assumed a sheepish smile. 'I thought he was holding a gun.'

Holden completed his examination of Kramer's suitcase Afu

and closed the lid. 'Ingenious. Ten watts' power – about three-hundred miles' range – possibly ten times that at night.'

'For Chrissake,' Gerrard muttered, taking the set from Holden and turning it over in his powerful fingers. 'All we've got to do now is find out who the bastard's been talking to.'

'You think he'll talk?'

'He'll talk,' said Gerrard grimly.

The determined note in the American's voice worried Holden. 'He's a spy and a murderer,' he pointed out. 'The British authorities are the right people to deal with him.'

Gerrard angrily stubbed out his cigar. 'Listen, Mr Holden, your government may own the *Tulsar* but she's still a US-registered ship and subject to US law. And under the law, I have the power to carry out any investigation I please. Right now I aim to find out from that murdering bastard who he is, who he's been talking to and why.'

Holden wrestled with his inner dilemma: to raise too many objections to the interrogation of Kramer might arouse the American's suspicions. On the other hand there was the danger that Kramer might talk and tell everything. If Kramer did confess, Holden wondered whether he would be able to talk himself out of trouble by saying that Kramer was lying. Everything depended on Kramer and the lengths Gerrard was prepared to go to in his questioning. He looked up into the American's grey eyes and guessed that the pressure Gerrard was prepared to put on Kramer would be considerable.

Holden nodded. 'Okay, captain. We question him.'

'Piet!' Gerrard yelled out.

'Cap'n?' the Afrikaner inquired, poking his head round the day-cabin door.

'You can release Lewis from the bow compartment. Tell him we've got the guy that killed his wife, and get Miss Britten to fix him up with a meal. We'll have our prisoner in now.'

Kramer was frogmarched into the cabin between two Lascar greasers who were none too gentle thrusting him into a chair. His hard eyes glared at the two men sitting opposite him but he gave no hint to suggest that he had recognized Holden.

'Name?' Gerrard fired.

Kramer's eyes flicked to Gerrard and blazed hatred from the depths of his straggling hair and beard.

'Name?' Gerrard repeated.

Kramer hollowed his cheeks and spat. The glob struck Gerrard in the face. The American lifted his wiry forearm to wipe the mess away and completed the movement by bringing the back of his hand hard across Kramer's face. Blood trickled from the corner of the German's mouth. His lips curled into a contemptuous smile.

'Name!'

Kramer's smile broadened but he kept his eyes firmly on Gerrard. At no time did he look at Holden.

'Piet,' Gerrard said to the Afrikaner who had just entered the cabin. 'Go fetch me a two-inch chisel and a heavy hammer.'

Gerrard sat back in his chair and watched the German carefully. The blood soaking into his whiskers gave his face the appearance of a grotesque, grinning mask.

Piet entered a minute later and placed a hammer and chisel on the desk.

'Thanks, Piet.' Gerrard picked up the chisel and ran the ball of his thumb along the gleaming edge, producing a thin line of blood. He nodded to the Lascars. 'Spread his left hand out.'

Kramer tried to struggle but the days he had spent in the lifeboat had weakened him considerably. The two sailors had little difficulty in forcing his hand down on to the desk.

'Hold his little finger out,' Gerrard commanded, holding the chisel in one hand and the hammer in the other.

The atmosphere in the cabin suddenly became very tense. Gerrard matched Kramer's smile with one of his own and rested the edge of the chisel across Kramer's little finger just below the knuckle.

'Well, fella,' said Gerrard cheerfully. 'I guess you don't have to be told what I'm planning. I'm going to chop your fingers off one by one until you decide to answer my questions.' He held the hammer poised two feet above the chisel's handle. 'Name?'

Kramer's mask-like smile became a glare of defiance.

There was a sharp crack as Gerrard brought the hammer down.

Holden muttered an involuntary, 'Christ.'

Kramer made not a sound but his arrogant expression changed to bewilderment when he saw the severed end of his little finger lying on the desk several inches from his mutilated hand. Blood was springing from around the shattered bone protruding from his knuckle.

'Now his thumb.'

The Lascars spread Kramer's thumb out on the desk.

'Name?'

Kramer stared down at the desk in silence. Holden's hopes that the German-born Afrikaner would be able to hold out began to rise.

'Cap'n –' Piet began.

'Shut up!'

The prisoner looked up at Gerrard with lustreless eyes. He suddenly shrank from the touch of cold steel as Gerrard rested the chisel's cutting-edge on his thumb.

'Paulus Kramer,' he croaked.

'Who were you transmitting to?'

Kramer didn't answer. Gerrard yanked Kramer's head up by his beard and repeated the question.

'A U-boat. For shit's sake do something about my finger!'

Gerrard caught Piet's eye and inclined his head to the door. 'And you,' he said to the Lascars. The three men left the cabin leaving Holden and Gerrard alone with Kramer who was desperately pressing his finger into his left wrist to stem the flow of blood.

'Let it bleed,' said Gerrard. 'It'll help keep it clean.'

Kramer relaxed his grip. Blood flowed afresh from the gory mess where his little finger had been. The finger itself lay palely in its own macabre pool of blood.

'What's the U-boat supposed to do?'

'Capture this ship,' said Kramer.

Holden decided to take part in the questioning in the hope that he would be able to lead Kramer off dangerous ground. 'Do you know what our cargo is, Kramer?'

'Yes.' The answer was spat out. The prisoner's spirit was returning. 'Gold. You've got to do something about my finger!'

'How did the Germans find out about the gold? Have they got spies in the Reserve Bank?'

Kramer saw the lead offered in Holden's question and seized upon it. 'Yes. Several.'

'Have you broadcast our position to this U-boat?' Gerrard asked.

Kramer nodded. 'But I swear to God that I don't know where the U-boat is. Please – my finger ...'

'How often do you talk to them?'

'Every night between midnight and three.'

Gerrard grinned. 'You're right-handed, Kramer? You wanna know why I was so considerate and worked on your left hand?'

Kramer made no reply.

'Because you'll need your right hand to talk to your U-boat friends at the usual time. You agree to that and I'll consider trying to sew your finger back on.'

# 18

CUCKOO TO EAGLE
TULSAR STOPPED WITH FOULED PROPELLER 9N 35W PLEASE GIVE YOUR POSITION AND ESTIMATED TIME OF INTERCEPT

Milland read through the signal again and gave it back to Sarne. He turned to Venner. 'And there definitely was no keying error in the fifth character of the text?'

'It's difficult to say, captain,' said the radio operator. 'He sent three times as he usually does. The error was there in the second transmission but not in the others. The trouble is that his Morse is so bad that it's hard to tell which are genuine errors and which are not. I needed all three of his transmissions to get the whole message down.'

'And it's the first time he's asked us for information on our position,' Sarne added.

Milland looked down at the chart. 'If Cuckoo's signal is genuine, we could intercept the *Tulsar* just before dawn.'

'*If* it's genuine,' Sarne commented.

Milland was undecided. Until *U-330* was within hydrophone range in order to get a fix on the *Tulsar*'s bearing, he was wholly dependent on the signals from the agent aboard the whaler for even the slightest chance of intercepting her. He carefully weighed the various considerations and came to a compromise decision:

'We'll treat Cuckoo's position of the *Tulsar* as genuine but we won't supply him with ours. We'll merely send him a brief acknowledgement of his signal.'

'Yes, captain.' Venner returned to his radio compartment.

Milland gazed impassively at Sarne for a moment before allowing his face to relax into a grin. 'Set course to intercept, Mr Sarne.'

The news that *U-330* was closing with her quarry swept through the boat in minutes. Bottles of beer, which Milland had strictly forbidden to be brought aboard, mysteriously appeared and were passed around by a jubilant off-watch crew.

Milland smiled thinly to himself as he hauled himself hand over hand up to the bridge. The lookouts were singing in perfect unison in the darkness, not allowing their song to interfere with their vigilance.

What the hell, Milland thought, deciding not to castigate them, they've earned it.

# 19

Jack Colby straightened up from the *Tulsar*'s Huff Duff set. 'Due north,' he announced. 'Range between a hundred and three hundred miles.'

Gerrard groaned. 'For Chrissake, Jack, can't you be more accurate than that?'

'That's pretty good,' said Holden. 'The Huff Duff is only accurate at providing a U-boat's bearing – not its range.'

'And it was a bloody short transmission,' Colby added.

'Jesus Christ!' Gerrard exploded. 'The bastard could be on top of us before dawn!'

Holden rose to his feet. 'Which means we had better set about putting my plan into operation right now.'

Gerrard gaped at the Englishman. 'You're not serious?'

'Why not?'

'It's a crazy idea, that's why.'

'Only if it doesn't work,' Holden murmured, moving to the door.

Josephine picked her way through the feverishly busy carpenters working under floodlights on the flensing deck. She had to shout at Holden to make herself heard above the sounds of nails being hammered into timber. Holden had his sleeves rolled up and was busily sawing through a plank. The industrious Englishman's shirt was clinging to his sweat-drenched body. The sight was even more surprising than all the unexplained activity because she imagined that Holden was not the sort of man to exert himself if it could possibly be avoided. Then she noticed Gerrard armed with a claw-hammer tearing the nails out of packing-cases. Holden stopped work when he finally noticed Josephine.

'Mr Holden. Would you mind telling me what's going on? I'm getting complaints from the passengers about the noise.'

'They'd be complaining even more if German U-boats start firing torpedoes into us,' was Holden's unhelpful reply.

'The noise is designed to frighten them away?'

Holden mopped his face with a silk handkerchief. 'How's Mr Lewis, Jo?'

'If he could get some sleep, maybe his temper will improve so that I can talk him out of his plans to sue the lot of you for wrongful arrest. Just what the hell is it you're building? A stage?'

'Something like that, Jo.' Holden resumed sawing and refused to be drawn further on the subject of the curious structure.

# 20

The cloud spreading from the west trapped the warmth rising from the ocean and layered the sluggish swell with a fine, warm mist. The night was unbelievably hot. Milland leaned on the U-boat's bridge coaming and wished that he could emulate the lookouts by stripping to the waist.

There was the sound of muted laughter from the foredeck where the off-watch crew had gathered to take advantage of the breeze generated by the speeding U-boat. The sensation of speed was heightened by the rolling clouds of mist that hurled themselves at the bridge, parting at the last second to avoid Milland and reuniting in the aft turbulence. There was a curiously dead atmosphere about the U-boat which Milland attributed to the cloying mist. Even the roar of diesel exhaust from the vent and the hiss and surge of water through the deck casing drains sounded muted and unreal.

'Control-room – bridge,' said Hans Fischer's voice.

Milland flipped the voice-pipe open. 'Bridge.'

'Time for another hydrophone sweep, captain.'

'Very good, Mr Fischer. Tell the chief to stop engines. I'm coming down.'

A minute later Venner settled his hydrophone headphones comfortably over his ears and switched on the first transducer. There were several of the sensitive underwater microphones grouped around the U-boat's hull which could be selected individually to pinpoint the direction of underwater noises.

Several minutes passed as Venner made minute adjustments to the knob that controlled the underwater microphone switches. Suddenly he tensed and pressed the headphones hard against his ears. 'I'm getting something. Very faint machinery or engine noises bearing one-eight-one.'

Milland's pulse accelerated. Virtually due south! The right direction! 'Range?' he fired at Venner.

'Can't say,' the radio-operator replied. 'It could be small engine thirty miles off or a large engine sixty miles off.'

Milland weighed up the problem. 'Well at least we've got a bearing on something. We'll run at maximum speed on the surface for another hour and stop for another hydrophone sweep.'

'Definitely a small diesel engine,' Venner announced an hour later.

Milland frowned. 'The *Tulsar*'s got a number of small diesels for her derricks and winches, but would the sound from one of those carry into the water? They're mounted up on deck.'

'How about an air-pump?' Sarne suggested. 'If they've got divers over the side working to clear a fouled propeller, the chances are that they're having to run an air-pump.'

Milland clapped his first officer on the shoulder. 'Of course! It's a damned air-pump!'

Venner checked the sound-level of the throbbing engine. 'In that case, I'd put its range at between ten and fifteen miles.'

'It's *got* to be the *Tulsar*,' Milland declared. 'Goddamn it, it's got to be!' He snatched down the crew address microphone and called Munt in the engine-room. 'Chief! Full speed ahead both!' He swung round to Fischer. 'Stand by with your gun crews, Mr Fischer.'

'Gun crews standing by, captain.'

'Boarding-party standing by,' Sarne called, not waiting to be prompted.

Milland rejoined the lookouts on the bridge. The gun crews emerged through the forward hatch and hurried to their respective weapons. Sarne and the twelve men that comprised his armed boarding-party were next to appear. All the men moved silently in their soft-soled shoes. They were well drilled in their various tasks – not a word was exchanged between them. After the boarding-party had inflated the U-boat's two dinghies, they sat down on the spray-drenched deck to be out of the gunners' line of sight once the shooting started.

'Control-room – bridge!' It was Venner's voice.

Milland acknowledged.

'Radar echo,' Venner stated. 'One-eight-four. Range six miles.'

'Chief!' Milland called. 'Stop engines! Half ahead on both electrics!'

125

There was a sudden silence from the diesel vent that was replaced by the soft purr of *U-330*'s electric motors.

'Range five miles,' Venner reported.

The grey U-boat ran on through the warm mist at a steady but silent eight knots.

'Have the searchlight sent up,' Milland requested.

Two ratings manhandled the heavy lamp through the bridge hatch and mounted it on the swivel bracket in front of the attack periscope. It was a cumbersome thing, rarely used because it had to be unshipped before the boat could dive, and the supply cable, which had to pass through the hatch, inevitably got in the way.

'Range three miles,' Venner informed. 'What's the tonnage of the *Tulsar*, captain?'

'Seven thousand. Why?'

There was a pause at the other end of the voice-pipe. 'These DT radar sets are pretty good on range,' Venner commented, 'but they're not so good on size indication. It seems a small echo for seven thousand tons.'

Milland chuckled. 'Be even smaller by the time we've shot away its radio mast and bridge.' Despite the bantering reply, there was no humour in his expression as he peered into the darkness. The mist was beginning to lift.

*It's all been too easy so far. Something's wrong!*

At that moment Milland heard the sound of the engine. Fischer heard it too and glanced expectantly up at the bridge.

'I heard it, Mr Fischer. You'll hold your fire until we're within five hundred metres as planned.'

Venner reported the range as one mile. Sweat trickled into the socket of Milland's artificial leg. He felt the leg shift out of position, moving the heel so that he felt off-balance and insecure.

*Dear God – not that. Not now.*

The engine was much louder. Thudding away in the thinning mist. It was the only sound in the night.

*There should be other sounds!*

Milland realized that he was letting his imagination take over his reason.

'Six hundred metres, captain.'

Milland's heart was hammering in unison with the unseen

diesel engine. His lips moved nearer the voice-pipe as he gauged *U-330*'s approach.

'Bridge – control-room! Now!'

The helmsman spun his wheel to port and at the same time Munt shut down the electric motors. Milland snapped the searchlight on just as the U-boat went about. He aimed the beam of light in the direction of the throbbing diesel engine.

'Fire!'

The big 104-millimetre was the first to open up. There was a flash and a boom followed by the whine of the shell arching through the night. Then the 20-millimetre added its quadruple yammer, spitting streaks of white tracer at the target.

Except that there wasn't a target.

Milland stared through the smoke – ignoring the fumes stinging his eyes. There was nothing there! Dazed, he heard Sarne call for decreased elevation. The main gun boomed another shell across the water. The 37-millimetre quick-firing gun joined in the racket. Fischer was yelling at the men passing heavy shells in a human chain from the ready-use lockers. Confused and bewildered, Milland swung the searchlight beam backwards and forwards. And then he saw it: instead of a 7,000-ton whaling-ship, illuminated by the beam was a makeshift raft fabricated from planks and oil drums. In the centre of the deserted raft was a puffing donkey engine. There was a banner strung the length of the raft that bore a hand-painted query made famous by Walt Disney:

WHO'S AFRAID OF THE BIG BAD WOLF?

The gunner manning the 20-millimetre followed the search-light beam. Splinters flew from the raft a second before the main gun scored a direct hit, blasting the raft to matchwood.

'Cease firing, you idiots!'

'Light to port!' yelled a lookout.

Milland spun round and stared in the opposite direction at the blinding light bearing down on the U-boat from less than fifty metres. The charging light separated. Frantically Milland swung the searchlight round, ignoring his displaced artificial leg. He caught a fleeting glimpse of what he thought at first was an E-boat. There were two of them.

'Open fire to port!' Milland screamed. 'Open fire!'

But the confused gunners were too late. There was a bright powder flash from the leading boat when it was within twenty metres of the U-boat. The distinctive sharp crack that followed the flash was a sound that Milland knew well – it was the sound of a harpoon-gun being fired. In that instant he realized with despair that the two craft were the *Tulsar*'s high-speed whale-catchers. The bulging warhead of the Svend Foyn harpoon struck *U-330* near the bow. The ensuing blast shredded the inflatable dinghies and swept Sarne and his boarding-party into the sea. The first whale-catcher sheered away, chased by tracer flashes from the 20-millimetre gun. But the gunner mis-judged the craft's speed and sprayed a seam of miniature waterspouts impotently into its wake.

The second boat came charging in. Milland saw what was coming – a shadowy figure was crouched over the harpoon-gun and aiming it straight at the conning-tower. Milland jabbed the Klaxon button and threw himself flat. The blinding flash and numbing concussion deprived him of sight and hear-ing for precious seconds. He struggled on to his good leg in time to see the last of the gunners diving down the hatch. He saw Fischer struggling in the water but was unable to make himself heard above the Klaxon's strident blaring.

The U-boat's diesels burst into life. *U-330* gathered way, rapidly building up the necessary momentum for the crash dive that the Klaxon had initiated. Already water was flooding into the ballast tanks. In the chaos it seemed certain that Munt was going to take the boat down without waiting for confirma-tion that the bridge hatch was closed.

Another explosion shook the U-boat. There was the sound of a high-powered petrol engine howling past the boat, but Mil-land wasn't interested; his immediate concern was to get down the hatch and close it before the boat was swamped. He crawled to the opening and dangled his legs down into the void while hanging on with one hand and groping for the hatch cover with the other.

The hatch refused to close.

*The cable! The bloody searchlight cable!*

'Hold it, chief!' Milland yelled. 'For God's sake someone disconnect the searchlight! I can't close the hatch!'

He could hear a commotion from the control-room. Someone was shouting about flood water. Grimly, he doubled the cable round his wrist and heaved in the desperate hope that he could tear the cable out of the searchlight. It broke free on his third attempt and fell about his shoulders. Thankfully he slammed the hatch shut and turned the locking handwheel a second before the bridge was flooded.

Without warning, *U-330* suddenly canted down by the bow nearly causing Milland to lose grip on the ladder. He could hear Munt below bellowing something about getting the door closed. Then there were noises that chilled his blood: the surging roar of water flooding into the boat, and the terrible metallic crash that could only be an engine breaking away from its mountings.

By the time he had dropped into the control-room and steadied himself on the crazily-tilting floor, *U-330* had dived past the 150-metre mark and was plunging out of control towards the ocean floor, three miles below.

# 21

Dawn was probing the eastern horizon when Gerrard throttled back alongside Holden's boat and grinned broadly across at the Englishman. 'Some sport, eh, Mr Holden?'

Piet, who was manning the harpoon-gun on Holden's boat, gave a booming laugh. 'Beats whales, cap'n.'

'How many hits did you manage, Mr Gerrard?' asked Holden. Brody centred the harpoon-gun on Gerrard's boat and called out: 'Three on the bow – all in the same place, like you said, Mr Holden.'

'Listen!' said Piet sharply. Holden shone the helm searchlight in the direction where Piet was pointing and picked out heads bobbing in the swell. There were seven men swimming with feeble strokes towards the two whale-catchers. Gerrard opened his throttle and eased his catcher alongside the struggling men. One by one Brody hauled them over the cockpit coaming. The seventh man was in a bad way; he gave a low moan when Brody grabbed his wrist. The man's hands were coated in oil causing Brody to lose his grip. The seaman made a grab at the man's collar and succeeded in tearing away his identity disc. Brody swore, tossed the disc in the cockpit and dived into the sea. He spent five minutes in a fruitless search for the missing German and climbed back into the whale-catcher, shaken and dispirited.

Holden manœuvred his craft and shone the light on each of the pinched, miserable faces in turn. 'An uninspiring collection,' he observed.

'Reckon they understand that throat-disease language of yours, Piet?' Gerrard asked.

Piet leaned across and addressed the survivors in Afrikaans. They replied with blank stares. Holden's excellent French produced the same result. Gerrard regarded them in contempt.

'How about English? Who speaks English?'

The men remained silent.

'They don't look much use,' said Gerrard, turning back to helm. 'Toss 'em over the side, Sam.'

'No!' said one of the Germans. 'That is forbidden. You cannot do that.'

Gerrard jerked the speaker to his feet by the lapels of his jacket. He noticed the single gold stripe below the five-pointed star on the man's sleeve. 'Can you speak English?'

'A little.'

Gerrard was surprised to see that the junior officer was scared of him. It was something he had not expected in a German.

'Name?'

'Leutnant zur See Hans Fischer.'

'Well, Leutnant zur See Hans Fischer, next time I ask a question and you remain silent, I'll kick your fucking Kraut ass all over the Atlantic Ocean. Do you understand?'

'*Jawohl, Herr Kapitän.*'

'Yes fucking sir!' Gerrard roared.

'Yes fucking sir,' Fischer repeated miserably.

Holden jumped down into the cockpit of Gerrard's boat and picked up the missing man's identity disc. 'Was Peter Sarne your commanding officer?' he asked Fischer after examining the disc.

130

'Cap'n!' Piet shouted.

The Afrikaner was pointing at the sea. Thirty yards from the two whale-catchers the surface was beginning to boil white. 'Air escaping from the U-boat, I guess,' Brody observed laconically.

The erupting bubbles spread rapidly until a sizable patch of the ocean was seething with life-giving air geysering from the unseen U-boat. The six survivors exchanged glances but remained silent as they watched the phenomenon. After a few minutes the bubbles gradually diminished and finally stopped, allowing the surface of the Atlantic to revert to its rolling black swell.

A picture formed unbidden in Holden's mind of the U-boat's remains, its crew and hull crushed by the inexorable pressure, gliding down to the ocean's abyssal floor. Gerrard appeared to be thinking the same thing as he stared down at the sea. Then he looked up and caught Holden's eye. He gave a crooked smile.

'Well done, Mr Holden. A crazy idea. But it worked like a dream, huh?'

'A measure of insanity has no countermeasures,' said Holden before climbing on to the coaming and jumping back into his own boat.

# 22

Milland ignored the pain in his stump from his heavy landing on the control-room floor. He clung to the back of the helmsman's chair and demanded to know what had happened.

'Pressure hull holed!' the helmsman answered.

The impact of the man's words cleared Milland's veil of pain. Before he could speak men were suddenly stumbling through the control-room. 'Everyone aft!' Munt's voice could be heard bellowing. 'Come on, you dozy bastards! Move! Move! Move!'

'Port engine off its mountings!' shouted a distorted voice from the loudspeaker.

Milland snatched down the crew address microphone. 'Motor-room! Group up and full astern both motors!'

The downward tilt of the boat steepened. Milland grabbed hold of Munt and hauled him up the sloping floor into the control-room.

'Fist-sized hole in the bow torpedo compartment,' the chief engineer panted. 'I've got the door shut and blown compressed air in which is stopping further flooding.'

'All ballast tanks blown,' a petty officer reported.

Milland glanced at the large depth-gauge above the planesman's head. The needle was steady at a hundred and sixty metres; the reversing propellers were arresting U-330's slide into the depths.

'The batteries won't hold for much longer,' said Munt, reading Milland's thoughts.

'How about plugging the hole?'

'It works in theory,' said Munt cautiously, 'but never in practice.'

'As it's our only hope, we'll try it,' said Milland cryptically.

'Now!' yelled Munt. He spun the locking-wheel and the bow torpedo compartment door burst open as though a bomb had gone off behind it, releasing a miniature tidal wave of seawater that nearly swept Munt's legs from under him.

Machin and Hoffman, two engine-room mechanics who had been selected for the task because of their considerable build, dived through the open door and were immediately up to their waists in water. The water gushing through the hole in the pressure hull appeared to possess the rigidity of an iron bar – twice it blasted the wad of cotton waste out of their hands as they struggled to wedge it into the hole. They succeeded in pinioning it in place on their third attempt but with water spraying around the edge of the plug like a giant watering-can rose.

Munt offered a silent, heartfelt prayer; Milland's improbable idea had worked because, by the grace of God, the hull had been holed in one of the few places where it wasn't obstructed by pipes and electric cables. He waded into the torpedo compartment and lifted the microphone off its hook.

'Okay, captain,' he informed Milland. 'You can start the pumps.'

At dawn *U-330*'s grey conning-tower lifted slowly above the surface of the Atlantic in time to greet the sun.

# PART THREE

**WINNING**

# 1

It was 11 April, two days after the attack on the U-boat; Milland was taking the loss of Sarne and Fisher badly and was in no mood for Munt's reasoned arguments. He ignored the chief engineer and concentrated on transferring U-330's position on to the chart. Munt waited patiently. Finally Milland looked up.

'We're seven hundred miles west of Dakar on the west coast of Africa, Munt,' said Milland calmly. 'If we hold our present course we'll pass west of the Azores, and west of the Azores is the course the *Tulsar* will take to stay out of range of the long-range bomber squadron at Bordeaux. I think you should return to the control-room now.'

Munt stood his ground. 'With respect, captain. With the port diesel smashed we can't make any more than this twelve knots. We can't dive with that plug in the pressure hull *and* we've lost twelve men *and* we've lost the element of surprise. If stopping the *Tulsar* is that important then we must signal the OKM.'

Milland's patience was dangerously near breaking-point. He controlled himself with considerable effort because Munt was now his acting first officer and was entitled to express his side of the argument. He stood and pulled on his cap.

'We maintain radio silence, Munt.' He paused and stared hard at the chief engineer. 'I will tell you this much. So long as I have a boat, a crew, and guns, I shall continue to obey my orders. Obedience to orders is expected of me just as I demand it of you.'

Munt donned his cap, returned Milland's curt salute and left the cabin nursing the growing suspicion that Milland's hard stare had been that of a man who was in danger of losing his sanity.

# 2

Josephine fell into step beside Holden as he was taking his customary early morning walk around the weatherdeck.

'Good morning, Mr Holden.'

Holden returned the greeting without altering his measured pace.

'As I've made clear to you, Mr Holden, I never ask for or expect favours.'

Holden leaned against the rail and inclined his head, listening to the two Ursuline nuns who were singing a hymn near the stern. Their soft notes perfumed the clear morning air. 'But you're going to ask one now?' he inquired.

'I've talked Mr Lewis out of suing you and Captain Gerrard for wrongful arrest even though you both deserve it, *and* I've spent hours heading off complaints from the other passengers over the time this voyage is taking. We should've docked in New York a week ago.'

'Don't blame me for our zig-zagging, Jo. For all we know that U-boat we sank may have been just one out of an entire pack of them.'

'I've explained all that. Even so, Mr Vanson is demanding to know why we're doing about ten knots when we could be doing fifteen or more.'

Holden resumed walking. 'U-boats have hydrophones – underwater microphones. The faster we go the easier we make it for them to hear us. So what's the favour?'

'I want to find out about my father. Mr Colby said it would be possible to send a short-wave signal to Western Union in Panama for forwarding to New York. When I asked him how much it would cost he said that the sending of messages required the captain's permission. I asked the captain yesterday and he said that it was up to you. As this is still a US registered ship – a neutral ship, Mr Holden – and I'm prepared to pay out of my own pocket to send the cable, I don't see –'

'I'll tell Mr Colby that I've no objection to your message being sent, Jo,' Holden interrupted. He pointed to Piet who was standing on the bridge, signalling to him. 'Excuse me, but I'm wanted.'

Holden entered Gerrard's day-cabin and was mildly surprised to see Fischer standing stiffly to attention before Gerrard's desk. The young German officer had his cap tucked under his arm and was staring straight ahead at the bulkhead. He had obviously taken pains to ensure that his once-sodden uniform looked reasonably presentable.

Gerrard waved a battered, glowing cigar in Holden's direction and said to Fischer, 'He's the boss. Tell him your problems.'

Fischer's eyes flickered sideways to the blond Englishman. 'We are war prisoners, you understand. It is right that we should be treated so. The man Kramer is a spy. We should not be shut in with a spy.'

Gerrard snorted. 'Kramer is nothing but a cold-blooded murderer.'

'You are too, captain,' Fischer retorted, gaining confidence. 'You sank a U-boat last year and now you sink my boat. You are American. Neutral. Is that not so?'

Holden began to feel uneasy; he wondered what Kramer had been saying to his fellow captors in the bow compartment and cursed himself for not foreseeing the situation earlier. 'Leutnant Fischer is right, of course,' said Holden, smiling at the German. 'Prisoners of war should not be locked up with civilians. It's against the Geneva Convention.'

Gerrard was not listening but was staring thoughtfully at Fischer. 'Who told you about the sub I sank last year?'

Fischer drew himself up. 'My commanding officer,' he said proudly. 'Kapitänleutnant Milland.'

Gerrard's chair fell forward. Hot cigar ash dropped on to the back of his hand but he ignored it. '*Who?*' he choked.

The American's reactions startled the German officer. 'Kapitänleutnant Milland,' he repeated nervously.

139

Holden had raised his eyebrows and was regarding Gerrard with interest.

'Kurt Milland?' Gerrard almost shouted.

Fischer nodded.

'You mean Kurt Milland was the captain of your U-boat?' Fischer was confused. 'But you knew of course? He told us that he had been selected for the command because he knew you.'

Gerrard absently brushed the ash off his hand. It was some seconds before he spoke. 'Kurt was my first officer on this ship. We were old buddies. In his last letter he said that he was a naval instructor. He never said anything about U-boats. . . .'

Gerrard's voice trailed into silence. Holden seized the chance to put a question that was foremost in his mind. 'Why send a U-boat to intercept us? Why not send something faster? Or was there something special about your boat?'

'It is not permitted for me to answer,' said Fischer sullenly.

'How did he manage with his leg?' Gerrard asked abruptly. 'Christ – you can answer that.'

'Never trouble,' Fischer admitted, wondering how to bring the conversation back to the question of Kramer. 'After time we never thought about it.'

Gerrard shook his head. 'Christ – he had guts. I saw his stump once after he'd stood a rough watch off the Falklands. It was a mass of blood and blisters. No complaints. Nothing.' The American lapsed into a brooding silence.

Fischer remained at attention, hardly understanding what Gerrard had said.

Holden beckoned to Piet who was hovering in the doorway and said to Fischer: 'You'll have to remain with Kramer in the bow. We have no alternative accommodation. I'm sorry.'

Fischer was about to complain about the strange metallic grating noises that he and his men had often heard in the bow but decided that the two men would not be interested. He allowed Piet to lead him away.

'Odd that the Germans should send a U-boat against us,' Holden observed when he and Gerrard were alone.

But Gerrard made no reply; his thoughts were with Kurt Milland and the hauntingly vivid image of his crippled U-boat sliding helplessly into the silent depths.

# 3

'Stop engine,' Milland commanded down the voice-pipe.

The exhaust vent was silenced and *U-330* lost way. Milland had judged the order well, for the U-boat came to a wallowing stop in the middle of the widely-distributed patch of garbage floating on the surface.

Two men armed with long-handled boathooks went down on their knees on the deck casing and began fishing the débris aboard. 'Careful with the paper!' Milland shouted. 'I don't want it shredded!'

The men carefully unwrapped the sodden fragments from round the ends of their boathooks and spread them on the deck.

'Mueller!' Milland shouted at a man who was watching his colleagues curiously. 'You can swim. Round up all you can!' He pointed to the remains of a carton floating some hundred metres from the U-boat. 'I want that.'

Mueller reluctantly removed his grey naval-issue U-boat overalls and dived naked into the sea. He surfaced and struck out for the carton.

Milland swung down the ladder from the bridge and stumped along the deck, holding on to the jumping wire. He stopped when he reached the two men and stared down at the items of garbage they had gathered. Most of the pieces of paper were in such a state of disintegration that it was not possible to determine their original purpose. A greaseproof wrapper for a five-pound block of South African margarine had survived well but there was no reliable way of determining how long it had been in the water.

The water all round the U-boat was dotted with vegetable peelings. Milland realized that trying to estimate how much time had elapsed since the garbage was dumped would give a very hit-or-miss result. Nor could he be certain that the garbage had come from the *Tulsar* on the basis of the margarine wrapper, because South Africa was one of the Allies' principal food suppliers.

He studied the bits of waste bobbing on the rolling swell.

The stuff was spread over an area roughly two hundred metres in diameter. He felt reasonably certain that had the garbage been in the water much longer than two days it would have been completely dispersed by the wind and current.

Mueller reached the side of the U-boat pushing the sodden remains of a large cardboard box. His colleagues helped him aboard and carefully laid his trophy out on the casing for Milland's inspection.

'Turn it over,' Milland ordered. 'Carefully, you idiots!'

One of the men gingerly peeled the limp cardboard from the casing and turned it over. The faded remains of a coloured label indicated that the carton had contained two dozen tins of South African peaches. Something had been pencilled on one of the carton's blank sides. Milland went awkwardly down on his good knee to peer closely at the pencilled characters. It was a scribbled delivery note. Judging by the hastily-formed letters, Milland guessed that the writer had been obliged to write the same thing on dozens of similar cartons. The delivery note said: TULSAR P/T NATAL D/BAN.

Without saying a word but his face set into hard lines, Milland gripped the jumping wire and pulled himself to his feet.

The three men watched his stocky frame stump back to the conning-tower.

He hauled himself back on to the bridge and flipped open the voice-pipe cover.

'Chief! Same course. Full speed ahead. Everything you've got.'

The rolling eased as *U-330* got under way again. Milland stared straight ahead where the U-boat's bow was aiming at the northern horizon.

Forty-eight hours, he thought. A thousand miles.

But his determination to catch and destroy his prey would not have been weakened had the distance between them been ten thousand miles.

# 4

Holden entered the *Tulsar*'s restaurant when tea and coffee were being served after lunch. He nodded to Herbie Lewis and placed an envelope before Josephine. 'Jack Colby's just received a reply to your message, Jo.'

Josephine tore the envelope open and read the signal. She crumpled the slip of paper and dropped it in the ashtray. 'I suppose you know what it says?' she remarked coldly.

'That your father has less than three weeks. I'm very sorry, Jo.'

'I don't want pity, Mr Holden. All I want is for this God-damn boat to get to New York.'

'There've been a lot of complaints, Mr Holden,' Herbie Lewis underlined for Josephine.

'Complaints I can deal with,' said Holden. 'Torpedoes are more troublesome.' He moved to the middle of the restaurant. 'May I have your attention please, ladies and gentlemen.'

The low buzz of conversation and the clink of china stopped as the passengers turned expectantly to the speaker. 'As you know, of course,' Holden began when he had everyone's attention, 'the *Tulsar* was bound for New York. But we've just received instructions from the owners that we're to dock at Falmouth in Cornwall.' Holden paused. A number of passengers, Josephine included, were gaping at him in frozen bewilderment. 'To get you home as speedily as possible, the company has booked first-class passages for you on an American liner sailing from Liverpool on –'

'Hold it. Hold it. Now just hold everything, Mr Holden.' It was Eli Vanson, cigar jammed in the corner of his mouth like a facial talisman, who had pushed himself forward. He was a man with a turn of phrase that was in no way inhibited or modified by the presence of nuns. 'Just what is this shit about us going to England?'

Holden wasn't given a chance to reply. In that instant the *Tulsar* gave a sudden, convulsive shudder and stopped, transferring its ten-knot momentum to its passengers and everything that wasn't fixed to the floor. There was screaming

pandemonium as passengers, tables and chairs were hurled forward against the bulkhead in a panic-stricken, struggling mass of waving arms and legs. Someone cried out:
'We've hit a mine!' We're sinking!'
Holden was badly winded by a crippling blow in the solar plexus. For a few seconds his consciousness was dominated by the need to suck air into his lungs. He rose to his knees and was nearly knocked sprawling by someone crashing past to get to the door. People were screaming as they struggled to disentangle themselves from tables and chairs and each other. Flesh was ground into the broken china that was everywhere. The well-ordered world of after-lunch coffee and conversation was snuffed out in less than two seconds and replaced by confusion and terror.

Holden climbed to his feet and pulled Josephine and Lewis clear of the blindly-stampeding mass of people trying to fight their way through the door. A minute passed and they suddenly realized that they were alone in the restaurant, apart from the two Ursuline nuns who were attending to a steward with a broken collar-bone.

'Are you all right?' the elder sister inquired.

The three appeared to have suffered nothing worse than minor cuts and bruises.

'What happened?' asked Lewis when he had recovered his spectacles from amid broken glass and china on the floor.

'Well, one thing's for sure,' Holden replied, leading the way to the door. 'It doesn't feel as if the ship's sinking.'

The *Tulsar* was lying stopped and rolling abominably in the heavy swell. Piet left the anxious knots of passengers and crew who were gathering round the lifeboats on the leeward side and hurried across to Gerrard.

'Bow compartment flooded, cap'n,' he said in answer to Gerrard's query. 'I guess maybe we've hit something pretty big.'

'Lucky you got the watertight door shut so quickly, Piet.'

Piet stared at Gerrard. 'It was shut already, cap'n, the prisoners –'

Before Piet could finish the sentence, Gerrard was racing down the side deck towards the bow. He leaned over the bulwark but the flare of the bow prevented him from obtaining a clear view of the bow's pointed stem where it met the waterline. The sluggish manner in which the *Tulsar* lifted to the swell felt exactly the same as the last time they had a flooded bow compartment after the ramming of the U-boat in the Indian Ocean. There was a dull grating from torn plates moving against each other every time the whaling-ship sank into a trough.

'No sign of a log or baulk of timber,' said Piet, joining Gerrard at the rail. 'So what did we hit?'

'Let's get this opened up, Piet,' Gerrard ordered.

The two men opened the hatch that gave access to the anchor-chain compartment that was located above the flooded bow compartment where Kramer and the six U-boatmen were trapped – possibly drowned.

Daylight fell on the great mass of galvanized anchor-chain and cable. There were two hundred fathoms of it – a little over twice the *Tulsar*'s length.

Gerrard signalled to the bridge to release the anchor. There was a loud clunk from the hydraulically-operated latches followed by a splash when the stockless anchor hit the water. It plunged down, its weight dragging the anchor-chain and cable through the hawsehole with a deafening roar.

The instant all the cable had been paid out, Gerrard jumped down. He dropped to his knees and pressed his ear to the steel floor. He could hear water surging back and forth in the flooded compartment. That meant that there was an air-pocket. He banged his fist down several times. A metallic tapping answered him. It was faint, barely audible above the noise of the grating plates and the sea, and yet it was too regular to be anything but man-made.

Gerrard secured the bowline around his waist while Piet passed the rope twice around the windlass.

Josephine and Holden looked on with the other passengers as Gerrard disappeared over the side of the bulwarks. Josephine leaned out and saw him fending his body away from the *Tulsar*'s stem with his feet. He mistimed one kick and sent himself spinning dizzily round. Piet kept the windlass turning slowly, gradually lowering Gerrard until the heaving green swell was reaching for his feet before falling away. One particularly heavy swell immersed him to his waist. When it bellied down, lifting him clear of the water, he had a brief glimpse of torn metal plates splayed outwards. He signalled to Piet to stop lowering him and stared at the point where the seething maelstrom met the bow's pointed stem. He cursed the foam that rendered the otherwise clear water opaque.

For a second the maddened foam was swept away by a clean, unbroken wave enabling him to see below the water-line and to appreciate the full extent of the disaster that had overtaken the *Tulsar*.

He made a circling motion with his finger for Piet to haul him up.

'It's the shit welding and riveting carried out by those clowns in Durban,' said Gerrard savagely when he was back on the foredeck. 'The plates have split right down the stem from waterline to forefoot and she's gaping open like a hippo on heat.'

Piet swore roundly in Afrikaans. 'Could we get them out through the split?'

'Not a chance. It's too small and they'd be cut to ribbons on the plates. The only way to get them out is through the floor of the anchor-chain compartment.'

'How, cap'n?'

'We cut a hole! How do you think?'

'As soon as we make even a small hole – whoosh! And their air-pocket is gone,' Piet pointed out.

Gerrard hadn't thought of that. 'Shit,' he muttered. He brooded for a moment. 'Shit,' he repeated. He looked up. Holden was regarding him thoughtfully.

'Any chance of carrying out the rescue operation while we're under way, captain?'

Gerrard gave a bitter scowl. 'At anything above two knots that plating is going to tear away from the frames. If the plates rip past the watertight bulkhead we're right up shit creek – the pumps could never cope. Sorry Mr Holden – looks like we're going to be stuck here awhile.'

An hour later Gerrard spread the plans of the *Tulsar* out on his desk for the benefit of Colby and Brody who were not as familiar with the whaler's design as Piet. Holden looked at them with interest and guessed that the freehand sketches

146

Gerrard had given him in Durban were copied from these plans.

'We know two things,' said Gerrard. 'First, that at least one of them is alive, and second, to get them out and to repair the bow we're going to have to lift the *Tulsar*'s bow clear of the water.'

'Right out of the water, boss?' Brody's expression of surprise was the best his prizefighter's features could manage.

'High and dry,' Gerrard confirmed.

'Crazy,' Colby muttered. 'You're crazy – you know that?'

Gerrard gazed levelly at his radio-operator. 'Apart from rescuing those men, we've got to lift the bow somehow to repair it. If we try to move in our present state, the chances are that water pressure will break down the watertight bulkhead or split the hull open past the bulkhead. Either way, our chances of remaining afloat are slim to the point of vanishing.'

'How about moving our cargo aft?' Piet suggested. 'Two hundred tons of lead on the slipway will lift our bow marks a good way out of the water.'

Gerrard had an uninspiring vision of the *Tulsar*'s gold sliding down the whale slipway and splashing crate by crate into the Atlantic. He caught Holden's eye and grinned. The Englishman didn't respond – he seemed preoccupied with other problems. Gerrard turned to Piet.

'How do you stop the crates sliding into the sea?'

'Easy,' said Piet. 'Wedge the first row. No problem.'

'One helluva lot of trouble shifting two hundred tons of lead, boss,' said Brody.

'Why don't we dump it?' asked Colby. 'Christ – what's two hundred tons of lead worth compared with this ship?'

'A lot if it'll help lift our bow out of the water,' said Piet.

Gerrard gazed speculatively at Holden. 'Do you have any ideas, Mr Holden?'

The Englishman smiled. 'I was thinking that two hundred tons of lead moved aft will make the rolling that much worse and there will be a danger of the ship rolling right over.'

Gerrard stared at Holden and relaxed into a grin. 'You know something, Mr Holden? For once you and me are thinking on the same wavelength. We're going to have to think of a sure-fire way of keeping the *Tulsar* stable.'

'How about floatation bags lashed around the bow?' Holden inquired.

'A great idea. The trouble with owners is that they're full of brilliant but impractical ideas. It just so happens, Mr Holden, that we're short on supplies of floatation bags.'

Holden was unmoved by Gerrard's sarcasm. 'The trouble with whalemen,' he observed boredly, 'is that they're usually short on imagination.'

For a moment Gerrard was sorely tempted to modify Holden's patronizing smile with his fists but the Englishman was no fool and ideas cost nothing to listen to.

'Okay,' said Gerrard wearily. 'Let's hear what's stewing under those golden locks.'

# 5

Five days later the long search was over.

Gerrard suddenly saw the silvery fountains of the whales' blows. He waggled his wings and climbed hard. The two catcher boats, following a routine that had always worked well, peeled away from each other and reduced speed to fifteen knots in order to make life reasonably tolerable for the harpoonists.

Gerrard positioned the seaplane above the sperm whales at a thousand feet and circled. He looked down. The catchers were sweeping in wide circles round the whales, closing into positions that kept them astern of the unsuspecting creatures. Piet's harpoonist was crouched behind his weapon – swivelling it towards the tail of the nearest whale. His left hand suddenly went up in the universal gesture of forward. Piet's catcher accelerated and swung to one side. As he overhauled the outside whale, the harpoonist's sights moved the length of its blue-grey back until they reached the massive, rounded prow of the head.

Gerrard saw the harpoon flash across the intervening distance and bury itself deep in the whale's brain. The explosive head erupted silently beneath the creature's spine resulting in what whalers called a 'clean' kill. One second the whale was an intelligent, living breathing, warm-blooded being. The next second it was a wallowing mass of profitable bone and tissue of which, the whalers said, everything could be turned into dollars except its blow. So sudden had been the whale's death that there had been no communication between it and its herd sisters; they continued their leisurely pace, not noticing that one of their number was being left further and further behind.

Piet's catcher veered away to allow his harpoonist to reload. Brody closed his launch in on the opposite side of the group. There was a brief puff of white smoke from the harpoon-gun that was snatched away by the wind. Another clean kill. The rope attached to the six-foot harpoon was paid out from a safety grill beneath the gunner's feet to reduce the danger of him becoming entangled and dragged down into the depths by a sounding whale. The Malay boys in the catcher's cockpit attached the end of the line to a large, bright orange buoy and heaved it into the water.

Piet's second kill was clumsy; the harpoon exploded against the bull's head, blasting an ugly crater in the blubber. In panic, the beast blew twice and sounded, its wildly thrashing tail beating the sea into a welter of foam before it disappeared. The three remaining sperm whales, a young bull and two cows, also sounded.

Gerrard guessed that the injured whale had dived too quickly to have charged its bloodstream with oxygen effectively; it was unlikely to remain submerged longer than ten minutes. Piet appeared to have thought the same for he steered his catcher to a point half a mile ahead of the spot where the whales had sounded. He swung his craft round in a wide circle while the harpoonist reloaded. But the gunner's second weapon was not needed; the dying whale appeared on the surface in the exact centre of Piet's circle and managed one feeble blow. Gerrard could see the sea turning red from the blood voiding from the terrible wound. Then the stricken creature went into its 'flurry' – the apt name by which whalers describe the death throes of an adult sperm whale.

Gerrard called Piet on the radio and congratulated him on the clean kills.

The *Tulsar* lay nearly an hour's flying time to the south. For several days it had been lying stopped – wallowing helplessly in the swell, at the mercy of the wind and any passing U-boat. Luckily they were well away from the convoy routes where U-boats were likely to be found. Now, at last, they had the means of carrying out the repairs to *Tulsar* to enable them to continue the seriously-delayed voyage to England.

# 6

The strain of having to run *U-330* without his two executive officers was beginning to tell on Milland. He glowered, unshaven and red-eyed, at Dieter Venner as though he suspected that his radio-operator was playing a practical joke on him.

'You expect me to believe such nonsense? You really think you can tell me that Robert Gerrard is catching whales? You think I'm stupid? You think he's stupid?'

'I'm merely telling you what I heard, captain,' said Venner evenly. 'I'm not saying that it was even the *Tulsar* I heard, but it was definitely someone radioing directions in English to a whale-catcher.'

'In the middle of the Atlantic – in the middle of a war?'

Venner wasn't prepared to argue. As an old hand, he recognized that Milland was suffering from end-of-patrol nerves in addition to the extra burden imposed on him.

'Well, Mr Venner?'

'Isn't there a whaling industry in the Azores, captain?'

'There is.' Milland glared forbiddingly at Venner. 'What of it, may I ask?'

'Perhaps it's one of their catchers?' Venner fervently wished that he hadn't heard the transmission.

'Have you ever been to Horta in the Azores?'

'No, captain.'

'The whalemen there are poor – very poor. They can barely afford fuel for their catchers.' Milland's voice suddenly rose to shout. 'They certainly can't afford radio and they don't speak English!'

Venner capitulated. 'Maybe I was mistaken,' he muttered. He pulled his headphones on and turned back to his switches and tuners.

'The mistake was mine in accepting you as my radio-operator,' said Milland harshly.

Munt picked that moment to enter the control-room from the engine room.

'May I have a word with you please, captain?' The chief engineer's usually amiable expression was absent. Even during the anxious moments when *U-330* had so narrowly avoided disaster, his good humour had never deserted him.

'Well?' Milland demanded.

Munt glanced at the helmsman and petty officer engineer sitting at their controls. 'In your cabin or the wardroom please, captain.'

Milland stood his ground. 'What is wrong with the control-room?'

Munt read and correctly interpreted the danger signals. His heart sank but there was no alternative; he had to keep Milland fully informed. It was his duty; Munt had a highly-developed sense of duty. He licked his lips and tried not to meet Milland's eyes, glaring with menace and lack of sleep.

'The diesel's running hot, captain.' Munt paused, but Milland said nothing, forcing him to press on. 'The oil pressure is down ten per cent which is causing the camshafts and valve gear to overheat. I've increased the water flow to the heat exchangers, which helped, but the temperature's still creeping up.'

Milland regarded his chief engineer coldly. 'So?'

'I want us to stop so that I can look at the oil-pump.'

Milland's face was devoid of expression. 'For how long?' He omitted Munt's courtesy title of 'chief'.

'Two hours, captain.'

'That is out of the question. We must continue at full speed.'

The curt rejection of his request justifiably angered Munt. The commanding officer of a U-boat had a duty to listen to and to accede to the reasonable requests of the chief engineer. Munt stared levelly at Milland. 'I'm not questioning your order, captain, but I would strongly recommend that the oil-pump is examined as quickly as possible to prevent damage to the engine.'

Milland took a step nearer Munt. The two men's faces were inches apart. Munt noticed the beads of sweat standing out on Milland's forehead. 'That's exactly what you *are* doing! Milland barked. 'You're questioning my orders. Why? Do you know what is at stake?'

'I know what's at stake, captain,' said Munt quietly.

His calm attitude seemed to enrage Milland even more. 'You think you can run this boat better, Munt? Mm? If you do, tell me how you expect this boat to carry out its duties when rolling about on the surface while you tinker with your engine. You know what we have to do, don't you? We have to capture the *Tulsar* and its gold. Or sink it. Something we can't do with our one engine stopped while you waste time tinkering –.' Milland realized that he was repeating himself and stopped in mid-sentence.

'We don't stand much of a chance of overhauling the *Tulsar* on one engine,' said Munt, trying to make his voice sound respectful. 'And none at all if the engine seizes up.'

Milland glared at Munt, suspecting insubordination. The chief engineer met his gaze without flinching.

'We press on at full speed,' said Milland stubbornly. Without waiting for a reply, he turned his back on Munt and swung his leg through the circular door that led to his cabin.

Munt caught Venner's eye. The radio-operator pointed a forefinger at his own temple and made a twisting motion, cunningly converting the suggestive gesture into a movement to brush a strand of hair away from his eyes.

# 7

By three in the morning the racket from the seamen working on deck was so intolerable that Josephine abandoned further attempts to sleep. She dressed and climbed the companionway to the flensing deck. Mr and Mrs Eli Vanson were also on deck, well wrapped against the near freezing wind and spray, and morosely watching a gang hoisting the cargo crates out of the hold and manhandling them down the whale slipway where a stout timber barricade prevented the crates from sliding into the sea. Josephine's eyes adjusted to the glare from the portable floodlights and she saw that the *Tulsar* was so low by the stern that half the slipway was flooded. Seamen working near the stern were up to their waists in the black, surging water as they struggled with ropes to make the crates secure.

'Have they got the men out yet?' Josephine inquired.

'Christ knows,' Eli Vanson muttered. 'Christ – what a crummy ship – not even the Goddamn crew know what the hell's going on.'

'It's not her fault, Eli,' said Mrs Vanson reprovingly.

Josephine left them arguing and picked her way forward, carefully judging each roll and noting the positions of handholds in advance.

Holden was leaning over the bow bulwark beneath a cluster of floodlights that had been swung out on booms to direct their light down at the water. Josephine joined him and looked down. The sight of the whales came as a shock: the huge carcasses, lashed around the bow, were grotesquely swollen to almost double their normal girth. As she watched, the bloated beasts dipped in the swell, and the ropes around their bodies tightened, cutting deep into thick, resilient blubber.

'Why are they such a size?' she asked.

Holden appeared to notice her for the first time. She was shocked by the fatigue that was showing in the Englishman's face.

'They've been blown full of compressed air,' said Holden.

'Why?'

'To provide enough buoyancy to lift the bows clear of the water.'

A man jumped out from below the bow's overhang and landed on the back of one of the whales, steadying himself with a flenser's pick. It was Gerrard.

'So they haven't got them out yet?' she asked, guessing what the answer would be.

'Not yet. Another two hours. Maybe three. I don't know.'

Suddenly Josephine's problems seemed of little importance and her smouldering anger with Holden over the change of the *Tulsar*'s destination was gone.

'Look,' she said in a reasoning tone. 'There's no point in you staying here for the next three hours and freezing to death. I'll unlock the passengers' galley and make us some coffee. Come on.' She took Holden's arm and was surprised by his acceptance of her authority. She led the way down to the restaurant and pushed Holden into an armchair. He sat unresisting and uncomplaining – his eyes ringed with exhaustion.

'Stay there. I won't be five minutes fixing the coffee. And I guess you'd like an orange juice as well?'

Holden smiled faintly. 'Just the coffee, Jo.'

She returned a few minutes later bearing a jug of coffee only to discover that Holden had slumped forward and was sound asleep.

There was nothing to do but make him as comfortable as possible, and sit sipping coffee, waiting for the dawn.

Two hours later the men working on the rescue operation were ready to cut through the floor of the anchor-chain compartment to reach the trapped men. Piet and Gerrard passed cold chisels and sledgehammers down to the men who were working in the confined space. A minute later, those passengers who had managed to sleep that night were woken by the resounding clamour of steel upon steel.

# 8

The rasp of the saw slicing into his shattered tibia brought Milland back to screaming consciousness; his spine arched like a bow with the agony.

'For Chrissake keep the chloroform drip going,' said a voice. The voice belonged to a pair of grey eyes between an unkempt mop of dark hair and a gauze mask.

Milland felt heavy hands on his chest that forced his shoulders on to the stainless steel table. Something was pushed over his nose and mouth. He tried to fight but the sickly sweet vapour filling his tortured lungs drained the pitiful reserves of strength left in his mutilated body. The pain, like molten lead being injected into his spinal column, began to fade although the sound of sawing seemed to get steadily louder.

'Christ, the bastard must have a casehardened steel shinbone.'

'How the hell should I know? I've never cut through one before. You let go of that artery and I'll start on you.'

Milland giggled to himself before drifting off to sleep. A minute passed and then they were shaking him.

'Captain...'

'Jesus Christ, what a mess.'

'I've seen worse.'

'Do I keep the drip going?'

'Captain!'

*For God's sake let me sleep.*

'Captain!'

Milland opened his eyes. The grey eyes and the gauze mask had gone. The man shaking him was wearing the grey shapeless tunic and baggy trousers of U-boat overalls. His shoulder mark bore the lightning flash insignia of a third-class radio-operator. He was one of Venner's men.

'I'm sorry, captain, but Mr Venner said to wake you. You didn't hear his call on the loudspeaker.' The U-boatman's eyes flickered nervously to the bulkhead-mounted loudspeaker above Milland's bunk.

Milland swore and sat up. He had taken to sleeping with

his artificial leg strapped in place. For a sickening moment as he stood he experienced the sensation of phantom toes. And then the familiar pain returned to his stump as it took his weight, causing the sensation to vanish abruptly. He ignored the radio-operator and ducked through the watertight door into the control-room.

'You sent for me, Venner?' The sharpness in Milland's voice was not due to his having just woken, it was now a permanent feature of his character.

The petty officer was wearing his hydrophone headphones. He swung round on his swivel stool when Milland addressed him. 'Yes captain. I'm picking up a faint HE on the keel microphones which I can't account for. If we could stop –

'Our own propeller noises? You woke me because you can hear our own propeller noises?'

Venner kept his voice respectful. 'Noises I *can't* account for, captain. If we stop our engine I could –'

'Out of the question,' Milland interrupted.

Venner spun his stool round to his console without saying a word. The helmsman looked quickly round at Milland and hurriedly returned his attention to the gyro-compass. There was an embarrassed silence in the U-boat's control-room that was disturbed only by the labouring beat of the partnerless starboard diesel.

'What sort of noise?' Milland asked at length.

'An irregular clanging. I don't think it can be machinery.'

'Bearing?'

'Dead ahead but I can't be certain, captain. There's too much cavitation noise around the microphones.'

Milland lifted the interphone off its hook. 'Munt,' he said, not bothering to identify himself, 'stop your engine.'

In the engine-room Munt recognized Milland's voice and mistakenly thought that his captain had at last seen sense. He thankfully shut down the diesel engine that he had been anxiously watching and two mechanics immediately set to work to remove the suspect oil-pump.

Venner carefully adjusted the hydrophone bearing indicator. 'It's definitely dead ahead. It's not machinery and it's not fish.' He removed his headphones and handed them to Milland who listened intently for a moment before returning them.

'You're right: a clanking noise. Man-made I'd say. How far?'

Venner didn't wish to appear indecisive but the truth was that he didn't know. To say that to Milland in his present mood would be inviting trouble. It was better to guess.

'Fifty miles, captain.'

Milland nodded. In a reasonable voice he said: 'Give me an accurate bearing.'

Venner settled the headphones over his ears and made a number of fine adjustments to the bearing indicator. It took him less than five minutes to establish that the curious noise was on a bearing due north of *U-330*'s position.

'Munt!' Milland barked into the interphone. 'Start your engine please. I want maximum revolutions.'

In the engine-room, Munt gaped at his two mechanics and shifted the interphone handset to his left ear. 'I'm sorry, captain, but you just gave the order to stop.'

'And now I'm telling you to start!'

'But I've got the starboard engine oil-pump stripped down.'

There was a pause, then: 'Did I say you could do that?'

'No, captain. But I thought –'

'You thought wrong, Munt!' The two mechanics could hear Milland's voice coming from the control-room without the aid of the telephone. 'I want that engine started within two minutes!'

'But, captain,' Munt protested. He broke off when he heard the click of the receiver being returned to its hook. Five seconds later Milland's powerful frame filled the watertight door opening. His eyes took in the dismantled oil-pump lying on the engine-room's tiny work-bench.

'I'm sorry, captain,' said Munt quickly. 'But another five minutes' running and the pump impellers would be completely chewed up. It'll take at least two hours to fit new ones.' He picked up the damaged components and held them out for Milland's inspection. Suddenly he felt very angry; he shouldn't have to justify himself or his actions – it was the captain's duty to accept the word of his chief engineer.

Milland stumped forward and knocked the impellers from Munt's hands. 'You disobeyed my orders when I specifically said that you were to keep the engine running!'

'But I thought when you ordered me to stop –'

'I'm not interested in what you *thought*!' Milland screamed, his face inches from Munt's. 'What concerns me is that you disobeyed orders!'

Munt fell silent. Milland suddenly regretted his boorish behaviour; he would need Munt's co-operation – but he wasn't going to apologize. 'We'll run on the electric motors,' he said, turning back to the control-room.

The order astonished Munt. Sustained surface running on the electric motors was strictly forbidden – there was the attendant risk of a U-boat finding itself with exhausted batteries and unable to dive should an emergency arise.

'Yes, captain,' said Munt respectfully. 'But such an order will require your signature in the engine-room log.'

The two men glared at each other in mutual dislike.

'Give me the log,' said Milland coldly.

Munt opened a locker and handed a hide-bound book to his captain.

Milland opened the log and scrawled his signature in the last column. 'You will also group up the batteries,' he said, snapping the log shut and returning it to Munt. 'I want every knot this boat can muster.'

The chief engineer replaced the book and shut the locker without speaking. Milland's order meant that both electric motors were required to drain the batteries at full load. Being a Type IXD, *U-330* had a range of a hundred and fifteen miles on her batteries at a top speed of only four knots. Which meant that after twenty-nine hours' running, unless he could repair the diesel, *U-330* would finish up wallowing helplessly on the surface like a dying whale – unless he did the unthinkable and deliberately disobeyed Milland's orders.

# 9

At noon, under a leaden sky that reflected the sombreness of the moment, the last of the bodies of the six drowned U-boatmen was hoisted out of the *Tulsar*'s bow compartment and laid out on the foredeck. The seventh and final body removed was Kramer's.

Gerrard and Piet started down in silence at the row of still forms and removed their caps. Kramer was easily recognizable by his bandaged finger and his straggling beard. Leutnant Fischer could be identified by the gold stripe on the tattered, blood-soaked remains of his jacket. Gerrard realized that he couldn't even remember the names of the other five. The sleeves of all the men's clothing were torn to shreds, and their hands and forearms were badly mutilated. An image formed in Gerrard's mind of the seven men tearing at the torn metal plating in their desperate but futile attempt to escape from the steel tomb of the flooded compartment.

The only sound from the passengers lined against the rope barrier across the foredeck was from the two nuns reading in muted tones from their missals.

'So what do we do with them, cap'n?' asked Piet at length.

Gerrard appeared not to have heard. Piet repeated the question.

'For Chrissake, Piet, I shouldn't have to tell you. We sew them up in canvas, weight them with lead, and bury them.'

Gerrard crossed to the bulwark and gazed down at the bloated sperm whales lashed around the *Tulsar*'s bow.

'We're going to have to be pretty damn quick fixing the bow,' Piet remarked practically. He pointed to a dorsal fin creating a V-wake as it homed in on one of the whales carcases. 'Mako,' he added, his tone expressing the sailor's traditional hatred and fear of sharks.

The primeval fish rolled over, exposing its pale belly, and drove its crescent jaws deep into the yielding blubber. Its sleek body gave a convulsive shudder and a mouthful of blubber was spooned neatly down the creature's gullet. The killing-machine shape of a hammerhead shark nosed cautiously at the smallest whale before withdrawing and then lunging, twisting its awkwardly-shaped head to one side. The triple rows of teeth sliced deep into the whale's flesh and clamped shut. From the state of all three whales, Gerrard could see that the sharks had been gorging themselves for some time.

'They'll be through the blubber soon,' said Piet phlegmatically, 'then whoosh. We lose air and the bow goes down.'

Gerrard cursed himself for forgetting the possibility of sharks deciding to feed on their buoyancy aids.

'There won't be time to fix the bow unless we catch more whales,' Piet observed.

'Christ, no – we wasted enough time looking for those three.' Gerrard thought for a moment. 'Supposing we cram those bales of coir into the bow compartment and shore them up against the split and then fother canvas round the bow on the outside?'

Piet nodded. Fothering was the ancient technique of stopping a major leak or repairing serious underwater damage by spreading a sail over the affected part of the hull and relying on water pressure and lashings to hold the canvas in place. 'Be okay if we jettison those crates, cap'n.'

'Hell, no. They go back in the hold.'

Piet's normally unruffled expression changed to one of disbelief. 'Are you serious, cap'n?' The *Tulsar*'s not built for that sort of cargo. If we hit weather and the crates get lively without those bales of coir round them ...'

'That's a chance we have to take, Piet. The crates go back just as soon as the bow's patched up.'

Piet knew Gerrard well enough to realize the futility of attempting to dissuade him from such a seemingly lunatic course. He merely shrugged and said: 'We'll need timber to shore the bales in position.'

'We've plenty of lumber.'

'We used it to make the barricade across the slipway.'

The mounting problems and the stolid Afrikaner's lack of imagination to solve them annoyed Gerrard. 'For Chrissake, Piet, chop up lifeboat six – the one that was damaged when we smoked Kramer out.'

# 10

'You've lost them!' Milland shouted, his red-rimmed eyes inches from Venner's face. 'Don't make bloody excuses – you've lost the bastards. Admit it.'

For an insane moment, Venner was sorely tempted to pull the hydrophone headphones back over his ears and shut out the ranting voice. Instead he kept his eyes averted from Milland by gazing fixedly at his console. The hardest part was maintaining a respectful tone.

'I can't hear something that's not making a noise, captain. And we don't know for certain that the noise we heard earlier was the *Tulsar*.'

'We've heard no convoy reports, Venner, or maybe you haven't been listening to the radio either?'

'The radio is switched on all the time, captain.'

Milland glared at his radio-operator. He was about to add a biting rejoinder when he became aware that the electric motors did not sound as if they were running at maximum speed. He glanced up at one of the main ammeters that indicated power consumption and immediately stumped aft.

In the motor-room, Munt heard his approach and quickly pushed the sliding control against the stops. The hum of the electric motors increased.

'Munt!'

The chief engineer turned from the control panel.

'Captain?'

'Why the hell aren't we running at full output?'

'We are, captain.' Munt was appalled by the dramatic change in Milland's appearance; it seemed that the staring, bloodshot eyes were those of a madman.

'Then why the hell are the ammeters in the control-room saying we're not?' Milland raged.

'I've just tried switching the battery banks around, captain. Some are more discharged than others.' He returned Milland's gaze, confident that he could not be proved a liar.

'You had better not be messing me about, Munt. By God, if you are I'll have you court-martialled.'

Munt waved his hands at the controls. 'See for yourself, captain. The controls are fully open.' He half expected Milland to take his word for it, but the senior officer moved to the control panel and studied the settings with an air of suspicion that Munt considered unforgivable. The chief engineer had taken enough. He pushed the watertight door to with his foot so that the mechanics in the adjoining engine-room would not overhear what he had to say.

'Would you have me court-martialled for offering some well-meant advice, captain? I don't think you're getting enough sleep and I think it's likely to impair your judgement.'

Milland wheeled round and glowered at Munt like a bull facing an impudent picador. He took a step towards the chief engineer. There was an anxious moment when Munt thought that Milland was going to strike him. He stood his ground and stared right back at the senior officer. Quite unexpectedly, Milland suddenly relaxed and nodded.

'You're right, Munt. Thank you for having the guts to tell me.'

A minute later, when he was alone, Munt decreased power. It was a hollow victory, he decided as he watched the flagging voltmeters – the instruments that indicated the condition of the U-boat's batteries. The simple story they told was that *U-330* was dying.

# 11

That evening a layer of cloud plundered the sun of the last of its warmth. There was an hour of daylight left. Gerrard glanced up at the whale-spotters' platform to satisfy himself that the Malay boys armed with binoculars were doing their job. Only three ships had been sighted since they had left Durban, which was hardly surprising because the war had swept most shipping into convoys and the *Tulsar* had deliberately kept clear of the convoy routes.

Jack Colby joined him at the rail. 'I see the fother's in place, captain. When do we get under way?'

'Just as soon as we ship those crates back into the hold, Jack.'

Colby unwrapped a stick of chewing gum. 'When do we make Falmouth?'

Gerrard considered. 'We won't be able to make much more than three knots with that fother in place otherwise it rips away. We're twelve hundred miles from Falmouth so I guess we'll be docking around 22 or 23 May. Why the sudden interest?'

'Just picked up a signal from New York for our purser,' said Colby laconically. 'Her pa's in a pretty bad way. Won't last two weeks. Doesn't look like she's gonna get to see him, does it, captain?'

Gerrard swore softly. 'Christ, Jack. What the hell can I do about it?' He leaned on the bridge rail and stared down at the carpenters who had dragged the damaged number six lifeboat on to the flensing deck. They were preparing to attack it with pry-bars as soon as Piet had removed the emergency rations and useful fittings.

'You want me to tell her?' Colby suggested.

Piet emerged from the lifeboat holding a scrap of paper and looking baffled. He climbed the steps up to the bridge where Gerrard and Colby were talking.

'Hell,' Gerrard muttered. 'I guess I'd best tell her.'

'Sorry to trouble you, cap'n,' said Piet, holding out the piece of paper. 'But I found this hidden under the lifeboat's duckboards. Maybe it belonged to Kramer but I think maybe not.'

Gerrard took the offered sheet and glanced at it. He stiffened with shock. 'Jesus bloody Christ.'

It was a sketched layout of the *Tulsar* with pencilled notes in his own handwriting.

Gerrard found Holden in the restaurant talking to Josephine.

'Good evening, captain,' said Josephine. 'A rare visitor. How much longer will we have to endure this God-awful rolling?'

Gerrard sat down and felt in his sweat-shirt pocket for a

163

cigar. 'We'll be through reloading the cargo about nine, then we'll be on the move again.'

'Delighted to hear it, captain,' said Holden, wondering at what could be amiss to drag Gerrard into the restaurant.

'Miss Britten,' said Gerrard. 'I guess your job must keep you pretty busy, huh?'

'Well – yes.'

'I think he means now,' Holden commented.

Josephine rose. 'Direct requests in plain English save time and prevent misunderstandings,' she said frostily, and left the restaurant.

Holden watched Gerrard carefully. 'You have a problem?' he prompted.

Gerrard made no reply but produced the sketch which he unfolded and placed on the table in front of Holden. Nothing in the Englishman's expression betrayed the fact that he had recognized the drawing immediately and that his brain had started working fast.

'So Kramer had it all along?' Holden observed mildly – it was a desperate gamble. 'Obviously you didn't search him that thoroughly when he was captured.'

The gamble paid off because Gerrard was taken aback by Holden's cool reaction to the sketch's appearance.

'It's the sketch I gave you in Durban,' Gerrard stated.

'That's right, captain.'

'Kramer had hidden it in the lifeboat.'

'That explains everything,' Holden murmured. 'Would you care for a cup of tea?'

Gerrard felt that the interview wasn't going according to plan. 'Explains what?' he demanded suspiciously.

'Why, it's only just turned up, of course. I would've thought that was obvious.'

'Now wait a minute. Just wait a minute. Are you trying to tell me that you can explain how Kramer got his hands on this?'

'I don't have to explain anything.' Holden's mind was still racing but he felt that he was gaining command of the situation.

'Goddamn it, you do, Holden,' Gerrard growled.

'My hotel room in Durban was robbed. Some money and a few papers disappeared. Nothing important because the useful stuff was always with me in my briefcase. A robbery carried out by Kramer or one of his minions no doubt.'

'So how in hell did he manage to find out about the gold?'

Holden shrugged. 'Kramer mentioned agents in the Reserve Bank.'

'*You* mentioned them – not Kramer.'

The atmosphere suddenly became icy. Holden regarded Gerrard with an expression of profound contempt. 'If you're thinking what I think you're thinking, captain, you would do well to remember whose idea it was to destroy that U-boat.'

Gerrard realized that the smooth-talking Englishman had a valid point. He lit his cigar to give himself time to think. There seemed little point in antagonizing Holden with unfounded accusations when it was likely that a good word from Holden would lead to him remaining the *Tulsar*'s captain after they had docked at Falmouth. Then he remembered something else.

'What about the time when Kramer was captured, Holden? If I hadn't knocked the rifle down, you would've killed him.

Holden gave a mirthless smile. 'If you hadn't knocked the rifle down, it would not have gone off. That was a remarkably stupid thing to do.'

Gerrard flipped some cigar ash into an ashtray. 'I guess I'd better get back to the bridge.'

'I guess you'd better.'

Gerrard returned to the wheelhouse. He was still suspicious and resentful of Holden. It would be best if he ensured that the Englishman was kept away from the radio shack.

At 9.15 pm Piet inspected the completed jury repairs to the *Tulsar*'s bow. The bales of coarse coconut matting were shored up against the torn plating in the bow compartment with planking cannibalized from the lifeboat, and the lifeboat's canvas cover was fothered in place over the outside of the damaged hull. It was time to start loading the crates back into the hold – an operation that could be carried out with the ship under way, provided the speed was kept down to less than three knots.

The remains of the three sperm whales were cut adrift for

the sharks to finish off, and the *Tulsar*'s engine-room tele-graph clanged for dead slow ahead both engines.

Gerrard thrust his hands into the pockets of his peajacket and stared through the wheelhouse glass into the darkness. 'Thank God we're moving again,' he muttered to Brody. The coxswain grinned. 'Been a long day, boss.'

# 12

---

*U-330* was creeping along on the surface at four knots, the maximum speed that Munt dared wring from the virtually exhausted batteries, when Venner picked up machinery noises on his hydrophones.

'Hydrophone effects bearing one-seven-zero, captain,' he reported. 'Dead ahead.'

Milland took the headphones and listened without speak-ing. 'Range?' he requested at length.

'Twenty miles,' Venner replied promptly to disguise what was a wild guess. 'It sounds like the same sort of engine noises that caught us before.'

Milland angrily banged the headphones down on Venner's table. 'Gerrard won't try the same stupid trick twice.'

'Some stupid trick,' Venner muttered to himself when Mil-land's back was turned.

Milland suddenly spun round. 'Did you say something, Venner?'

'No, captain.'

'If you have a contribution to make, then I'd like to hear it please, Venner.'

What the hell, thought Venner. He said: 'If it is the *Tulsar*, captain, she's not moving very fast but we don't stand a chance of catching her in our present state. So why not stop and let the chief repair the diesel if he can and give the batteries the chance to recover?'

Venner did not flinch from Milland's hard stare. 'You think you can run this boat better than me?'

'I didn't say or imply that, captain.'

'But you thought it, Venner. Very well – we will try your method.'

Milland picked up the interphone and called Munt.

At 3 am, after five hours' work making new oil-pump impellers, Munt surprised himself and the rest of the boat when he managed to coax the diesel engine into life.

A minute later, Milland tumbled into the engine-room still tightening the harness of his artificial leg. He stared at the throbbing engine and clapped Munt on the back.

'My God, chief, that's the sweetest sound in the whole world.'

'But I don't know how long it will hold out for, captain – the oil pressure is only half what it should be.'

'Never mind, chief. Never mind. It'll give us six knots.' Milland paused with one leg through the watertight door and gave his chief engineer a delighted grin. 'By the way, chief, I'll be recommending you for a Knight's Cross when this mission is over.'

Venner was woken two hours later by one of his ratings. 'Those hydrophone effects are much nearer, Mr Venner, but there's something odd about them.'

Venner swung out of his bunk and made his way forward to the control-room, yawning and rubbing sleep from his eyes. He flopped into the swivel chair with a muttered 'this had better be good' and pulled on the headphones. Suddenly he was wide awake and listening intently while the rating eyed him nervously.

'See what I mean, Mr Venner? It's not steam engines and it's not diesels.'

Venner listened carefully for a few more seconds. He smiled. The rating was entitled to be puzzled because ninety per cent of the world's merchantships were driven by some form of reciprocating engine whereas the sound in the hydrophone headphones was a curious humming.

'Steam turbines,' said Venner, laying the headphones on the table.

The rating goggled at him. 'Then it *must* be the *Tulsar*! Shall I wake the captain?'

167

'For God's sake no,' Venner replied with feeling. 'Let the poor bastard sleep.'

# 13

The whale-spotter's platform was over a hundred feet above sea-level. Gerrard lowered his binoculars and eyed the Malay boy in scornful disbelief. 'So where is this smoke now, Tommy?'

'Boss – I see smoke there. I swear, boss.'

The platform was swaying through a gut-churning thirty-degree arc, forcing Gerrard and the lookouts to hang on to the safety rail.

'Smoke, boss,' said the Malay boy glumly, seeing a one-dollar bonus slipping away. 'Black smoke. Not cloud.'

Gerrard sat down, hooked his legs around a stanchion, and used both hands to hold the binoculars steady. It was then that he saw it – a faint strand of black against the grey, heavily overcast sky. It lasted for less than a second and was shredded by the wind. Then there was another wisp of rapidly-thinning black. Cloud didn't behave like that.

'You see it, boss?' the Malay boy asked hopefully.

'Yeah, Tommy. I see it now. I'll tell Mr van Kleef to add a dollar to your pay.'

The boy's eyes mirrored his delight and relief. 'A ship below horizon I guess, yes, boss?'

Gerrard nodded. 'I guess, Tommy.' He opened the box that housed the interphone and called Piet in the wheelhouse. 'The boy's right, Piet – it's a ship. We'd better make some distance between it and us. Hard left. Ten knots.'

'You're crazy, cap'n!' Piet's voice rasped in Gerrard's ear. 'The fother will rip away at anything above four knots!'

'Just do as I say, you Goddamn obstinate Dutchman!'

# 14

'Munt! We're making too much smoke!'

'I'm sorry, captain,' the chief engineer's voice answered from the voice-pipe. 'Cylinder two injector's not working properly – we're blowing unburnt fuel.'

More thick, black smoke spewed from the U-boat's exhaust vent and was carried into Milland's face, momentarily obscuring his view of the ship's masthead that had edged up above the horizon. The smoke cleared and he could discern a whalespotters' platform. It was the *Tulsar*! It had to be the *Tulsar*!

'Bridge – radar!' he shouted down the voice-pipe.

Venner's voice answered immediately. 'Radar – bridge.'

'State your target.'

Venner reeled off the course, range and angle on bow figures concluding with 'speed three knots'.

Milland strived not to show his wild excitement to the lookouts. Three knots! They'd have the *Tulsar* in range within the hour!

The grey U-boat ploughed towards its victim at a steady six knots, driven by its labouring diesel. Milland's ear was tuned to the engine's uneven beat, willing the sick diesel to keep going with an intensity that drained the saliva from his mouth.

He lifted the binoculars to his eyes. The upper decks were now visible. He could even see the seaplane. The Northrop monoplane was the one thing that removed any lingering doubts as to the ship's identity.

Curiously, the elation and excitement that had whitened his knuckles with the intensity of his grip on the binoculars was no longer there. He found himself gazing at the *Tulsar*'s familiar lines with a calculating objectivity that surprised him, for he had convinced himself that the sight of the whaling-ship was sure to arouse long-banished emotions – a yearning for the past, when he had been a whole man and not a cripple.

In the confused pattern of his thoughts, one objective stood sharp and clear: he would have to kill the American. It had been Gerrard's eyes that had stared down at him as he lay half drugged on the stainless steel table. It had been Gerrard's hands that had held the saw that had removed his leg. Gerrard had been good on first-aid but how could he have been certain that it had been necessary to amputate his leg? And then there was the gravest doubt of all, one that only haunted Milland during moments of the blackest depression: could a surgeon have saved the leg if Gerrard had sacrificed seven days of that lucrative season by turning back to port?

Venner's voice broke in on his thoughts.

'Radar – bridge. Target's range six miles. Course steady. Speed steady.'

Milland acknowledged. At that moment the diesel engine stopped and *U-330* began losing way.

'There's nothing I can do about it,' Munt snapped in response to Milland's bellowed demands. 'The cylinders are nearly at melting-point and the pistons have seized and that's that!'

'What speed can we make on the batteries, damn you!' Milland shouted back.

'They're down to forty volts. Three knots for another hour if we're lucky.' Munt's terse reply omitted the customary 'captain'.

'Very well. Keep the electrics grouped up,' said Milland curtly and snapped the voice-pipe cover shut.

The electric motors cut in and *U-330*'s speed crept up to a little over three knots. A watery morning sun broke through the cloud and fanned wedge-shaped beams across the swell. Milland cursed his U-boat's torturously slow progress. Through the open hatch by his feet he could hear the sluggish whine of the electric motors draining the pitiful reserves of the batteries.

'Eleven thousand metres,' Venner reported.

Milland lifted his binoculars. There was something odd about the *Tulsar's* bow. For a few seconds the splash of blue around the whaler's forefoot puzzled him. And then he realized that it was one of the lifeboat covers. The *Tulsar* had hit a mine or had been damaged by a torpedo from another U-boat and had been obliged to fother her bow! No wonder she was moving so slowly. He snapped the voice-pipe cover open.

'Bridge – radar! Gun crew on the double!'

The forward hatch clanged open. The steel-helmeted crew led by Machin climbed on to the deck casing and moved to the main gun. The men were well drilled. Within fifteen seconds they had removed the tampon and locking pins, cleaned the thick, corrosion-inhibiting grease from round the breech and loaded it with a 104-millimetre shell from a ready-use ammunition locker. More shells were passed on to the casing by a human chain.

Machin looked expectantly up at Milland hunched over the conning-tower's spray lip. 'Standing by, captain.'

'Thank you, Machin. Target should be in range in thirty minutes. I shall want you to try for that aerial array above the bridge.'

Munt's head appeared in the bridge hatch. 'Permission to come on bridge, captain?'

Milland assented and growled: 'Why aren't you nursing those damned motors?'

'There's nothing more I can do now, captain – they will run until the batteries are exhausted and then we're finished.'

Milland nodded to the *Tulsar*. 'Once we've captured her, we can transfer the crew and scuttle the boat. It will have served its purpose.'

Munt looked with interest at the whaling-ship that had eluded them for so long. 'I thought it would be bigger, captain.' Milland handed Munt his binoculars. The chief engineer examined their target for a few moments. 'What about that seaplane, captain?'

'Gerrard won't be able to fly it off from this swell.'

'Looks like she's picking up speed.'

Milland snatched the binoculars back and frantically refocussed them. The *Tulsar* had suddenly acquired a bow-wave.

'Radar – bridge!' shouted Venner. 'Target has altered course ninety degrees to port! Speed ten knots!'

Milland stood transfixed as he slowly lowered the binoculars. His expression was suddenly haggard with the realization that he had had victory within his grasp and it was now being snatched away. There was no longer the slightest hope of catching the *Tulsar*.

# 15

Holden studied *U-330* for a minute and returned the binoculars to Gerrard. 'So we didn't sink the damned thing after all,' he observed.

'If it's the same sub,' Piet pointed out.

'It's the same,' said Gerrard laconically.

'Cap'n,' said Piet earnestly. 'That sub's hardly moving. Couldn't we reduce speed to five knots? That fother won't hold at this speed.'

'We maintain this speed,' said Gerrard flatly.

Holden cleared his throat. 'I've just looked at that fother, captain. Mr van Kleef is right – it won't hold.'

Gerrard ignored the Englishman and turned to the radio shack. 'Jack!'

Colby poked his head out of a window. 'Captain?'

'There's a sub out there, Jack.'

The Canadian's eyes went round with alarm. 'Friendly?'

'Not unless it's changed sides. If it starts shooting, no distress calls with our position until the water's up to your waist. Okay?'

Colby paled. He acknowledged and withdrew his head quickly as if he expected the U-boat to start firing immediately.

Gerrard turned to Holden. 'Are you prepared to obey my orders?'

Holden gave a disarming smile. 'That depends.'

'Find Miss Britten and tell her to get all the passengers below and to keep them occupied. I don't want anyone on deck. Understood?'

'Understood,' said Holden with an acquiescence that took Gerrard by surprise.

'You know something, Piet,' said Gerrard sourly, watching Holden join Josephine on the flensing deck where she was talking to a group of passengers. 'I don't trust that Limey bastard an inch.'

# 16

*U-330*'s batteries finally expired. Munt quickly cut the starboard electric motor so that the tiny trickle of current was available to the port motor. It kept turning for another minute. The voltmeter pointers were resting on the zero stops. He threw the main lighting switch, plunging the entire U-boat into darkness. Faint shouts of protest reached the motor-room.

The starved electric motor picked up a few revolutions for a second and then stopped. Munt angrily shut the motor down and restored the enfeebled lighting. Thanks to his crazy captain, *U-330* was now at the mercy of the wind and the waves and would be easy meat for even the RAF's lumbering Sunderland flying-boats should one chance upon them.

On the bridge, Milland swore when the motors stopped. He was about to bawl down the voice-pipe when he suddenly realized that haranguing Munt would serve no useful purpose. The *Tulsar* was dwindling towards the horizon; all he could do was gaze after it in despair and frustration – emotions that the years had made familiar companions.

Piet leaned far out over the bulwark and gazed down in mounting alarm at the fother. The hopelessly over-stressed canvas was splitting. He could even hear the loud cracks of the parting fabric above the sound of the *Tulsar*'s bow crashing into the swell. He turned and waved frantically to the bridge. At that moment the fother parted; the wind tore the two halves of canvas away from the hull and sent them flapping and straining at their lashings. One of the coconut bales inside the bow compartment must have collapsed under the sudden load because Piet could hear the dull roar of water flooding through the gaping hole. There was the faint clang of telegraph bells and then the *Tulsar* was losing way.

'Just say "I told you so" and I'll wring your Goddamn thick neck,' Gerrard warned when he joined Piet at the bulwark. 'How long to fix another fother?'

'Forty minutes, cap'n.' Piet was staring out to sea.

'Jesus Christ! Those gunners will be punching their initials in our hull with that four-incher before then!'

'I don't think so cap'n,' said Piet stiffly. 'The sub's stopped as well. What do you make of that?'

Gerrard raced up the steps to the wheelhouse and snatched up a pair of binoculars. Piet was right. The U-boat had stopped. It was not showing a bow-wave.

Both vessels were warily eyeing each other across an intervening six miles of grey, neutral Atlantic; both were unable to move.


Josephine politely disentangled herself from Eli Vanson. The sugar magnate was lecturing her and anyone else who cared to listen on his ambitious plans to turn an army of lawyers loose on the *Tulsar*'s owners just as soon as he got back to New York. She was about to suggest to Holden that she ordered the cooks to prepare an early lunch when the *Tulsar*'s engines stopped and the ship began to slow.

'What's happened?' she asked.

'The damned fother's split,' Holden replied with an uncharacteristic flash of irritation.

Josephine followed him to the door. 'Those bales they crammed into the bow will hold, won't they?'

'God knows, Jo, but you've got to keep everyone in the restaurant in case that U-boat gets within range.'

The American girl regarded him with large, serious eyes. Her conscientious attitude to her job meant that she felt personally responsible for the safety of the passengers. 'For God's sake – it's day-time – they must be able to see the Stars and Stripes on our hull. Surely they won't torpedo us?'

'No – they won't risk torpedoing us,' said Holden. 'That might sink us. They want to capture us. You see to the passengers. I won't be long.'


'Their fother's ripped in half!' Milland cried jubilantly to Munt. 'They've had to stop!'

Munt studied the *Tulsar* through a pair of binoculars. He could see men working around the whaling-ship's bow, cutting the damaged canvas away. 'But they're two miles out of extreme range, captain,' he pointed out. 'It might just as well be ten miles.'

Milland laughed. 'She's got a hundred times our top hamper, Munt.' He grinned delightedly at his chief engineer's baffled expression. 'The wind, Munt! You're forgetting the wind!'

'Jesus Christ! The bloody wind!' Gerrard suddenly shouted. He leaned over the bridge rail. 'Piet! Can we go astern?'

'No! I've got men in the water!' the Afrikaner yelled back. He returned his attention to the Malays, who were struggling to keep their heads above water and fend their bodies away from the *Tulsar*'s jagged hull plates while at the same time battling with a perverse lifeboat cover that refused to sink so that it could be drawn under the whaling ship's forefoot.

Holden emerged on deck and gazed thoughtfully out to sea at the U-boat. The gap between the two vessels was closing, he decided. He thrust his hands into his pockets and moved slowly aft, bracing his weight alternately to the left and right as the heavy swell shifted the deck like a living thing beneath his feet. He paused and looked up at the seaplane that was lashed by the floats to its platform.

'Radar – bridge!' Venner's voice announced over the bridge voice-pipe. 'Target's range eleven thousand five hundred metres.'

Five and a half miles, thought Milland. The gap was inexorably narrowing. Nothing could save the *Tulsar* now, *nothing*! He leaned over the spray lip.

'Machin! If the wind holds, she'll be in range in about forty minutes!'

'Piet! For Chrissake get those clowns out of the water!' Gerrard's voice boomed over the crew address system. 'I'm going astern in five minutes!'

Piet left the bulwark and mounted the steps to the bridge with an ability that belied his bulk. He burst into the wheelhouse and glared at Gerrard.

'Listen, cap'n. Those boys damn near drowned getting that fother under. We need another twenty minutes.'

In all their years together Gerrard had never seen Piet so angry. The usually stoic Afrikaner's eyes were bloodshot with exhaustion and yet alive with defiance.

'For Chrissake, Piet – in fifteen minutes we'll be in range of the four-incher if we keep drifting like this. We've got to go astern.'

'May I make a suggestion, captain?'

Gerrard spun round. Holden was smiling at him. The Englishman had entered the wheelhouse from the day-cabin.

'What in hell do you want, Holden?' Gerrard demanded belligerently.

Holden kept smiling. 'I'm anxious to share your problems, captain. I have a suggestion to make. A somewhat bright idea, I fancy.'

Gerrard was scathing. 'Oh yeah? Like the last one that was supposed to have sunk that U-boat?'

'An even more brilliant idea,' Holden replied lightly. 'I'm sure you'll be fascinated by it.'

The wind blowing from the south-west where the *Tulsar* lay seemed to carry the taint of whalemeat. Milland dismissed the smell as the product of his imagination – like the sensation of phantom toes that tortured his senses when he was tired.

'*Tulsar*'s lowering a boat,' one of the lookouts called.

Milland raised his binoculars. One of the whale-catchers was being lowered down the backdrop of the huge Stars and Stripes painted on the side of the *Tulsar*'s hull. The small craft cast off and the wind unfurled what appeared to be a white sheet. There was a vaguely familiar figure at the helm.

Gerrard!

'Looks like a flag of truce, captain,' said Machin.

This time Milland was not going to be caught out by Gerrard's treachery. 'Man the AA gun!' he barked at the lookouts. 'Quickly, you idiots! Bring it to bear on that launch!'

Two lookouts jumped down on to the wintergarten deck. One dragged a snaking belt of 20-millimetre ammunition from a ready-use locker and fed the end into the breech of the anti-aircraft gun while the other swung the quadruple barrels down and aimed them at the whale-catcher now speeding towards the U-boat.

Gerrard saw the multiple barrels tilt towards him and swung the launch round in a wide circle so that the white flag fixed to the transom staff would be clearly seen. He spun the wheel through his fingers until the catcher was back on course for the U-boat.

Milland sourly misconstrued the circling manœuvre as a typical piece of Robert Gerrard bravura. The American's casual stance at the helm – one hand resting on the wheel and one foot planted nonchalantly on the coaming – very nearly brought Milland's pent-up rage from weeks of frustration to the boil. For an insane, blinding instant, he was possessed of an overpowering urge to push away the men manning the anti-aircraft gun and to open fire on the one man who had been the sole cause of his misery and repeated failures. It was the white sheet that held his reason together, thus restraining him from taking the fateful action.

He watched in silence as Gerrard steered the launch round to the U-boat's leeward side and approached the stern where *U-330*'s deck casing raked down to water-level. The lookout swung the anti-aircraft gun down, keeping the launch centred in his sights.

Milland was surprised to see how much Gerrard had changed during the years since he had last seen him; the denim trousers and faded sweat-shirt were exactly the same but the weathered face beneath the same unkempt mop of hair had aged noticeably. The grey eyes were as alert and cunning as ever, quickly absorbing every detail of the U-boat but ignoring the flared multiple barrels of the gun that were pointing straight at him.

Two ratings tossed a line to Gerrard which he deftly caught and made fast while they fended the launch away from the U-boat's vulnerable saddle tanks. The two craft rolled in harmony in the same swells.

'Permission to come aboard, captain?'

Milland signalled to the ratings who then steadied the

whale-catcher to enable Gerrard to jump neatly on to the deck casing. He looked up at Milland who was leaning on the wintergarten rail beside the anti-aircraft gun and gave a perfunctory salute.

'Good morning, Kurt.'

Milland's slight hesitation was because he hadn't spoken English for a number of years – even though the acknowledgement was virtually identical to German.

'Good morning.'

'May I join you or do I crick my neck?'

Milland stepped back from the rail. Gerrard grasped one of the stanchions and vaulted up beside Milland as though he were deliberately demonstrating a prowess he knew Milland could never emulate. He even leaned back on the rails, his hands resting on them as if the U-boat was his personal property.

'What's wrong with your engines, Kurt? You've got us all baffled on the *Tulsar*.'

'State your business,' Milland growled.

Gerrard noticed that everyone was watching him; no one was paying attention to the *Tulsar*; all was going according to plan. He gestured to the whale-catcher. 'We picked up some of your crew after you went down. We put them in the bow compartment which later flooded. I figured the decent thing to do was to turn them over to you for burial.' Gerrard saw little point into going into the exact details of how the U-boatmen lost their lives.

Milland looked down at the launch. A number of shapeless forms laced up in canvas were lying in the cockpit. Gerrard didn't understand what Milland said to his crew but they immediately set about transferring the bodies to the U-boat and laying them carefully on the deck casing. Milland leaned against the rail and gave a curt order. A rating unlaced the end of one of the canvas sleeves and drew the material down. Milland stared at Leutnant Hans Fischer's face for a moment without speaking and told the rating to close the bag. He turned to Gerrard.

'I suppose I should thank you, but there seems little point as you were responsible for their death in the first place.'

Gerrard gave a faint smile. 'You've not changed, Kurt.

You're still the autocratic bastard we all used to know and love.'

Gerrard's irony was lost on Milland. 'Perhaps you have changed,' said the U-boat captain stiffly.

'In what way, Kurt?'

'I didn't think Robert Gerrard was a man to deliberately ram and sink a U-boat killing forty men.'

The American's half smile and relaxed attitude abruptly vanished. His grey eyes hardened. 'That was after U-boats started torpedoing unarmed passenger liners, Kurt.' Gerrard didn't wait for a reply but ducked through the railing and jumped lightly on to the deck casing. He brushed past the ratings who were fending off the launch and dropped behind the helm.

'Gerrard!' Milland called down as the American cast off and operated the whale-catcher's self-starter. 'As you have done the decent thing, I will also do the decent thing: I won't open fire until you have returned to your ship.'

Gerrard's reply was drowned by the roar from the whale-catcher's exhaust. Milland watched the receding figure hunched over the launch's helm and wondered why he suddenly no longer seemed to hate Robert Gerrard.

'Captain!'

Milland turned.

'Message from the chief, captain,' said Machin. 'The diesel has cooled and is no longer seized. He thinks he might be able to start it.'

Milland did not reply. He was staring at the *Tulsar*. Something was wrong – there was something different about it. And then he realized what it was: the seaplane was missing from its customary perch above the whaling-ship's deck.

Gerrard swept the whale-catcher around the *Tulsar*'s stern and stopped beside the seaplane that was bobbing on the surface with its engine warmed up and running smoothly. Piet was balanced precariously on one of the aircraft's floats. He caught the rope that Gerrard tossed to him and drew the two craft as close together as the swell permitted. The two men quickly changed positions: Piet dropped his bulk behind the whale-catcher's helm while Gerrard scrambled into the seaplane's cockpit and pulled the canopy shut. He spared one glance down at the cluster of explosive-head harpoons that had been lashed to each float and pointing ahead. Satisfied that all was well, he opened the throttle.

The machine dipped a wingtip into the rolling swell as it began taxi-ing towards the *Tulsar*'s bow. Piet followed at a distance in the whale-catcher like a dog following its master into battle.

Gerrard rounded the bow and had a brief glimpse of *U-330*'s low profile before the seaplane plunged like an ungainly duck into a trough. He opened up to maximum power. The propeller became a spinning disc of light, sucking spray off the broken water and creating a whirling cloud of mist in the wildly bucking machine's wake. But the experienced whalemen on the *Tulsar* knew that the seaplane stood no chance of getting airborne under those conditions.

There was a grating of damaged metal when Munt operated the diesel engine's compressed air starter. The engine turned over several times but refused to fire. The two mechanics watched in silence as he checked the fuel-level in the filter. There was another explosive hiss of compressed air that was smothered by the shriek of damaged crankshaft bearings. Munt closed his eyes and kept the starter turning. It didn't require much imagination to visualize shattered piston rings scoring deep into the engine's cylinder walls. Quite suddenly the engine started.

Milland allowed himself a second's elation at the sight of water boiling past the hull before calling down a course to the helmsman that swung the U-boat's bow round until it was heading towards the *Tulsar* at a steady three knots.

'Watch the sky for that damned seaplane!' Milland raged at the lookouts. He guessed that Gerrard would be attempting a take-off away from the *Tulsar* – using the whaling-ship's bulk as a screen. He cursed himself for not seeing Gerrard's visit for what it was: a cunning ploy to distract attention while the seaplane was launched.

'Range four miles, captain!' called Machin who was peering through the main gun's range-finder.

'Open fire when you're ready,' Milland ordered.

One of the gunners quickly spun a handwheel. The barrel of the big gun slewed smoothly round on its well-greased bearings until Machin had the *Tulsar*'s image square in his sights.

The seaplane's whirling propeller racked into the water and gunned spray over the canopy. Gerrard lost sight of the U-boat for the third time and then caught a glimpse of white smoke belching from the U-boat's main gun when the next wave nearly stood the seaplane on its tail. He had no idea how far Piet was behind in the whale-catcher; the important thing was to keep his eyes fixed on the U-boat, now less than a mile away. He risked a quick inspection of the floats to ensure that the harpoons were still securely in place. The rivet-breaking roller-coaster motion meant that the air-speed indicator was useless, but he estimated his speed at around forty knots.

He was one minute from the U-boat.

Milland spotted the seaplane leaping from a crest like a hooked marlin when it was half a mile off the U-boat's quarter. The anti-aircraft gun was brought into action and the sustained roaring of its belt-fed barrels was added to the intermittent boom of the main gun pounding the *Tulsar*.

'Higher! Higher, you idiots!' Milland screamed, seeing miniature waterspouts lacerate the water in the charging seaplane's path. At that moment, the machine dipped below the swell and was lost to sight. It re-emerged seconds later in a cloud of propeller-driven spray having closed the distance between it and the U-boat by two hundred metres. The man operating the multiple-barrel gun over-corrected his aim and sent lightning darts of tracer spraying into the sea to the seaplane's left.

'Idiot! Idiot! Milland raged. He lurched forward to the wintergarten rail and screamed abuse at the gunner.

Confused by the noise and smoke, and the burning hot shell cases dancing out of the breech, the gunner stopped firing in order to take a fresh aim at the madly-twisting target. He resumed firing a continuous burst and succeeded in chewing the seaplane's wing-tip to splinters.

'Hit the fuselage!' bellowed Milland.

The seaplane was within a hundred metres and seemed unstoppable. Suddenly its engine was plainly audible above the gun's staccato racket. In fury, Milland jumped down on to the wintergarten deck. He ignored the sharp snap of pain in his stump from the jolt and pushed the gunner away. A spent shell case rolled under his artificial leg causing him to lose his balance temporarily. By the time he was in position behind the gun, the seaplane was a roaring nightmare within fifty metres and coming straight at him. He took careful aim and pulled the trigger.

At the precise moment that Milland started firing, Gerrard judged that the seaplane was near enough. He lifted his legs over the edge of the cockpit and levered his body out on to a wing root. The water, inches beneath his feet, was a blur. If he miscalculated his jump, he would be decapitated by the tailplane. At that moment the aircraft suddenly seemed to start falling to pieces around him. He tried to shift his weight on to the float. A searing pain stabbed savagely into his shoulder. The shock caused him to lose his handhold. He retained consciousness just long enough to thrust away with his feet from the disintegrating seaplane.

At twenty metres, Milland's careful firing could do nothing to destroy the seaplane's hundred feet per second momentum. One float broke away from the wing, causing the entire machine to slew round so that it struck *U-330* amidships instead of near the bow. Ten harpoons exploded simultaneously. It wasn't a large explosion but it was enough to blast a foot-wide hole in the U-boat's pressure hull just below the water-line. The harpoon-laden float that Milland had shot away drifted against the side of *U-330* and the force of that explosion lifted Milland bodily over the bridge coaming and tossed him into the sea.

The sudden inrush of water swept Venner from his stool. Even before he had climbed to his feet there was a foot of black water in the control-room. He ignored the mad scramble of bodies trying to climb the bridge ladder and the roar of water erupting through the hole. Instead he pulled on his head-

phones, encoded a succinct distress call on the cipher machine
and set his radio to transmit.

# 17

Admiral Wilhelm Fritz Canaris, head of the Abwehr, left the
Reich Chancellory building at 10 pm and hurried to his car.
The driver jumped out and opened the rear door. Canaris
climbed in beside Strick, settled back in the seat and tossed
his high-peaked cap on the floor.

'Well?' inquired Strick as the car moved off.

'Naturally he was disappointed that *U-330* had failed in its
mission.'

'Failed?' echoed Strick. 'But we've got the *Tulsar*'s position!
I don't call that failure. Surely you didn't tell the Führer that
we've failed?'

The tyres of the Mercedes hissed wetly through the darkened streets. Canaris reached into an inside pocket and spread
a copy of *U-330*'s signal on his lap. He switched on the reading-
lamp and passed the fateful slip of paper to his companion.
'Read it again,' he said.

The words had been printed on Strick's memory since he
had first been shown the signal an hour earlier, but he reread
the terse message.

U330 TO BDU
POSITION GRID SQUARE AH2867. UNDER ATTACK.
SINKING

'You see?' said Canaris. 'There's nothing in that to suggest
that *U-330* was sunk by the *Tulsar*. And even if it was, with
her top speed of twenty-six knots, she would be miles away
by now.'

Strick began to get angry. 'But that's why it is imperative
that we despatch a radar-equipped ship to search for the *Tulsar*
now! The purpose of your audience was to persuade the
Führer –'

'I learned something just now,' Canaris interrupted, giving Strick an impish grin. 'I suppose that must sound odd coming from the head of the intelligence service, but Grand Admiral Raeder is remarkably adept at keeping his conniving schemes to himself. It appears that for some time the Grand Admiral has been nursing an ambition to send a heavy surface force into the Atlantic to challenge the Royal Navy. Quite insane, of course, and the Führer has rightly refused to allow such nonsense. But to placate Raeder, the Führer has allowed him to dream and scheme.'

'What does that mean?' asked Strick.

'All the operational planning required to send a significant naval force into the North Atlantic is complete and has been for some while. Codes, lines of command, supplies – all the thousand and one tasks have been carried out. It's even got a code name – Operation Rheinübung.'

Strick made a despairing gesture with his hands. 'Then why, in the name of God, didn't you persuade the Führer to give Raeder the go-ahead?'

Canaris looked at his watch. 'The Führer will be speaking to Raeder about now. He will be telling the Grand Admiral to order Admiral Lütjens to put to sea as soon as possible. Naturally, Raeder won't be given the real reason why Rheinübung is receiving his assent until Lütjens' task force has broken through into the Atlantic – perhaps not even then. I have a feeling that the Führer may communicate with Lütjens direct.' Canaris paused. He had enjoyed his little game with the cold-blooded economics professor. He smiled at Strick's expression of astonishment and added: 'Did you know that the Führer paid Lütjens a visit two days ago?'

'Lütjens is putting to sea?' Strick managed to blurt out.

Canaris nodded. 'His entire task force will move to Korsfjord when they're ready and wait for the right moment to break out into the Atlantic.'

Strick could think of nothing to say. Admiral Lütjens flew his pennant from a very special warship. With its 41,700 tons displacement, massive 'Wotan' armour-plating and eight 15-inch guns, it was one of the most powerful warships in the world. Its lurking presence at Gotenhafen on the Baltic where it was beyond the reach of the RAF was a constant, nagging threat to the British, who dreaded the terrible damage it could inflict on the Atlantic convoys if it broke out. It was well known that they would do anything and resort to any subterfuge to tempt it out into the North Sea where they would be able to hurl several battleships and cruisers against it. Even its name symbolized Germany's might and prestige.

It was called the *Bismarck*.

# 18

Milland opened his eyes and stared up at the deckhead in the *Tulsar*'s sick bay. He knew every light, every girder – every detail of that deckhead was permanently etched on his consciousness. Even the lines of rivets were part of the pattern. In terror, his hands went to his sides and felt the cold smoothness of stainless steel beneath the mattress. He started up on his elbows.

'No!' he croaked. 'No!'

'Easy there,' said a voice.

Milland turned his head and saw Gerrard. The American grinned.

'Hi there. How are you feeling, Kurt?'

'My leg ... my leg ...' Milland babbled. 'Is it –? Is it –?'

Gerrard thought his former colleague was referring to his artificial leg. He said reassuringly: 'Your leg's fine, Kurt. Can't say the same about your U-boat or my seaplane.'

'U-boat?' The German stared up in bewilderment. 'U-boat?' he repeated. And then the fog cleared from his mind. He allowed his aching head to drop back on to the pillow. '*U-330*,' he muttered.

Milland closed his eyes for a minute and opened them again. 'Tell me what happened.'

Gerrard removed the bandage from Milland's head and examined the ugly bruise on the German's temple. 'Guess you had yourself a spot of concussion, Kurt.'

'What happened!' Milland suddenly shouted. He pushed himself up on his elbows again and grimaced in pain.

'I charged you with the seaplane. There were harpoons – '

'After that.'

'We both ended up in the sea. I'd stopped a splinter in the shoulder but the water brought me round. Next thing I found myself hanging on to your collar until Piet picked us up in the catcher. Remember Piet? He wants to look by later.'

'How about my men?'

Gerrard remained silent.

'Well?'

'I'm sorry, Kurt.'

Milland stared up at Gerrard. 'Not even one?'

Gerrard placed a fresh lint over Milland's temple and unrolled a clean bandage. 'I guess they were as lousy swimmers as they were gunners. Piet searched around for three hours.'

Milland's eyes were fixed on the deckhead lights. 'You won't get the *Tulsar* to England,' he said in a flat, detached tone. 'I've failed but there will be others. They'll throw everything at you.'

Gerrard eased Milland into a sitting position and started tying the bandage around the German's head. 'Done pretty well so far, Kurt.'

Milland made no reply.

'How did your people find out about our cargo?' Gerrard asked, making the inquiry sound like a chance, conversational remark. He continued winding the bandage around Milland's head. 'Well, I don't blame you for not talking, Kurt. But we caught your guy Kramer.'

'I guessed,' said Milland sourly. He suddenly remembered that Admiral Staus had told him that there were *two* agents aboard the *Tulsar*. From what Gerrard had said, it was certain that the second agent hadn't been caught. The first agent was Kramer. What was the name of the second agent – the passenger? It had been typed on his sealed orders which had gone down with *U-330*. An English name. He cursed the blow on his head. For Christ's sake what had his name been? The name! The name!

Gerrard finished tying the bandage. The door of the sick bay opened and a slightly-built, fair-haired man wearing a well-cut suit entered. His aristocratic features reminded Milland of the British actor Leslie Howard. Milland tried to remember if Leslie Howard had such intense blue eyes.

'How is he?' the man inquired.

'He's tough,' said Gerrard. 'Just like all whalers.'

The man offered his hand to Milland. 'How do you do, Captain Milland. My name is Ralph Holden.'

Milland met the stranger's unsettling eyes. He gave a slow smile and shook the offered hand.

'I'm pleased to meet you, Mr Holden.'

# 19

The hours of daylight lengthened as the *Tulsar* pushed northwards at two knots. The sub-tropics had been left far behind, and blustery winds alternating with driving squalls forced the bored passengers to remain below decks where Josephine did her best to keep them entertained.

Occasionally the two Ursuline nuns ventured out on deck, their black habits flapping like the cloaks of demented witches in the biting wind that held the promise of worse to come. Mr and Mrs Eli Vanson waged an acrimonious truce against each other over endless card games in the restaurant because the bar had run dry. Herbie Lewis thought about Rose, and the former newly-weds were sustaining the electric aftermath of a bitter row.

Kurt Milland sat in the guarded cabin that had been assigned to him and wondered when Holden would attempt to contact him. He spent hours on his bunk brooding about his failure. After an exercise walk that had included the flensing deck, he had noticed the new cargo hatch, and his brooding changed to scheming.

On the afternoon of 17 May the *Tulsar* was sighted five hundred miles south-west of Lisbon by a long-range Focke-Wulf belonging to the Aufklärungsstaffeln (reconnaissance) squadron. The big four-engine machine was scouring far out into the Atlantic in search of a Gibraltar convoy that was believed to be taking an extreme westward route.

The FW 200's crew studied the *Tulsar* through binoculars and noted the giant Stars and Stripes banner on each side of the hull. Lone sailings by whaling-ships belonging to neutral countries were not their concern but there had been nothing else to report so they plotted the *Tulsar*'s position, course and surprisingly low speed, and radioed the information to their base at Bordeaux.

By one of those coincidences that was to have far-reaching consequences, their signal was received at Bordeaux at the same time as a general alert from Oberkommando der Luftwaffe requiring all lone sailings to be reported to the naval high command. The order was immediately obeyed, with the result that the intelligence on the *Tulsar* was radioed to Admiral Lütjens on the *Bismarck* within the hour.

Such were the intricate preliminaries that were ultimately to decide the fate of the mighty leviathan and exhaust the meagre balance of the *Tulsar*'s luck.

# 20

Shortly after 10 am on 18 May a flight of four snub-nosed, single-engine FW 190 fighters under the command of their renowned *gruppenadjutant*, Oberleutnant Paul Kassel, landed at Bordeaux after a long flight from the Luftwaffe test establishment at Rechlin.

Once the pale blue aircraft were under cover the admiring ground crews were able to take a close look at the new machines and bombard Kassel with demands for autographs which he laughingly supplied with a series of exuberant flourishes from a gold fountain pen presented to him by Reichmarschall Hermann Goering.

The debonair Kassel's four machines were pre-production FW 190 A-4's and were the creation of Focke-Wulf's brilliant designer, Kurt Tank. They were each fitted with four 110-pound bombs on a fuselage bomb-rack together with wing-mounted cannons and external long-range fuel tanks. Goering had proudly described the new aircraft as having 'the speed of a fighter and the punch of a bomber'. His purpose in despatching Paul Kassel's flight to Bordeaux was to steal a march on the despised Kriegsmarine. Kassel's Wurger-gruppe – 'Butcher Bird Squadron' – were required to find and destroy the *Tulsar*.

On that same day, a thousand miles to the north-east, the mighty *Bismarck* quietly slipped away from her Baltic anchorage.

From both ends of the continent of Europe, inexorable forces were closing on the diminutive whaling ship.

# 21

The weather deteriorated rapidly over the following week. The low-pressure fronts overhauled the *Tulsar* and slowed her to a virtual halt with mountainous seas that reared up and burst over the jury-repaired bow with a force that made Piet uneasy. He had just returned from an inspection of the fother and was standing on the the bridge with Holden when the two men heard the faint drone of aircraft engines.

'They sound like the same ones we heard yesterday,' Holden commented. He searched the leaden cloudbase but there was nothing. The wheelhouse door opened and Gerrard stepped on to the bridge. He listened for a few seconds.

'You reckon they're looking for us?' Piet inquired.

'Christ knows,' Gerrard answered. 'Maybe that big four-engine job did spot us after all the other day.'

'A certainty,' said Holden.

'Okay,' said Gerrard with finality. 'We increase our speed and alter course – just in case those bastards plotted us.'

'Cap'n,' said Piet anxiously, 'I'm telling you that fother won't take any more speed.'

'Another three knots, Piet.'

'No, cap'n.'

'For Chrissake, Piet. We're asking to be bombed out of the sea if we stick to this speed.'

The Afrikaner's voice suddenly was hard. 'Cap'n Gerrard. Why are the Germans busting themselves to stop us?'

'I have a suggestion to make,' said Holden abruptly. 'A slight increase in speed will help, but do we have any paint?'

Piet gaped at Holden. 'Paint?'

'Paint.'

Piet forced his uncooperative mind to dwell on the subject. 'Maybe three hundred gallons of red primer but no top coat.'

'And brushes?'

'Plenty of brushes,' Piet replied, bewildered.

Gerrard suddenly realized what Holden was thinking and started laughing.


Ten miles to the east, Paul Kassel decided that there was little point in continuing the search that day in the worsening visibility. He switched on his throat microphone and spoke to his three comrades.

As one, the four hungry Butcher Birds turned for home.


Josephine burst out laughing. 'You're kidding? No – you're not kidding.'

'They've been complaining that they're bored,' said Holden. 'Now's their chance to do something useful.' He prised the lid off a five-gallon can of paint and stirred the contents.

'It's primer,' said Josephine.

'So?'

'One thing I do know from my father's hardware store is that you're not supposed to paint primer on top of top coat.'

'Have you had any more news about him, Jo?'

'No.'

Holden decided that her emphatic tone indicated that the subject was not to be pursued. He straightened up. 'Will you tell the passengers or shall I?'

'I'll tell them,' said Josephine. 'But I have this theory that Mr Eli Vanson will blow his stack.'

Eli Vanson blew his stack.

'I'm to what!' he bellowed at Josephine.

'Help with the repainting of the ship,' Josephine said for the second time while counting slowly up to ten to contain her temper. Eli Vanson had been nothing but trouble since Durban. She turned to the other passengers. 'It doesn't have to be done carefully. All we have to do is slap it on as quick as possible. There's more than enough brushes for all of us and the crew, and the crew will do the more difficult work of painting the hull.'

Eli Vanson's vehement protests were interrupted by the elder of the two Ursuline nuns. She took two brushes from Josephine, gave one to her companion, and told Josephine that they were ready to start work.

Persuading the rest of the passengers to help was easy after that.

By mid-afternoon, not only had the *Tulsar* changed her colour from pale grey to dark red, but she had also changed her appearance: several lifeboat covers had been stitched together and stretched tightly across the open divide of the whale slipway – the one feature that unmistakably identified the ship as a whaler.

# 22

The following morning, 20 May, Paul Kassel held a brief conference with his three fellow Butcher Bird pilots.

'Our only fix of the *Tulsar*'s position is now three days old,' he told his men. He placed a finger on the chart of the North Atlantic off France. 'We know that she was moving north at two knots – fifty miles a day she's making – therefore she cannot be more than two hundred miles from that position unless she has increased her speed.'

'She must have done so,' said one of the pilots. 'We've covered every square mile ahead of her last position. Either that or she's now heading west.'

The four men spent another ten minutes discussing their search tactics before walking out to their waiting fighters.

Kassel was worried because he had promised Goering that the Butcher Birds would be tasting the *Tulsar*'s blood before the week was out.

He was even more worried that afternoon when they landed back at Bordeaux after a fruitless five-hour sortie. They had seen and photographed two ships and neither of them had resembled the *Tulsar*.

Two hours later, the refuelled Butcher Birds took off again and headed north to the tiny grass airfield at La Rochelle.

The new base brought a disastrous change of luck during the next few days. On 23 May Paul Kassel's number two aircraft hit a pothole dug in the field by Breton saboteurs and smashed an undercarriage leg, and on 25 May number four's BMW engine was beset by the usual BMW problem of overheating that led to the seizure of the motor's lower cylinders.

On 26 May, after having flown some twenty sorties over the Atlantic, he and his remaining fighter transferred to Guernsey Airport in the occupied British Channel Islands where they were obliged to share the limited facilities with sympathetic Luftflotte 3 personnel who were secretly delighted that one of Goering's blue-eyed glamour boys was having a rough time.

But the setbacks merely served to strengthen the indomitable Kassel's resolve to find and sink the *Tulsar*.

# 23

At 9.10 am on 27 May, when the *Tulsar* was approximately five hundred miles south-west of Brest, a low irregular rumble was heard from the north.

Gerrard spun round in his chair in the wheelhouse. 'Hey, Sam,' he called to Brody at the helm. 'Did that sound like thunder to you?'

'Queerest thunder I've ever heard, boss.'

Gerrard pulled on his oilskins and sou'wester. 'That's what I thought.'

Piet too had heard the noise and was climbing on to the bridge when Gerrard stepped out of the wheelhouse into the driving rain.

The low, menacing noise was repeated. It seemed to roll right round the horizon so that the two men had some difficulty in locating the direction of the sound.

'What do you make of it, cap'n?'

Gerrard peered into the squall-laden spray. Visibility was less than two miles. 'Well, it sure as hell isn't thunder, Piet.'

'The weather's getting very English,' Josephine observed while she and Holden were eating breakfast.

Holden frowned and held up a finger for silence.

'What's the matter?' Josephine was puzzled by Holden's sudden tense expression. The normally dispassionate face was alive with anticipation. He uttered one word:

'Guns.' And then three more: 'By God! Guns!'

'Guns,' said Piet. 'Big bastards.'

Gerrard had already reached the same conclusion. 'How far?'

'Could be fifty–sixty miles if they're 15-inchers. You could hear 15-inch guns being fired at Simonstown from off Cape Aghulas.' Piet listened for a few moments. 'Battleships or heavy cruisers maybe.'

'Or both.'

Piet nodded. Despite the appalling conditions on deck, men

were gathering along the bulwarks and were staring in the direction of the ominous thunder.

The unseen battle was still raging an hour later.

'Christ, it must be one helluva dispute,' Gerrard muttered.

By 10.10 am the interval between each crashing salvo and the next was noticeably longer. By 10.20 am there was only the occasional roll of cordite thunder. There was renewed spate ten minutes later that lasted for less than two minutes and then there was silence.

Piet and Gerrard remained at the rail for a long time, saying nothing. There seemed little doubt that many fellow sailors had been killed or were dying beyond the horizon.

Just how many was not revealed until shortly before nightfall when the *Tulsar* found herself steaming through a vast area of oil, wreckage and floating bodies wearing Kriegsmarine uniforms. There were hundreds of them and more were languidly reaching the surface around the *Tulsar* when she stopped.

Nothing was said by the men and women lining the rail and gazing down at the ghastly spectacle. There was nothing that could be said; it was a scene that made the mechanical business of assembling words into sentences impossible.

A lifebelt was fished aboard by a Lascar on Holden's orders. Gerrard joined the group at the rail and watched as Holden went down on one knee and turned the lifebelt over. Through the layer of wartime grey paint, it was possible to discern the single, unequivocal word that the lifebelt had borne in peacetime: *Bismarck*.

'What's the matter, Mr Holden?' Gerrard inquired amiably.

Holden stood. 'Why should anything be the matter?'

'Oh, nothing. It's just that I thought your hands were trembling a shade when you turned the lifebelt over.'

'She was a capital ship – one of the largest in the world,' Holden replied.

Gerrard grinned. 'Sure. Makes you wonder how many ships she took down with her.'

# 24

Oberleutnant Paul Kassel's luck changed when a U-boat returning to Lorient after a two-month patrol that had exhausted its torpedoes reported sighting a ship that fitted the description of the *Tulsar*. The only thing that was wrong was the colour. The *Tulsar* was not red but Kassel attributed this to a decoding error.

At 3.20 pm on 28 May, an hour after receiving the report, the two Butcher Birds took off from Guernsey and headed west out into the Atlantic.

After a quarter of an hour the two fighters dipped down through the cloudbase and were surprised to discover a British Flower class corvette four miles dead ahead. The sudden appearance of the two Luftwaffe fighters upset the sensibilities of the small warship – HMS *Shepherd's Purse* – for it immediately let fly at the intruders with its anti-aircraft guns. Kassel flew so low over the ship that he could actually see the gunners frantically swing their weapons round to keep him in their sights as he roared over their heads. He chuckled to himself and guessed that there would be baffled exchanges on the corvette as to why the plainly-visible bombs under the Focke-Wulf's wings hadn't been released. He glanced back and realized with a cold shock that he was alone. He turned the other way in his seat and saw his companion Butcher Bird hit the water and break up. His attention was drawn to the port wing of his own aircraft and the five regularly-spaced holes that should not have been there. The corvette's firing had been more accurate than he had supposed – a fact that was confirmed ten minutes later by his instruments indicating low oil pressure.

The visibility improved as he flew west. The cloud lifted and enabled him to climb to a thousand feet. He spotted the *Tulsar* heading north-east and immediately put the Butcher Bird's nose down towards it. The ship was red, but it was definitely a whaling-ship – not even the clumsy attempt to camouflage the slipway could disguise that fact. He came in low. He could see men frantically running and pointing. Some had the good sense to throw themselves flat.

Only one bomb of the four released by Kassel hit the *Tulsar*. It burst through the deckhead aft of the wheelhouse and exploded, blowing out the sides of the wheelhouse and every pane of glass. Brody threw himself flat at the moment of impact and was protected from the blast by the heavy pedestal of the gyro-compass. Piet van Kleef actually saw the bomb pierce the wheelhouse roof from his vantage point on the spotters' platform and immediately assumed that Sam Brody had been killed. He saw Gerrard run along the weatherdeck and climb the twisted steel steps to the bridge.

Kassel cursed the three bombs that plunged harmlessly into the water beside the *Tulsar* without exploding. He wheeled his aircraft round to examine the whaler and was surprised and infuriated to discover that the ship was still moving.

His engine began labouring, which was hardly surprising since his oil pressure reading was a little above zero. There was no time to even consider strafing the ship with his cannons. The important thing now was to nurse his Butcher Bird back to Guernsey. He circled round on to an easterly course and listened anxiously to the note of his faltering engine.

Five minutes later his anxiety changed to bitter anger when he found out that his radio was not working. Goddamn that corvette and the chance that had found it for him! He could not even radio the *Tulsar*'s position. At that moment his engine stopped.

There was nothing left for him to do but to check his parachute harness and slide back the Focke-Wulf's bubble cockpit canopy.

He wondered what his chances were of being picked up by an E-boat.

Gerrard and Holden stood amid the wreckage and gloomily surveyed the devastated remains of the wheelhouse.

'Jesus Christ,' Gerrard breathed. He picked up a small tangle of metal that had been his sextant and dropped it in disgust. 'We haven't even got a Goddamn sextant now.'

'What about Kramer's sextant?' Holden asked.

'It was in the chart-table drawer. You tell me where the chart-table is and I'll tell you where Kramer's sextant is. Gyro-compass knocked out, telegraph out, not one chart left – Jesus, what a God-awful mess.'

'Helm's still answering,' said Brody cheerfully. 'Trouble is, boss, I don't know what course I'm steering. Could be heading back to Africa.'

'I'll get Piet to get a compass out of a lifeboat,' said Gerrard.

Josephine appeared in the entrance that had once led to the day-cabin. She was trying to balance a tray of steaming mugs of coffee in one hand and cling to the door frame with the other. Holden quickly took the tray from her and held her steady.

'Are you okay, Jo?'

Josephine's face was ashen. 'Just fine,' she said with forced good humour. 'I guess the excitement is getting a little out of hand, huh?'

'Is everything still okay below?' asked Gerrard.

Josephine nodded. 'Those two nuns are real angels. They're pacifying everyone including Mr Vanson and he's not sure how to take it.'

# 25

The day after the bomb attack consisted of an unremitting battle against the gale-force winds and huge seas like male-volent mountains that reared up in the *Tulsar*'s path and hurled themselves down on the canvas-shrouded bow in a welter of foam and fury. One sea had barely roared through the scuppers before the next thundered down on the battered foredeck.

Gerrard's worries were remorselessly added to with each heavy sea. Would the fother hold? How in the world could canvas take such punishment? Would the lashings securing the crates stand up? But the worst of all – something that really frightened him – was not knowing where he was except that he was close to land. The behaviour of the seas, coming at the *Tulsar* from all directions, told him that he was near land. It was land that destroyed ships, rarely the sea. For the first time in his seafaring life he was lost. He had no charts – all had been swept into the sea by the bomb blast – and no navigating instruments apart from a hand-bearing compass removed from a lifeboat. Desperately he tried to recall details from the charts of the Cornish coastal areas, but they were a part of the world he had never sailed before and no snippets of information were permanently stored in his mind. He knew that the north and south coasts of Cornwall were wild and rocky, and that there were precious few coves or inlets that were not exposed to the full fury of the Atlantic. Reduced to crude basics, the sailing directions for entering the English Channel from the south were turn right a hundred miles after Ushant. Choosing the moment to turn right was going to be the most momentous decision of his life.

Nightfall brought stronger winds that howled through the gaps in the canvas lashed down over the smashed wheelhouse. The material dementedly flapped and banged, making helm orders impossible to convey without yelling in the helmsman's ear.

By 2 am the rolling was worse and the sea more broken and unpredictable. Gerrard lay exhausted on his bunk, unable to sleep as he listened for the sound of crashing crates in the hold that would mean the end.

# 26

Milland brought his artificial leg down with all his strength on the back of the Lascar's head. The seaman collapsed unconscious over the tray of food he was setting down on the table.

Certain that someone must have heard the crash of cutlery and metal dishes, Milland dragged himself across the floor to the cabin door and pushed it shut. He waited in silence, sitting on the floor with the empty leg of his trousers tucked underneath him. He risked a quick glimpse outside. The darkened corridor was deserted. He picked up his leg and saw that he had hit the seaman too hard; the ankle joint was broken – a jagged mess of torn metal and sheared rivets. He cursed his stupidity and flung the useless limb across the cabin in bitter frustration. Without the leg he was helpless – the only way he could get about was by crawling.

There was an ivory-handled knife in a sheath on the Lascar's belt. Milland unfastened the buckle and withdrew it. The blade was six inches long and honed to razor-sharpness.

He sat brooding for a quarter of an hour, wondering what to do. It was the vicious rolling of the ship that gave him the idea. The leg didn't matter. If he had to crawl, then that was exactly what he would do.

He pushed the knife into his belt, searched through the Lascar's pockets, and found what he was looking for: a box of matches.

Milland waited for two minutes in the shadow of a ventilator inlet while his eyes adjusted to the darkness. He was constantly drenched by breaking seas but didn't care; the important thing was to keep a tight grip on the matches so that they remained dry and to study his objective carefully, one of the circular blubber hatches that were located around the edge of the flensing deck. He wondered how they were locked. But wondering was no use – there was only one way to find out. . . .

The hinged hatch was secured by a simple pin and eye latch. He pulled the pin out with some difficulty and opened the hatch. It was heavy and the task was not made easier by the appalling motion. The sustained booming of seas crashing against the hull effectively masked the creak of rusty metal. Milland's arms were called upon to do much more than a man with both his legs. As a result, they were exceptionally powerful. It required no great effort on his part to hang down into the chasm, gripping a rung with one hand while lowering the hatch with the other. He felt about in black space with his leg. There were no more rungs. He pulled some coins from his pocket and dropped them. The sharp clatter beneath his feet told him that he had about four feet to fall. He released his grip and fell sprawling on to what felt like a timber crate. The next roll sent him tumbling off the crate. He managed to break his fall by grabbing the ropes that lashed the crates to the hold's floor.

He was too dazzled by the flare from the first match to see anything clearly. The second match revealed that he was exactly where he hoped he was – in the bullion hold, surrounded by crates stacked ten high and stretching along the narrow passage-way for as far as the feeble light from the match could reach. It was a sobering moment. He was completely surrounded by gold; billions of marks' worth of gold: the entire wealth of the mighty British Empire.

And one sharp knife could send the lot to the bottom. In the ponderous rolling, a dozen crates cut loose would crash into other crates and break them loose, which would in turn smash and splinter into each other until the entire cargo was a sliding, living mass that would eventually burst through the side of the hull or cause the *Tulsar* to develop such a list that she would inevitably broach to.

One sharp knife . . .

He jerked the Lascar's knife from his belt and set to work sawing at the straining lashings. First one rope parted, then another. He didn't need matches to see – just slash and hack at every rope within reach. Never in history would such a simply-performed act of sabotage have such far-reaching consequences.

He heard the upper crates sliding and felt an entire column tilt as the ship rolled. He intensified his already demented activity. The creaking and groaning from above his head was louder. Another rope parted, this time with a loud twang.

He heard the column of crates begin to topple and desperately crawled clear along the passage-way just as they came crashing down. The pool of light from a match showed that the crates had jammed themselves together into a solid, unyielding mass. He pulled himself upright and tried to dislodge the crates by pushing them, but to no avail. Sweat streaming down his face, he sank to the floor and rested. The *Tulsar* suddenly hit a particularly heavy sea. Before he could move, the crates came to life. They were breaking free and crashing all around him.

# 27

It was getting light when Piet hauled his glistening, oil-skinned bulk up the pitching remains of the steps that led to the bridge. He clung to the temporary safety rail with both hands. 'Pumps not holding!' he bellowed above the shrieking wind at Gerrard. 'Thirty-nine inches of water!'

Gerrard looked at the big Afrikaner in dismay. That amount of water in the bilge sump was serious. 'For Chrissake, Piet – get a party on the hand-pumps!'

'What in hell do you think I've been doing!' Piet yelled back. 'It doesn't make any difference!'

He got no further for Gerrard saw the charging green mountain and screamed out. Piet spun round in time to see the mighty sea hurl itself against the *Tulsar*'s side with stupendous force. The whaling-ship heeled violently and Gerrard had to hang on to Piet to save himself from being tossed into the seething maelstrom below. The foredeck was completely buried under countless tons of raging water. Piet thrust Gerrard against the rail and held him there until the American grabbed a handhold. Gerrard knew this time was going to be different; this time the *Tulsar* was not going to recover – she was going right over.

For endless seconds the two men clung with fear-induced

strength to the rail – oblivious of each other in their fierce determination not to be swept to certain death.

Miraculously, the *Tulsar* began to right herself but the motion was too slow – too uneven. Gerrard's feet, finely tuned to the feel of his ship, sensed tremors coursing through the deck plating as though the ship was being pounded by a mighty sledgehammer.

'Cargo's broken loose,' Piet croaked.

There was a momentary lull in the deafening, mind-numbing roar of water through the scuppers. Then Gerrard heard a new sound – heavy crashes from within the ship that could only be caused by the crates breaking loose in the hold. The crashes were perfectly synchronized with the reverberating booms of the massive rolling seas pounding against the hull.

The *Tulsar* did not complete her self-righting but remained listing heavily to port as if she was cowering from the seas that were seeking to destroy her.

Holden grabbed hold of Josephine's arm to prevent her losing her balance on the restaurant's sloping floor.

'Listen!' he said. 'Gerrard's going to have to give the order to abandon ship. You've got to get all the passengers on deck now. Get the crew to help. Check every cabin – but get them all out!'

'We can't!' Josephine snapped in anger rather than fear. 'He's got to give the order first. Maybe we'll be okay.'

'Don't be such a crazy bitch! Look at it! Gerrard's got to give the order!'

'What about you?' Josephine demanded.

'I've got something to do, now for God's sake stop arguing and get those passengers out of their cabins!'

Holden left Josephine and made his way to his cabin – steadying himself against the bulkhead as he walked on the sloping floor. He entered his cabin and dragged Kramer's Afu radio-transmitter out from under his bunk. He glanced round the inside of the cabin and guessed that the surrounding steel would screen the signal. He decided that he would have to operate the transmitter in the open.

'Steering's gone!' Brody screamed at Gerrard through the glassless wheelhouse window. The *Tulsar*'s head fell away and a sea rolled up the ramp provided by the hull's starboard flank. The list to port became more pronounced. Jack Colby appeared below. With the engine-room telegraph and interphone out of action, the radio-operator was relaying messages between the engine-room and the bridge.

'Cooling pipes are bust!' he yelled. 'They've shut down the turbines!'

Brody licked his lips and let the useless wheel spin through his fingers. 'That's it then, boss?'

Gerrard stared straight ahead into the eye of the storm for a few seconds and then roused himself. 'That's it, Sam. . . .' He reached for the crew address microphone and remembered that it was no longer there. 'Piet! Pass the word! We're abandoning ship!'

Holden scrambled up the steep slope of the starboard weatherdeck and crouched under a lifeboat. He could hear the calls of the crew and passengers as they mustered on the port deck. He released the catches on Kramer's radio-transmitter, opened the lid and tossed the coil of antenna wire over a davit before switching the set on and waiting for it to warm up.

A weak morning sun broke briefly through the cloudbase. It needed only one person to climb to the starboard deck and he would be seen.

A minute passed. The headphone began to hum. Holden's frozen fingers slipped on the Morse key. He blew on them and grasped the ebonite knob firmly, and started transmitting.

A sea suddenly swept up the port deck and knocked Herbie Lewis off his feet. 'Hang on to the ropes!' Piet yelled at the passengers through a megaphone. 'You all hang on and you'll be okay!'

Josephine helped Herbie Lewis to his feet, then went to the aid of Eli Vanson who was in danger of losing his footing. For once the sugar magnate was not complaining. He, like the rest of the passengers, was cold, wet, and frightened. His wife was hanging on his arm and upsetting his balance.

'It would be easier for Mr Vanson if you held on to the safety line,' Josephine shouted above the wind. But the terrified woman merely stared blankly and tightened her grip on her husband's sleeve. She hardly acknowledged Josephine's presence as Josephine checked that her Mae West lifejacket was properly tied in place.

Piet shambled along the deck holding a clipboard containing sodden papers. 'Have you all the passengers, Miss Britten?'

'All except Mr Holden,' Josephine answered. 'I've no idea where he is.'

'I want all the passengers in the whale-catcher!' shouted Gerrard. 'All passengers to the whale-catcher! Come on! Move! Move!'

The high-speed launch was luffed out on its davits and lowered until it was level with the listing deck. Two Indian seamen stationed themselves against the bulwark and helped each passenger in turn to scramble off the treacherously-sloping deck and jump down into the launch's open cockpit.

'All passengers except Holden accounted for!' Piet yelled in Gerrard's ear.

'How about the crew?'

'One deckhand and the German prisoner. I'm just going to fetch them.'

Gerrard had forgotten Milland. 'I'll get them, Piet. You stay with the passengers. Tell Colby to start loading the crew into lifeboats.'

The Lascar Milland had knocked unconscious was recovering when Gerrard found him. He confessed that he had no idea where Milland was. Gerrard roundly cursed the man and half dragged, half pushed him out of the cabin before going in search of Milland.

Mrs Eli Vanson screamed in terror as the first wave threatened to tip the whale-catcher on to its beam ends. Piet started the launch's engine and swung it away from the stricken *Tulsar*. For the first time Josephine was able to appreciate the magnitude of the disaster that had overtaken the whaling-ship; the *Tulsar* was listing at an angle of more than thirty degrees and was settling deeper in the water by the bow.

Josephine stood up in the cockpit. She had to hold on to the coaming with one hand and shield her eyes from the spray with the other. She pointed at the lifeboat that Jack Colby was loading with crewmen.

'Where's Mr Holden?' she yelled at Piet.

'Cap'n's looking for him. There's nothing to worry about,' the Afrikaner replied, concentrating on keeping the launch's bow aimed into the seas.

Gerrard dropped down the rope into the hold and shone the torch around. He was deafened by the splintering crashes of crates charging into each other and cannoning against the inside of the hull. He leapt clear of a crate that came hurtling straight at him. There was blood on the floor.

'Kurt!'

The *Tulsar* heaved – a movement that provoked a tangle of crates to detach themselves from where they had piled up against the inside of the hull and to go sliding and grating into the middle of the hold. It was then that the beam of light from Gerrard's torch picked out an arm protruding from beneath a mass of crates that had jammed themselves into a corner. Keeping a wary eye on a crate that was threatening to break loose, Gerrard hooked his fingers under the crate that was lying across the trapped man. He waited for the right moment and managed to tip the crate to one side. The trapped man was Milland. The lower half of his body was pinioned under crates and Gerrard knew there was no chance of shifting them. He went down on one knee beside the German.

'Kurt!'

Milland was still breathing. He opened his eyes and stared up at Gerrard. There was no expression in his lustreless eyes. His lips moved. Gerrard bent over him to hear what he was saying.

'She's finished?'

'She's finished, Kurt. You've won.'

Milland turned his head, trying to see the chaos he had caused. What he couldn't see, he could hear. He gave a satisfied smile.

'Funny,' he muttered.

'What is, Kurt?'

The German coughed and grimaced in pain. 'Having... having your ship smashed up by gold.'

205

The *Tulsar* pitched sharply and increased its list. Two crates hurled themselves against the hull within six feet of Gerrard and Milland. A plate burst open and seawater roared through the fissure. In desperation Gerrard again tried to dislodge the crates on top of Milland. After two minutes of frantic effort he gave up and slid to the floor beside Milland to get his breath back.

'Robert ...'

'Yeah?'

Milland struggled to form a sentence. 'I'm sorry about Cathy.'

'Yeah.'

The crates withdrew from the side of hull in harmony with the *Tulsar*'s motion and hurled themselves back at the fractured steel. More plates buckled outwards, unleashing fresh cascades of water. One side of the hold was now flooded and was a mass of jostling boards from shattered crates. The crates above Milland moved slightly, forcing a cry of pain from his punctured lungs. He moved his hand and caught feebly at Gerrard's peajacket, drawing him close.

'Ask him something for me,' Milland croaked.

'Ask who?'

'Holden. Ask him why he didn't contact me ... why he didn't help.' Milland's voice trailed away. He closed his eyes. His breathing was suddenly more laboured.

'Why should Holden help?' Gerrard cupped some seawater in his hand and splashed it on Milland's face. 'Kurt! *Why should Holden help you?*'

Milland's lips moved. Gerrard bent right over until his ear was a few inches from Milland's mouth. He heard the dying man say, 'Holden was our second agent. . . .'

Holden felt the *Tulsar* give another tremor. The deck was angled at nearly forty degrees as far as he could judge in the driving, blinding spray. He decided that it was time to stop transmitting. He switched the radio off and jerked the antenna wire down from the davit.

'*Holden!*' a voice bellowed behind him.

He turned. Gerrard had an arm hooked round a stanchion and was aiming the Lee Enfield rifle straight at him.

'Just give me one opportunity to blow your head off, Holden, and my God I'll take it.'

'What do you want me to do?' Holden inquired calmly.

The coolness in the Englishman's voice infuriated Gerrard to the point where he was tempted to pull the trigger and kill Holden out of hand. 'Close that case.'

A sea burst over the *Tulsar*'s side and nearly swept the suit-case-radio from Holden's grasp. He closed the lid and watched Gerrard carefully.

'Now what, captain?'

Gerrard gestured with the rifle. 'This way.'

Holden stumbled along the sloping deck towards Gerrard.

'Okay. Now down the deck.'

The flensing deck had become a steep ramp that led straight down into the maddened sea that was raging white against the bulwarks. The whale-catcher with Piet at the helm was danger-ously close to the *Tulsar*'s leaning hulk.

'On your ass!' Gerrard shouted.

Holden sat and slithered down the drenched deck. He reached the bulwark and felt Gerrard's weight crash into him. The two men were up to their waists in water. Gerrard was still holding the rifle. He signalled to Piet who then nosed the whale-catcher's wildly pitching bow in as close as he dare to the *Tulsar*.

'Throw the radio first!' Gerrard ordered.

Herbie Lewis was clinging to the whale-catcher's harpoon-gun. He indicated that he was ready to catch the suitcase. Holden tossed it to him. The Canadian caught it neatly and passed it aft.

'Now you!' Gerrard shouted.

Piet edged the whale-catcher nearer while Holden crouched on the bulwark. He judged the narrowing gap and jumped, landing clumsily on the whale-catcher's small foredeck. Herbie Lewis grabbed him by the shirt and the other passengers reached out and dragged him unceremoniously into the cockpit. As soon as Gerrard was also safely aboard, Piet put the launch hard astern and pulled away from the *Tulsar*.

Josephine knelt beside Holden and helped him into a sitting position.

'Get away from him!' Gerrard yelled. 'No one is to speak to him!'

'Don't be so silly, and don't point that gun at me!' Josephine retorted.

Gerrard hauled Josephine away from Holden and thrust her beside the two Ursuline nuns. 'He's a spy, Miss Britten. And I say that no one is to speak to him.'

'Do as he says, Jo,' said Holden wearily.

Piet steered the whale-catcher towards Jack Colby's lifeboat which was a hundred yards clear of the *Tulsar*. Josephine was about to defy Gerrard but decided against it. Also, the unfamiliar motion of the smaller boat was beginning to make her seasick.

A tow-line was thrown from Jack Colby's lifeboat and secured to the whale-catcher's Samson post. There was a loud crash from the *Tulsar* and Josephine was astonished to see the side of her hull burst open along a line of rivets. The second crash split the hull plates sideways. It was as if there was a crazed bulldozer inside the ship trying to smash its way out through the hull. She saw Gerrard standing in the stern staring back at his ship's death throes. Two more crashes followed in quick succession. The hull suddenly burst open. A wooden crate fell out of the wound and plunged into the sea. Several more followed and suddenly there was a cascade of splintering crates raining down into the water in one sustained splash.

The stream stopped and it seemed that the *Tulsar* was trying to right itself. But the end came very quickly: two heavy seas battered the ship on to her beam ends. One of her propellers appeared momentarily above the foam and was then lost to sight as the stern slipped under. The bow, still with the fother in place, lifted high above the broken water as if the ship was attempting to climb out of the seas that were trying to engulf her. The bow paused, undecided, and finally abandoned the unequal struggle.

The *Tulsar* sank at 2.55 pm on 30 May 1941.

Piet kicked the gear lever into neutral. Passengers and crew on both craft gazed in silence at the patch of bubbling white water that marked the spot where the *Tulsar* had disappeared.

'What course, cap'n?' Piet asked. He had to repeat the question.

Gerrard shrugged. 'East. North-east. South-east. Christ only knows where we are.'

The Afrikaner spun the wheel until the compass was indicating due east.

The weather began to moderate by 3.30 pm. The wind veered round to the south-west and dropped. By 5 pm the sun was shining and the spirits of the survivors rose as a patch of blue sky expanded from the west.

At 5.10 pm the *Shepherd's Purse* found them.

# 28

Lieutenant-Commander James Keron, Royal Navy Volunteer Reserve, commanding officer of His Majesty's corvette *Shepherd's Purse*, looked up and smiled warmly as Gerrard was shown into the cramped wardroom. The American's appearance after a night's sleep and a bath and shave had improved decidedly since he had been picked up the previous afternoon.

'Good morning, captain,' said Keron affably, standing and shaking Gerrard's hand. 'Please sit down.' 'My steward's been looking after you, I trust?'

'Fine,' said Gerrard, sitting at the table. He glanced quickly around. Sunlight was streaming into the wardroom. Outside was the hammer and clatter of a shipyard working under wartime pressures.

'Eleven's a little early for pink gins don't you think?' said Keron cheerfully, pouring two cups of coffee from a jug. 'Actually I can't stand anything except beer but I have to keep quiet about it otherwise they'd make me resign my commission.'

'Is this Falmouth, commander?' Gerrard's tone was brusque. He was in no mood for the naval officer's pleasantries.

'But of course. We docked at oh-four-hundred.'

'Why wasn't I woken up earlier?'

'Because you were sleeping like the proverbial top, old boy.'

'Where is everyone?'

'In a local hotel. They're all being well looked after – but no one's allowed to talk to them.'

'And Holden?' Gerrard inquired, sipping his coffee.

'Under arrest, of course, in view of what you told me.'

'What will happen to him?'

'If he is what you say he is, he'll most likely be hanged.' Keron looked up at the door. 'Ah – come in, captain.'

A thin, distinguished-looking man wearing a charcoal-grey suit entered the wardroom. He was carrying a GVIR-created briefcase.

'Captain Steven Houseman,' said Keron, introducing the stranger to Gerrard.

'If you would kindly leave us for a while, I'd be most grateful,' Houseman said crisply when the introductions were over.

'I'll see that you're not disturbed, sir,' Keron promised, and left Houseman and Gerrard alone.

Houseman sat down and lit a cigarette from a gold lighter. He stared hard at Gerrard for some seconds before speaking. 'I've just flown down from London, Mr Gerrard, since speaking to Lieutenant-Commander Keron on the phone this morning.'

He opened his briefcase and removed some papers. 'Tell me about the *Tulsar*'s cargo, Mr Gerrard.'

'Two hundred tons of gold,' Gerrard replied, matching Houseman's brusqueness.

Houseman sighed. 'I had hoped that sleep might have modified your imagination, Mr Gerrard.'

Gerrard began to get angry. 'What the hell's that supposed to mean?'

'It's a polite way of calling you a liar, Mr Gerrard. Do you honestly expect anyone to believe such a crazy cock and bull story as the one you told Commander Keron? Do you really think we're such idiots as to fall for it?'

It took all Gerrard's self-control to keep his temper in check. 'If you talk to your Treasury –'

'I have,' Houseman interrupted. 'While I'm not prepared to discuss our gold movements with you, I can tell you that we never have moved gold out of Durban, we don't plan to, and if we did, we most certainly would not move our bullion on a US-registered ship.'

'For Chrissake, why do you suppose the Germans planted two agents on my ship? To count the whales they thought I might catch?'

Houseman smiled thinly. 'Ah, yes. Your two spies. Kramer and Holden.'

'You've seen Kramer's radio, haven't you?'

'Oh yes. Very interesting. Obviously he learned of your plans to sail for England and decided to stowaway. A professional agent. But he's dead.'

Gerrard clenched his fists and unclenched them. He realized that Houseman was deliberately goading him and decided not to give the arrogant Englishman the advantage by losing his temper. 'And there's Holden! A professional if ever there was! I even caught him using Kramer's radio and Kurt Milland himself said that Holden was an agent. What have I got to say to you people to convince you that I'm telling the truth, for Chrissake!'

Houseman closed his briefcase and stood. 'I've a number of inquiries to make, Mr Gerrard. You will be moved to a police cell until I'm ready to talk to you again.'

'I want to see a lawyer,' said Gerrard dully.

'That won't be possible.'

'I've a right, for Chrissake!'

Houseman moved to the door. 'Under the Defence Regulations all the rights are ours. We can hold you indefinitely without trial. And if we do decide to take action, we have the right to hold trials in camera, to pass sentences in camera, and to carry out executions in camera at Exeter Prison or anywhere we choose.'

Gerrard stared back at the cold eyes and suddenly realized that he was scared.

'There's something else I'd like you to think about,' Houseman continued. 'You say the bomb dropped by the German fighter knocked out your radio shack? You were picked up a hundred miles south-west of Land's End after being in lifeboats for just over two hours. Did it not occur to you that you were rescued remarkably quickly? The truth is that two shore-based radio stations were able to pinpoint your position by radio direction-finding from the sos signals transmitted by Mr Holden.'

\*　　\*　　\*

Two civilian policemen from the Cornwall Constabulary called for Gerrard an hour later and drove him to Falmouth police station in a black Wolseley. He was escorted to a bare, ten-foot square cell and given a wartime prison-issue meal of fish pie and boiled cabbage.

The coach stopped inside the wired compound and a smartly turned-out corporal in khaki battledress hauled the coach's door open.

'Everyone out, please, ladies.'

Josephine followed the two Ursuline nuns down the steps and turned to help Mrs Eli Vanson.

'Where are we?' Josephine asked the corporal.

'Somewhere in England, miss,' the NCO replied as he signed the WRNS driver's clipboard. 'If you'd all follow me please.'

The bride who had been separated from her husband in Falmouth burst into tears for what Josephine estimated was the twentieth time since the long drive had begun.

'For God's sake someone else look after her before she sets Mrs Vanson off,' said Josephine irritably to no one in particular.

The nuns gathered protectively around the girl and managed to calm her.

'This way please, ladies,' said the corporal impatiently, mounting the steps leading to a long, wooden hut.

Josephine was the last to enter the depressing building. As she did so, she glanced back. There was something familiar about the outline of the magnificent building that rose above the trees to dominate the skyline. It was a building she had seen in books and movies. And then she realized what it was: Windsor Castle.

'My God,' she said to herself. 'We must be in Windsor Great Park.'

Houseman didn't see Gerrard again until 6.30 pm. His manner was even more frosty than it had been in the morning. He sat at the table opposite Gerrard in the police station interview-room and opened his briefcase. He came straight to the point.

'We've been in touch with your agent in Durban, Mr Gerrard. According to him the *Tulsar* was loaded with two hundred tons of lead on 23 February last in Durban. We've also checked with the mining corporation at Broken Hill in Northern Rhodesia and they have confirmed that they despatched a trainload of lead ingots to Durban on 21 February.'

Gerrard looked bored .'That was the cover for the gold that Holden fixed. No one else but he and I knew about it.'

'And the Germans you say he told about it,' Houseman pointed out, his voice tinged with sarcasm.

'Have you talked to him?' Gerrard asked.

'Oh yes. His references are impeccable. He even had an identity card on him.' Houseman's smile was icy. 'In fact, of all of you, he was the only one entitled to enter the country.'

The interview dragged on for two hours, going over the same questions with Houseman dissecting the same answers. At 8.30 pm Houseman stood up and returned his papers to his briefcase. 'The issues are quite simple as far as I'm concerned, Mr Gerrard. On two occasions you used your vessel to conduct a personal vendetta against U-boats – highly commendable as far as His Majesty's Government is concerned. What is not commendable is that you should claim that you were carrying gold belonging to this country in what we can only construe as an attempt to pressurize the government into underwriting the loss of your ship as a result of your foolhardy ventures.'

'For Chrissake, will you listen!' Gerrard suddenly shouted. 'If you do nothing about Holden you're turning a German spy loose in this country! And if all the English are as stupid as you, then I guess you're getting no more than you deserve.'

Houseman regarded Gerrard with contempt. 'I'm sorry, Mr Gerrard, but it hasn't worked. We've checked Mr Holden's credentials most carefully. He's a top civil servant at the Treasury. He's never been to Germany nor has he ever had contact with Germans or pro-German sympathizers during his frequent visits to the United States.'

Gerrard realized the uselessness of further argument with the arrogant Englishman. Houseman had made up his mind and nothing would make him change it. 'Okay,' he said tiredly. 'So what's going to happen to me?'

'You're to be deported back to the United States on the first available ship, Mr Gerrard. In view of the fact that you have disposed of two U-boats, it has been decided not to bring charges against you.' Houseman chuckled. 'You see, Mr Gerrard? We're not ungrateful.'

The interviewing officer smiled at Josephine. 'No, Miss Britten, I promise there are no more forms to fill in but I would be grateful if you would kindly answer a few questions about your background.'

The next ten minutes seemed totally unreal to Josephine; the interviewing officer politely asked the most unbelievable yet searching questions. He wanted to know what her father's nickname had been for her when she was a little girl; he wanted to know the colour of the outside of the hardware store and even the name of the nearest delicatessen. Each time Josephine answered a question, the interviewing officer made a pencil mark that was neither a tick or a cross on a long, typed list. The next question was in complete contrast to the preceeding questions.

'Thank you, Miss Britten. Could you tell me what cargo the *Tulsar* was carrying?'

'Lead.'

'Thank you. How was it carried?'

'In large crates.'

'I see. Did you see the crates being loaded aboard?'

'No.'

'Did you ever see the crates?'

'No. Yes! When they burst out of the ship's side before it went down.'

'But you never saw the contents of the crates?'

'No.'

Josephine was about to ask the purpose of the unusual questions but the interviewing officer suddenly closed his file.

'Thank you, Miss Britten.' He opened the drawer of his desk and placed a buff envelope in front of Josephine. 'I presume you're anxious to return to New York?'

'That is a classic understatement,' said Josephine icily.

The interviewing officer looked sympathetic. 'A passage has been booked to New York for you, Miss Britten, and all the other passengers on the *Tulsar*. I'm afraid that we can't say when because sailing dates are confidential. You've all been booked into a London hotel in the meantime.

214

'You mean that I'm free to go? To leave here?'

'Yes, of course.' The interviewing officer handed Josephine another envelope. 'Don't forget this. There are some temporary identity papers in here. A bus is due soon to take you all to your hotel, although I understand that there's a young man waiting for you outside.'

The young man turned out to be Ralph Holden.

# 29

All the passengers from the *Tulsar* were gathered at Euston station waiting for the announcement that heralded which platform the Liverpool train would be leaving from. Josephine sat on a station seat next to Holden. They had been waiting an hour, saying little and watching the endless streams of men and women in uniform passing to and fro. Mrs Eli Vanson arrived with her husband in tow and gathered about her a knot of passengers anxious to hear the latest gossip.

'My dears,' she was saying. 'You know how difficult it is trying to find anything out? Well, I heard that it's an American ship – a proper ocean liner with restaurants and bars and a swimming-pool and a hairdresser's salon. . . .'

'Is it a proper liner, Ralph?' Josephine asked.

'So I understand.'

'Do you think you'll ever be able to give me straight answers to straight questions?'

'I don't suppose so. But I might.'

'There you go again. No wonder London is a hotbed of rumours.'

Holden laughed and then became serious. 'Jo . . .'

She sensed his hesitancy and looked sharply at him. 'What's the matter?'

'A message came through this morning about your father.'

'From my mother?'

'Yes.'

Josephine closed her eyes for a few seconds. 'He's dead, isn't he?'

'Two days ago ... I'm very sorry, Jo.'

'I did my best to get to him in time.'

Holden covered her hand with his. 'He'd understand.'

'Mr Holden?' said a cold, impersonal voice.

Holden looked up at the stranger. 'Yes?'

'Houseman,' said the stranger stiffly. 'Captain Steven Houseman. I've been instructed to deliver a certain gentleman into your charge.'

The two men inspected each other's identity cards and shook hands. 'I've been expecting you, captain,' said Holden. 'Where is he?'

Houseman beckoned to three men who were standing some fifty yards away. They came forward. Josephine gave a gasp of surprise when she saw them.

The man in the middle was Gerrard.

It was when Josephine left the reserved compartment on the train to see if the restaurant car was emptying that Holden hooked his hands together at the back of his neck and grinned at Gerrard.

'I suppose I owe you some sort of explanation. The trouble was that you were so eager to shop me to anyone who would listen after we were picked up. It was something I hadn't quite bargained for. Not that I blame you, of course.'

'Just who the hell are you working for, Holden?'

'The winning side.'

'For Chrissake, can't you ever give a straight answer?'

'You're the second person to make that complaint today.'

'Will you answer me one thing? Just what did we carry in the *Tulsar*'s hold?'

'What did Houseman tell you?'

'He said it was lead.'

'He was right.'

Gerrard stared at the Englishman. 'Then for Chrissake why did you tell me that it was gold?'

'And I told the Germans we would be carrying the gold. I met Kramer in Cape Town before we sailed and convinced him that we'd be shipping it on the *Tulsar*. The Germans didn't need much convincing that someone would be carrying it because they knew it was in South Africa and they knew that we had to get it out somehow.'

'So it's still in South Africa?'

'No. It was collected from Cape Town on 10 January by a United States cruiser. The USS *Louisville* was the real transporter of Churchill's gold. It went direct to America to pay our cash and carry debts. All £42 millions' worth of the stuff – the last of our reserves. There's not so much as a single gold bar in the Bank of England vaults now. It's all gone.' Holden paused and gazed out of the window at the passing scenery. 'Not that we need it any more,' he continued. 'Roosevelt has pushed his Lend-Lease bill through Congress and now we're getting all the munitions we need for nothing. Roosevelt has done exactly what he said he would do – he's eliminated the dollar sign from the conduct of the war.'

Gerrard's face was white with anger. 'So I was the sucker who was the decoy, huh?'

'No. You were more than that. We thought that if we deliberately fed the Germans with the story that the *Tulsar* – a fast ship – was carrying the gold, then there was a chance that we might be able to lure out some of their big ships to hunt you down. God knows why they initially sent a U-boat out. That's why I was anxious to knock it out of the hunt. Of course, we never dreamed that we would winkle the *Bismarck* out of her hidey-hole.'

There was a long silence.

'Jesus bloody Christ,' Gerrard muttered at length.

'Kramer turning up on board the *Tulsar* was something else I hadn't bargained for,' Holden admitted. He smiled. 'It just goes to show – the best-laid plans and all that ...'

Gerrard nodded slowly. The pieces dropped into place. Suddenly everything made sense. 'How many knew about the plan?'

'Less than six including myself.'

'But not Captain Houseman?'

'Especially not Captain Houseman,' said Holden with feeling. 'No imagination.'

Josephine entered the compartment. 'I managed to book a

217

table for three in ten minutes,' she said triumphantly. She frowned and looked at Holden and Gerrard in turn. 'Hey – you two. Have I missed out on something?'

It seemed to Josephine that there were as many people crowded on to the pier to say farewell to the ocean liner as there were passengers gathering round the gangways to go aboard. Already the streamers were spooling down from the towering decks into dozens of eager, outstretched hands.

'Where's your baggage, Ralph?' Josephine inquired.

'I haven't got any, Jo.'

'But you must have something. You can't go like that.'

'I'm not going to New York.'

Josephine stared blankly at Holden. 'But I thought ...'

Holden shook his head. 'I came along to say goodbye, Jo. Why? What did you expect?'

A porter seized Josephine's two small bags that she had purchased in London and piled them on to a trolley.

'I don't know,' said Josephine slowly. 'I thought ... hell, it doesn't matter what I thought.'

Holden took her arm and guided her to the gangway that was boarding first-class passengers. 'I've got your address in New York,' he pointed out. 'So if I do ever go ...' He left the sentence unfinished.

'Is that likely?'

'It all depends on President Roosevelt.'

'Why?'

'The Crown agents have an office in Manhattan. If America enters the war I'll be posted there.' He smiled down at Josephine and took her hands in his. 'I made them promise me that much.'

The gap between the pier and the liner slowly widened and the thousands of paper streamers linking the great ship to the land tightened, and then snapped. The wind scattered the broken strands and sent them tangling among the cheering crowds lining the quay and the ship's rails.

Josephine waved frantically but Holden was no longer looking up at her. The last she saw of the Englishman in his own country was his fair hair as he pushed through the crowds, making his way back to the terminal building.